THE LAST NOWEN

·RICK DUFFY·

First edition 2024
Published by Greening River

ISBN 978-1-7351954-6-9 (paperback)
ISBN 978-1-7351954-7-6 (ebook)
ISBN 978-1-7351954-8-3 (hardback)

www.rickduffy.com

THE SIGIL MASTERS SERIES

The Sigil Masters

Dark Reckoning

The Last Nowen

Who looks outside, dreams
Who looks inside, awakes

— *Carl Jung*

CONTENTS

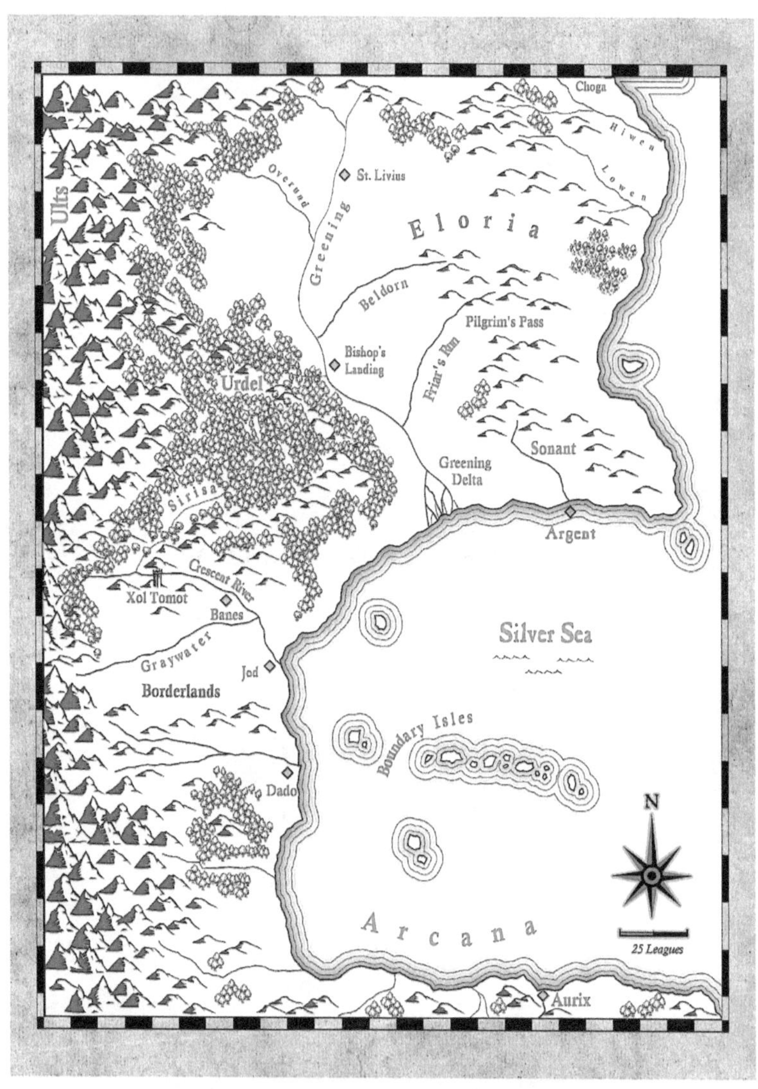

Close-in map, 1 league = 3 miles

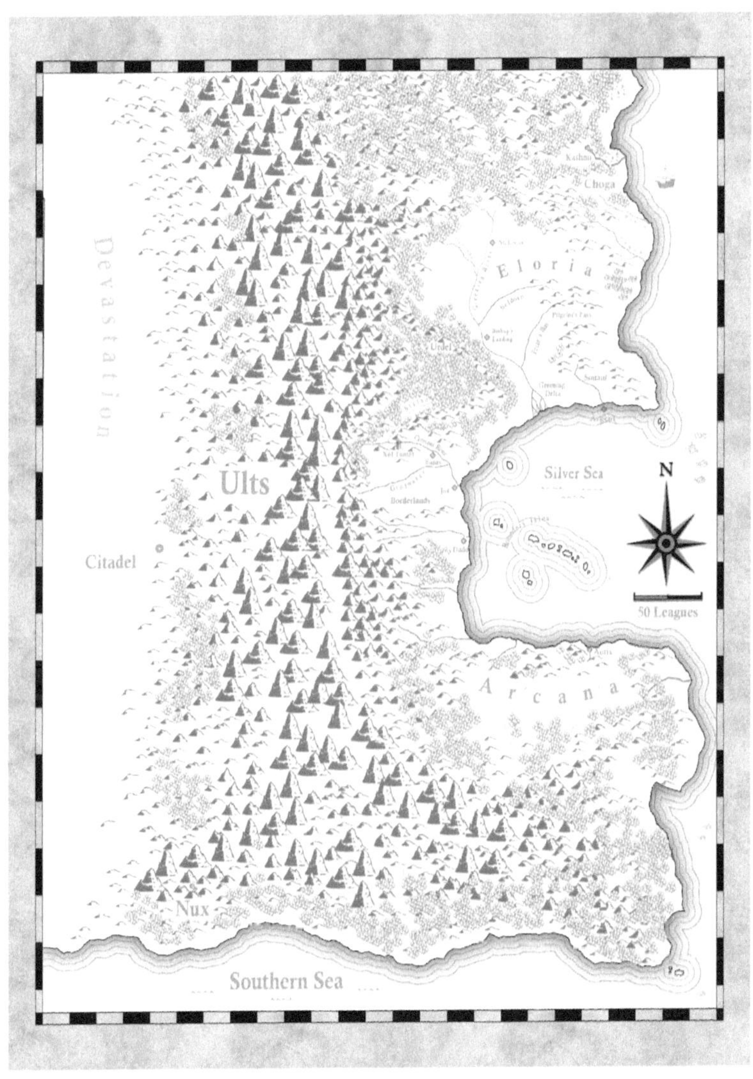

Wide map, 1 league = 3 miles

(Immortus & center of Devastation = 1000 leagues west)

PART ONE

THE DEEP WORLD

CHAPTER ONE

BLASTS FROM THE storm shocked Enio's skin and stung his eyes. But he gripped the *Sea Dog's* wheel and plunged through the night. All the while, the mainsail hung impossibly stiff, sparkling like crystal snow—the same as the deck, mast, and rigging. If Enio didn't know better, he'd swear he rode a ship of ice.

The going was terrifying—and exhilarating.

But the going where?

Memories rushed his mind, each shredded like the night. The last thing he remembered was being possessed by Cronus. Enio had escaped from that loathsome prison, yet afterwards, nothing made sense. Faces he couldn't place. Magics unknown and unimagined. He grasped now at dreams, and at nightmares.

Shaking his head to clear his thoughts, he shielded his eyes against the tempest and searched for a horizon. To starboard, below the dark, rushing clouds, was that the first glow of dawn? No, yet the feeling was somehow warm and comforting. Enio stretched out his senses, from his nose to his fingers, from his teeth to his toes. Then, in the cellar of his bones, a touch so soft it barely registered.

He wasn't alone.

And adding to this, the smell of rich crawtad soup—ridiculously out of place on the helm of the *Sea Dog* in a storm. Perhaps some foolish recollection from his childhood. But instinct insisted it was something more.

With all his strength, he turned the boat that way.

The winds shifted to aft and sped him along. Blurry stars peeked through thinning clouds, so he focused there, hoping for a clue to his location. Then, to his amazement, he found those weren't stars at all. Whatever they were, they were unravelling.

Enio watched in awe. Their rainbow rays broke into burning droplets. That was the spray stinging his face, filling the air and the crystal sails. He reached through a mist of the glowing specks. They collected on his skin and sank beneath, sending a thrill of power through his chest and limbs.

The night calmed. He thought he heard whispers and voices. Leaving the wheel, he peered over the rail. A mob of canoes now surrounded him, each also of crystal, each carrying a ghostly passenger holding up an unlit candle.

Enio tried to shout. *Ahoy! Ahoy!* But droplets of fire streamed from his mouth and along his vision, as if guided by his eyes. The motes of flame collected near one of those unlit candles. It flared into golden life.

He laughed with surprise and focused on another. That candle lit too. As his gaze glided from boat to boat, candle to candle, the shining motes flew to and from each wick, lighting them in a great, lustrous wave.

Then, in the corner of his eye, something flashed.

Purple hells! In his distraction, he'd missed an oncoming vessel, as large as his own.

He dove back to the wheel—too late! His crystal ship smashed into the other, and his entire world shattered.

CHAPTER TWO

PAR WANDERED ALONE through the busy streets of Argent. He'd struggled all morning to keep his spirits up. Was he asking too much from life? To have Enio healed? His friend still hadn't spoken. To see Lani again? She hadn't returned from the sea. Whether on the streets, or on the rocky shore, or beside Enio's quiet bed at the Mercy House, Par's loneliness only deepened.

It hadn't helped when, this morning, the Father Abbot had told him to get lost.

Yet that was his own doing.

Though Enio had remained unresponsive for the past week, Par had taken him to the Summer Festival. The Eminence himself had kicked it off, and as the crowds held up their candles, all their wicks burst to brilliant life in a great, lustrous wave. It was one of the most impressive invocations Par had ever seen the Eminence perform. Then after the ceremony, the Eminence said he hadn't done it.

Enio hadn't raised as much as a finger, but Par felt the candles had somehow been lit by him. So this morning, the Abbot decided to examine Enio in private. He dismissed everyone: the nurses, the Reckoners, the Confessors, and Par.

That might mean renewed hope for Enio. And as Par continued through the city, he had to admit there was more to be thankful for. The Eminence had proclaimed those unable to invoke the gods would now be treated as equals. It seemed as if the city had been holding its breath, waiting for just that change, but no one had spoken for fear of their neighbors. It turned out most of their neighbors had wanted the exact same thing.

Yes, Par told himself as he turned a corner, the future held new promise.

Three more seconds into that future, something crashed at his heels.

Par stumbled and spun. A dirty clump of broken pottery lay in his footsteps. A blotchy-faced old woman sneered from a window. "Abomination!" She slammed her shutters.

Like the pot, Par's fragile mood crumbled. He'd already learned, from behind-the-back whispers, that not everyone celebrated the Eminence's new proclamation.

But he pulled himself together and hurried on. Midday had arrived; he needed to check on Enio. Besides, Par had been working on a way to prove, at least to himself, that Enio's mind and soul were still intact. Par felt quite brainy to have thought of it.

He'd yawn at Enio.

Not a squeaky little yawn, but a face-splitting, tongue-wagging, tooth-curling yawn. Nobody could resist those. His friend would react and yawn back.

The black iron gates of the Mercy House stood open and unguarded. A worker on a ladder labored to remove the bars from the windows. Places like these were no longer prisons.

Par strode inside—the attendants knew him well by now and didn't question his business. Once upstairs, he stopped outside Enio's door to practice.

Yawn.

YaaaaWWWWnnn.

YaaAAAWWWWWWWwwnnn.

That should do it.

He knocked and pushed into the room. "I'm back."

Enio, in his feathered cap, sat on the windowsill. He smiled and waved.

Par froze in shock.

Spreading out his arms, Enio hopped from the sill. "Hey, Par. Look what—"

Stupor broke into joy, and Par bolted forward.. "Enio!"

The Father Abbot leapt from a chair near the bed. "Par, wait!"

But Par was upon his friend.

And through him.

And sailing out the window.

He shouted and flailed, but a cushion of air stopped him before he hit the pavement. It lifted him back up to the window and set him beside the Abbot, who was invoking. Enio stood a step away, wavering like smoke. Another more solid Enio lay motionless on the bed, eyes closed, his feathered cap still on the nightstand.

The Abbot ended his invocation. "Par, are you unharmed?"

Par stood dumfounded, catching his breath, looking from one Enio to the other. He poked a finger at his upright friend's transparent chest.

Enio slapped at the finger, but his shadowy hand passed right through it.

The Abbot said, "The Reckoners and Confessors have been delicate with Enio's treatment. Yet I felt he was stronger than they gave him credit for. So I decided to bestow a sigil on him, which is always a soul-to-soul affair. If he noticed my attempt, locked deep in his mind as he may be, he might make a grab for it."

"I saw it and reeled it in," Enio said, his voice, like his form, a bit airy. "Then I filled it with lumina. And here I am." He made a ghostly hop.

Par glanced at the physical Enio on the bed, the body still unmoving. "I don't understand."

"Do you remember," the Abbot said, "the time when I projected your image in a prison cell? And once, long ago, projected my own into the cemetery below the abbey?"

Par nodded.

"I have just given that sigil to Enio."

"But his body…" Par pointed to the Enio on the bed. "It's still not moving."

"Yeah," Enio's voice lost its cheer. "Maybe I can do something about that."

His wavering form glided across the room, the feet not quite touching the floor.

Par moved to follow. The Abbot held him back.

Enio stood beside the bed; the face of his solid self seemed like a blank page. His smokey finger reached out to touch his physical hand. As it passed inside, the fleshy hand twitched.

"Hmm," Enio said. He leaned down and pressed his face into an ear.

Par grimaced. Looking into your own ear just seemed wrong.

Enio pulled out. "Dark in there."

"I bet," Par said.

After a quick frown at Par, Enio turned back to his own body and with a sudden lunge dove in and disappeared.

Par gasped.

Golden light flashed around Enio's entire form and blinked out. The limbs began to tremble, then to shake.

"What's happening?" Par said with growing alarm.

"Hold him." The Abbot grasped an arm. Par grabbed the other.

The body arched and kicked.

Par mounted the bed and knelt beside his friend, pressing him down.

The mouth opened and screamed.

"Abbot!" Par shouted.

Before the Abbot replied, the muscles relaxed. The mouth closed. The chest rose and fell normally.

Then the eyes opened. They focused on Par.

"Your…" Enio cleared his throat.

"What?" Par bent closer.

"Your… knee. It's breaking my rib."

"Sorry." Par backed off. The Abbot did, too.

Enio gazed at the ceiling. He took a deep breath and rose onto his elbows. One wobbled. He propped himself up again. "I feel funny. Slippery inside. Maybe I got in backwards."

"But you're awake and aware," the Abbot said, smiling. "That's the important thing. How can we help? Are you hungry? Perhaps some lunch?"

Enio looked at his hand; flexed the fingers. "No, I need to stretch my muscles first. Move around. Get some air."

"It would be better if you took it easy for a while."

But Enio slid his legs off the mattress and lowered his feet to the floor. "Anyone seen my boots?"

The Abbot sighed. "Try under the bed."

While Enio searched, the Abbot spoke quietly to Par. "I'd hoped Enio would accept the sigil, but I didn't imagine he'd be able to use it without more practice."

"Does that mean anything?" Par said, hoping for some reassurance.

But concern troubled the old man's eyes. "I don't know."

That wasn't the answer Par expected. "What should we do?"

"You go with him. But don't push him. When he first saw me, he didn't remember my name. I suspect he has more healing to do."

Enio found his boots and fumbled them on. He staggered to his feet. Par tried to help him up, but Enio waved him off.

"I'm fine." Enio grabbed his feathered cap and shuffled to the door.

Par followed after a brief "Thank you" to the Father Abbot.

The man forced a grin, but Par detected a lingering worry there.

And as for not pushing, how would Par keep Enio from pushing himself?

CHAPTER THREE

Enio stumbled down the corridor.

Par caught up. "You sure you're good?"

"Just a little stiff, like a puppet."

The words gave Par a chill, considering how recently Cronus had been in control of Enio's body.

But his friend added, "I mean, like my brain is talking, but my muscles are hard of hearing."

At least that wasn't Cronus. "Weird."

"Yeah. Don't worry about it." Enio found his stride and continued more easily. "Which way is out?"

"Wasn't the Abbot going to order lunch?"

"Then let him eat it. I want to check on the *Sea Dog*."

"It's still in Arcana. Lani said the stags would bring it."

Enio turned. "Lani's here?"

"I talked to her once, near the shore."

"Great. Let's go there."

"She hasn't been back." Par had checked every day.

"Let's go anyway. I need that sea air."

There seemed no use in arguing. Besides, Enio wasn't a prisoner; he might go out alone. Better if Par stayed with him.

They left the Mercy House and passed through its black iron gates to the sunny lane. Enio looked both ways. "Which is faster?"

"Follow me," Par said.

The way he took wasn't the fastest, but it avoided aggressive flowerpots. As he trod the grungy streets and alleyways where they'd once scraped out a living, Par's spirits lightened, and he couldn't help but talk and talk. He told all that had happened during Enio's recovery, including the Eminence's new proclamation.

They reached a thin, lonely arch in the eastern walls. The bay beyond sparkled silver beneath the noonday sun, and a bracing, salty breeze brought back happy memories of their days on the *Sea Dog*. After scrambling over slick, mossy stones away from the piers, they came to a rocky, barren stretch.

Par halted. "This is where Lani found me."

They chose a dry place to sit, beyond the shadow of the high walls. The surf whispered in and out before their boots. Enio took a deep, loud breath, as if inhaling the aroma of a grand feast.

Par pointed farther down the shoreline, toward rising cliffs where the city walls didn't reach. "Up there. See that place?"

"With the trees?"

"It'd be a nice spot for a cottage."

"Yeah," Enio said. "If you had the money."

"Lady Agatha said she'd help."

"Lady who?"

Par eyed his friend. They'd traveled leagues across land and sea with that woman. She'd even given him that dumb cap. "You're kidding, right?"

For a moment, Enio seemed uncertain. Then he laughed. "Oh. Lady Agatha. Sure."

Before Par could ask about that mental slip, Enio added, "Good view. Gets a lot of wind, I bet."

"The wind might keep us from being bothered."

"Us?"

"Well," Par said, "if you wanted to stay there."

Enio shrugged. "Bothered by who?"

Par kept his gaze on the cliffs. "People who don't like the new proclamation—or me."

"Not everyone is going to love you, Par."

"I know, but they sure could hate me a little less."

"Used to be that everyone felt that way about, uh…" Enio paused.

"A feeble?" Par nudged his friend.

Enio nudged back. "You know what I mean. Some won't ever change."

"I guess, as long as they leave me alone."

"You and Lani, you mean."

Par looked back at Enio.

His friend smiled. "Have you told her?"

"Told her what?"

"Don't be stupid. You know what."

In fact, the entire situation still had Par confused. The last time he'd seen her, she'd kissed him.

Sort of.

And he'd kissed her back.

Sort of.

He still wasn't sure what it meant. He hadn't told anyone, not even Enio, about the kiss part. But he really was stupid if he believed he could hide his worries from his best friend.

"It's not that simple, Enio. She's a nymph, or half-nymph, and still has to choose between life on land or in the sea. Besides, she said she might transform into something."

Enio's face lit. "Like what?"

But Par didn't want to think about that part.

His friend didn't seem to mind. "A sea stag?"

"Stags are male," Par said.

"Oh. Right."

Taking a deep breath, Par asked, "What if she chooses the sea?"

Enio picked up a stone and lobbed it into the waves. "Tell her you want her to stay. Simple."

"It's *not* simple. She thinks she can be a bridge to the Deep World. Even the Abbot says that's pretty important. I'm not sure what to do."

Enio considered. "Have you tried poetry?"

"On the Abbot?"

Suddenly, Par found himself in a headlock. "Hey!"

"On Lani, dumbass!"

Par laughed, not only at the friendly scuffle, but because Enio could manage it.

"Just tell her." Enio let him go. "Or hide in your hillside fortress forever. What are you afraid of?"

"Nothing. You don't understand."

"You're smart, Par, but you think too much." Enio stepped to the surf and let it lap his boots. "She gave me that Sea Call sigil, remember? But I never used it." He gave his wide, broken-toothed grin. "What better time?"

"That's a great idea!" Par had forgotten about that sigil. Then again, should Enio be invoking in his condition? "But I'm not sure the Abbot wants you using sigils yet."

"He didn't say not to."

That was true. Still, Par should probably object more.

But he didn't.

Enio moved ankle-deep in the water. He stiffened. His face puckered, and he grunted a few times. A faint green spark leapt out of his ear, then fizzled with a dismal *phut*.

He jolted and looked around. "What was that?"

"You made a spark. But it went phut."

"What?"

"Phut. Did it work?"

"No."

"I guess the Abbot's right. You need more rest."

"Maybe." Enio twisted a finger inside his ear. They remained quiet, surrounded by the murmur of the sea and cawing gulls looking for a meal. Par took the moment to appreciate just being with Enio again. That his friend was back.

Finally, he said, "I always knew you were in there, Enio. I stayed with you."

Enio hesitated. "The whole time?"

"Except for a quick trip through the Threshold. Vex wanted the Luminary's ring that I left in the Citadel. Otherwise, yeah."

"Thanks."

"You'd have done the same. I'm glad you're better. I got scared—"

"Don't get mushy."

Par grinned. He didn't need to say more.

Then, more softly, Enio said, "But I wasn't anywhere near *in there*."

"What does that mean?"

"I was on the *Sea Dog.*"

Par frowned, hoping his friend wasn't losing it.

"Well, I'm not sure." Enio continued. "I was piloting a boat under the strangest stars I'd ever seen."

The Abbot had once speculated that Enio, or at least his soul, was adrift in the Higher Realms. Par had been there once himself, and he'd seen more than stars, like bright realms of light, and other, darker ones. "What else did you see?"

"People."

"What people?"

Enio closed his eyes. "They had candles. I made them light."

That confirmed Par's suspicions from the Summer Festival.

When the crowd's candles mysteriously lit, Enio had somehow been responsible.

"I have other memories," Enio added.

"Tell me."

"I was lying on a table with a bunch of crusty old guys around me."

"That was in the chapel," Par said, "where they tried healing you."

"I saw you there too."

Par could only nod. He had cried there.

"And before that, mountains."

Mountains? There were the Ults, but they were days away. "Do you mean the cliffs of the ruling quarter, or the ones across the bay?"

"No, not here. All rock and snow. Then a long, cold valley."

"What valley?"

"And something about a thirsty moon."

"A what?" Par asked.

"I don't—" Enio squeezed his eyes tighter. "I can't remember."

Par's concern rose a notch. First forgetting Lady Agatha, and now this? "Maybe the Abbot should check you again."

"I'm fine."

Not wanting to push any further, Par let the topic end. "We can try Lani tomorrow."

But Enio kept on, his voice now almost a whisper. "And I remember bones. Moving bones. Walking bones. You were there. You said you thought I'd dreamt it."

Par forced a nervous laugh. That's just what he was thinking. "When I was little, I dreamt a monster lived in the latrine and—"

"A monster," Enio repeated. "From the sea, with black fangs and eyes of green fire..." He trailed off.

"Not just a dream." Par peered hard at his friend. "A nightmare."

Enio took an unsteady breath and opened his eyes. He flashed an embarrassed smile and spoke the way a summer day demanded. "I had a lot of those dreams. In one, you and I were on the shore when an earthquake—"

Right then, the ground began to shake.

They grabbed each other to keep from falling over.

The shaking increased. They hunkered down. Shouts came from the city walls. People scrambled along the ramparts.

But as quickly as it had arrived, the tremor passed.

Par's eyes met Enio's. "Did you… do that?"

"Me? Are you nuts?"

They raised themselves back up. Par looked at the walls; thank the gods no one had fallen. He took a moment to catch his breath and let his nerves settle.

Enio brushed himself off, took another deep breath. "Smell that?"

Par sniffed and wrinkled his nose. "The weeds, the mud, or the rotting fish?"

"Nothing better. Hey, didn't you say the Abbot was getting lunch?"

"Yeah. Let's get back. I want to find out what just happened."

"And I'm starving for a bowl of crawtad soup." Enio glanced at the walls. "Which way again?"

Chapter Four

Par hurried with Enio back through the city. Fortunately, there seemed no major damage from the tremor. But people remained uneasy, many peering from doorways or around window curtains. Who could blame them? Par had never heard of a quake in Argent.

When they reached the Mercy House gates, the Father Abbot was coming out.

"You boys all right?" he asked.

"We're fine," Par said. "What's happened?"

"Some panic inside, a few bumps and bruises, nothing serious."

"I meant the quake."

"I wish I knew."

A thought hit Par. "Before we defeated the Ortu, the Aubade of Arcana threatened to bring down the cliffs of Argent. Do you think—"

"No, I can't imagine the Aubade would attack during this time of peace. But I will mention it to the Eminence. He's summoned me on another matter."

There was also Enio's dream. Par nudged his friend. "Didn't you have something to tell the Father Abbot?"

"Oh, right. We changed our minds about lunch."

"That's not—" Par began.

"Good," the Abbot said. "They're a bit busy inside. Let's find a street cart."

They started down the lane, Enio setting a quick pace. But Par couldn't let this drop. He lagged with the Abbot and lowered his voice. "Father Abbot, I'm worried Enio had something to do with the tremors."

The Abbot lowered his as well. "How so?"

"He was telling me things he dreamt while he was still unconscious. As he mentioned an earthquake, right then it happened."

"Indeed?" The man hesitated. "Is there anything else about him that worries you?"

"He still can't invoke. And he's unsteady sometimes, a little confused with directions and names. Otherwise, he's his old self. He tried to headlock me."

The Abbot smiled. "He was bedridden for several days, so some disorientation is expected, and any progress is good. Perhaps he will allow me to examine him further."

They caught up to Enio who had stopped at a street vendor's cart. A bald man shaped like a pickle barrel stood behind a tub of bubbling oil. Golden fried foods hung dripping from strings.

Enio sniffed at the oil. "I feel like I haven't eaten in a week."

"Not on your own," Par said.

The Abbot jingled a change purse. "Eat your fill. Lunch is on me."

"Thanks," Par answered with Enio. Par picked out a fried fish on a stick. The Abbot selected some kind of brown muffin. The barrel man didn't serve crawtad soup, but Enio filled a paper basket with nearly one of everything. They sat on a bench along the lane. The city had calmed, and the foot and horse traffic were picking up again.

As they ate, the Abbot said, "Enio, Par tells me you've had some interesting dreams?"

Enio nodded, batter crumbling from his mouth.

"Would you tell me what you remember?"

Without seeming too concerned, Enio told of his nightmare visions and the quake. When he finished, he wiped his mouth. "Gods, that was good." A monstrous belch followed his words. He eyed the Abbot. "Sorry."

"Quite all right. I'm glad to see your appetite has returned."

"Feels like I grew a second stomach."

Par was still pondering the dreams. "Could the quake have been a coincidence?" Even as he said it, the question rang as unlikely.

"Perhaps," said the Abbot. "But the answer may lie deeper within Enio. Deeper than we've so far looked."

Enio noticed the stares from Par and the Abbot. His eyes widened. "Oh, no you don't! I've had enough with people digging in my skull."

"I sympathize," the Abbot said. "And I realize how unnerving it can be. We each have our secrets, though they are not as uncommon as we might believe. But if you'd just allow—"

"I said *no*." Enio's tone, not to mention his face, gave no room for argument.

"I only want to help," the Abbot added gently.

Enio sighed and his expression softened. "Look, I can't, not now." He shifted his gaze to Par. "Everything is good. Cronus is gone. My memories are mine again."

A quiet pleading showed in those eyes. Enio had suffered unimaginable mental torture at the hands of Cronus, and later, at the Immortus, even allowed that man to possess him, the only way to invoke a crucial sigil and save them all from the Ortu. Par understood why Enio was done with people rummaging in his head, despite promises to tread easy.

"I understand," the Abbot said. "But—"

"Father Abbot," Par cut in, "maybe we can find another way."

The Abbot paused. "Yes, well, for safety's sake, we shouldn't ignore it. I expect the Eminence will want to discuss the quakes when he sees me. I will mention your vision to him."

Enio opened his mouth.

"And I will tell him," the Abbot added quickly, "I don't recommend further treatments at this time. I am his High Sigil Master. He will listen to me."

Enio closed his mouth.

"So what's next?" Par asked.

"Why don't you two go back to the Mercy House? I'll let you know what the Eminence says."

"Good. I feel like a nap." Enio yawned.

Par resisted joking about a nap at midday. It must be all the excitement.

Chapter Five

Not only did Enio conk out the rest of the afternoon, he slept late into next morning. Par roused him at lunch—to tell him they'd been summoned before the Eminence.

Enio frowned. "About my dreams?"

"The coachman didn't say, but the Abbot won't let anyone in your head. So get dressed. Unless you're not up for it?"

"Me?" Enio puffed out his chest. "I'm great, body and brain."

After a brief meal, they rode a fancy black carriage up to the governing sector. Enio slumped back, eyes closed. Traveling past stiff guards and through tall gates, they circled the bright central fountain, passed the shining triple-spired High Temple, and halted at the grand palace.

Par nudged Enio. "We're here."

But now Enio yawned and turned away. "I need five more minutes."

"What happened to that great body and brain stuff?"

"Not my morning brain. Couldn't they wait until after lunch?"

Par yanked him up. "You ate breakfast for lunch."

A guard escorted them through the lofty foyer, then to a roomy, windowless chapel. Par had been to the palace, but not this chamber. Candles burned on a raised altar, creating a solemn globe of light in the otherwise dark room. A trio of tall, velvety chairs loomed behind the altar. Behind those rested a fourth chair, throne-like on a raised dais. The room was mostly empty, except for a single row of simple wooden chairs in the center facing forward, and shadowy benches lining the walls.

The guard pointed to the wooden chairs. "Wait there." He left and closed the door.

They sat. Immediately, Enio slumped down. "Wake me when…"

He was out.

Par was beginning to worry about his sleepy friend. But he remembered the Abbot's words. He was still recovering.

After several more minutes, the doors to the room creaked. Par turned. For the first time, he noticed someone sitting on a side bench, hidden in shadow. The figure stood. He was dressed formally, with a frilly collar and cuffs: the clothing of the wealthy, or important. His posture and the set of his chin suggested an adult, but he seemed near Par's age. A palace servant? Still, it was creepy how he'd waited and said nothing.

The white-robed Father Abbot stepped through the doors.

Par stood too. "Good morning, Father Abbot."

The Abbot, eyes ahead, gave a slight head-shake and kept walking. Two others followed, also in white: the noble Lady Melora and the black-bearded Lord Simeon. They, along with the Father Abbot, were the three most important officials in Eloria under the Eminence. They strode past Par and around the altar, stopping before their fancy chairs.

The Abbot cleared his throat. "The Most High Pompeius Maxima Arcalus, Fondiscate of the Divine, ruler of Eloria."

Unlit candles along the walls flared to life. Par winced at their sudden brightness. Then the Eminence entered, his robes flowing like liquid gold in the bright candlelight. The fancy-dressed boy near the door bowed deep. Par bowed too. The man passed and continued to the highest chair.

A quiet snore came from Enio, who was still seated. Par nudged him with his foot. No change.

Then a brief flash sparked beneath Enio's chair.

Enio leapt to his feet. "Ow!"

"Shh," Par hissed.

Enio brushed his pants and looked around. "Oh, sorry." He made a brief bow, then side-whispered to Par, "Something bit me."

Par glanced at the Abbot, who returned an innocent smile.

The Eminence sat. Everyone did the same. Enio brushed his chair first.

"Before we begin," the Eminence said in a strong, friendly voice, "I want to acknowledge Enio's progress. The news is quite gladdening. And I understand he's had a dream that may be of import?" He nodded to Enio. "Please, speak freely."

Enio seemed much more attentive now. "Uh, I remembered an earthquake from my dreams. I was telling Par about it when one happened."

"Eminence," said the Abbot, "is it possible, given the nature of Enio's trauma and possession, that he may have gained some talent for prediction?"

"I very much doubt it," the Eminence said. "No known magic permits the viewing of what lies before us, though certain conjurations allow one to make a good guess."

"Might Enio have performed one of those conjurations?"

"Let us hope not." The Eminence's words darkened. "For that is the magic of the diviners."

"Divine magic?" Par asked. That didn't sound so bad.

"There is nothing *divine* about them," the Eminence said. "It is a magic of the Lower Realms."

All Par knew of the Lower Realms was the Ortu, which consumed the energies of the Higher Realms. Alexander Vex had once mentioned other magics without any other details. "Then diviners can see the future?"

"Not exactly. They discern the lost echoes of the dead. This sometimes brings knowledge that can help to predict…"

The Eminence trailed off a moment. "Enio, what else did your dreams show you?"

Enio rubbed his face. "The rest were like crazy nightmares."

"Please, tell us."

"If you say so. Monsters, maybe? Walking bones. Smoking red pits."

"Smoking pits?" Par whispered.

"Just remembered," Enio whispered back.

Lord Simeon, charged with defense and commerce beyond Eloria's borders, spoke up. "Near these pits, did you see large numbers of travelers among tents and wagons?"

"Oh… yeah, I think I did. In the mountains."

"Very curious." The Eminence peered intently at Enio. "Your dreams may, in fact, hold some truth, for we have had reports of similar migrations. This warrants further study."

Enio stiffened, but the man added. "To be clear, I do not mean inside your head, until you permit it."

With that, Enio let out a quiet breath of relief.

"In any case," the Eminence said, his gaze now including Par, "it supports the original purpose of this meeting. We've been contacted by the kingdom of the sea, the Deep World."

Par's heart skipped a beat. That's where Lani was.

The man went on. "Their ruler, the Asrai, acknowledges our victory against the rise of the Ortu. She has broken her long silence with our world, for she believes we are in new danger."

Par glanced at the Abbot. His lips had tightened.

The Eminence continued. "Hers is not the only land that noticed your deeds at the Immortus. So did the cults and tribes who use the magic of the Lower Realms. The Dark Tribes."

"They want revenge on us for stopping the Ortu?" Par asked.

"No, Par. An evil follower of Ortu had acted without their knowledge or consent, and his success would have meant misery to all. Yet your actions also brought the countries of Arcana and Eloria closer in friendship than we've ever been."

Before Par rested on his laurels, the Eminence added, "The Asrai believes the tribes of the Lower Realms now band together to defend themselves."

"From what?"

"From us," said Lord Simeon. "They see our friendship with Arcana as a threat. We've intelligence of widespread movement among the Dark Tribes. We suspect they are gathering an army."

"And there are whispers among the people," said Lady Melora, responsible for the welfare within Eloria's borders, "of an increase in travelers offering the telling of fortunes and selling strange charms, all forbidden by the Rule."

"So they caused the quake?" That made more sense to Par than Enio doing it.

"It would require power that we have never seen them channel," she answered. "But we do not know."

The Eminence spoke again. "And because of all this, the Asrai wishes to explore diplomatic relations, even hinting at an alliance. This is why we are here. She requests we send a delegation."

Par's heart skipped another beat.

"Shall I prepare an escort?" Lord Simeon said. "Perhaps a fleet of navy ships."

"No, my friend. She's made her wishes clear. Our delegation will be brought on Enio's *Sea Dog*."

"The *Sea Dog*?" Enio said with a start. "But it's still in Arcana… isn't it?"

"It arrived last night," replied the Eminence. "They trust you, Enio—they say you've visited them once before. In fact, they suggested you captain it, if you feel up to the trip."

"You bet I do!"

Par's excitement spiked. "Me too."

"Not you, Par."

It took a moment for the Eminence's words to take root. "Not me?"

"I'm sorry. They welcome only those who can commune with the élan." The Eminence looked past them all.

The boy that had waited near the door strode forward. He passed Par, his chin still high. He stopped before the altar and made a sweeping bow. "Eminence."

Par eyed this fancy-dressed person. Even the tuck of his saffron socks was perfect.

"This is Rafael," the Eminence said, "a young but talented diplomat from Jod and the Borderlands. I, and the Majesties of Arcana, agree he can speak on behalf of both our nations."

"Excuse me," Par said, his other interests getting the best of him, "but are you sure they didn't mention me?" Lani surely would have told them he'd want to come.

"The emissary was quite specific."

"Emissary?"

"She who delivered the invitation. Lady Alehilani."

That was Lani! Par stumbled out the words. "Did she—did she ask to see me?"

"No. She and the sea stags arrived with Enio's vessel in tow. She delivered the message and left."

Did that mean she'd decided to live in the sea after all? Could she not tell him herself? Or did she not even think it worth mentioning? Par didn't know what else to say.

With a rare bit of admiration, Enio gestured to Rafael. "He can use the élan?"

Focusing forward, his words clear and precise, Rafael said, "Eminence, if I may?"

The man nodded.

Rafael turned to face Par and Enio. "Attend, good fellows." He raised his hand, palm up, before his heart. As a faint gold glory shone around his head, a flame sparked to life, floating above his palm. "My most natural ability is with lumina. However…" His glory shifted to green, and the hovering fire became a flame of emerald.

Par had known no one capable of more than one type of magic, except Enio. But if, like the Eminence said, the Deep World knew and trusted Enio already, why this new guy? Par studied Rafael, with his high dress, perfect features, and hair so shiny he could pose for a tapestry.

And Enio: messy hair, mouth hanging open, broken side teeth, a little something hanging from a nostril.

Oh.

Rafael closed his palm and snuffed the flame.

"Um," Enio began, "want to trade sigils?"

Rafael turned back to the altar. "When shall we leave, Eminence?"

"First thing tomorrow. The guards will see the others out. My council and I must attend further to these matters."

Everyone stood and bowed, though Par didn't notice who bowed to whom. He couldn't believe what had just happened. Enio and Rafael were going to the Deep World, and Par wasn't?

He was being replaced?

But Enio didn't seem to mind the upgrade: before they were escorted back to the carriage, he tried again to trade sigils with Rafael. All Par knew was that he had until tomorrow to convince the Eminence, or the Abbot, or *somebody*, to allow him to go along. Considering that this new problem with the cults of the Lower Realms was a direct consequence of his actions at the Immortus, it only made sense he should be included on this trip. Besides, who better to keep an eye on Enio?

Not to mention, he had to tell Lani the things he needed to say before her final decision.

If he could figure out just what those things were.

And if it wasn't already too late to say them.

Chapter Six

P AR COULDN'T SAY he was surprised when Enio's top priority after meeting with the Eminence wasn't food, or sleep, or even finding a tavern.

It was walking the decks of the *Sea Dog*.

The Abbot had other duties but ordered a carriage to take Par and Enio to the navy shipyards. Lord Simeon penned a warrant to allow them access.

And Enio didn't snooze once during the ride. While they traveled, Par tried to discuss the Deep World, but Enio hung out the carriage window the entire trip, focused only on seeing his boat again. As they turned along the piers, Enio was beside himself. "Where is it? Par, can you see it?"

Par sat back, arms crossed, impatient for Enio's attention to his own problems. "The only thing I see is your skinny rear."

"There!" Enio shouted.

Par pushed next to him.

Tucked away in a corner of the shipyards floated the *Sea Dog*, its sails wrapped around the spars, the bowlines tight. Par hadn't seen the boat since they'd left it in that snug little cove along the coast of Arcana, and he couldn't help but share Enio's delight.

The carriage stopped. Enio lunged out the door and ran along the pier.

A stout guard holding a pike, the tip high and sharp in the sunlight, stepped in his way. "Halt. What's your—"

In a surprising burst of energy, Enio leapt. A silver glory, or a small part of one, sparked out his ear with another sad *phut*. He crashed into the guard, who dropped his pike. Enio tumbled across the dock.

The guard drew a sword instead. "Stop right there!"

Par ran up, waving the warrant. "Permission from Lord Simeon!"

Still somewhat flustered, the guard frowned at the paper and its official seal. His sword lowered as he read.

"Oh," the guard finally said, then made a brief bow. "My apologies. But he ran into me."

Enio had already disappeared.

"It's not your fault," Par said, and started again down the pier.

"Maybe next time, show the warrant first?" the guard added.

Par would certainly try.

He reached the *Sea Dog* and scurried up the gangplank. Enio emerged from the cabin, panting and smiling.

"How's it look?" Par asked.

"Perfect. Beautiful." Enio held out his hand. The two Lustering pendants they'd stashed before entering Arcana rested in his palm. Par hadn't thought about them since. He draped his around his neck. The cool metal pendant rested over his heart. Enio donned his too.

"What was that you tried to invoke?" Par said.

"The flying sigil Vex gave me."

"Phut again?"

"I guess." He darted aft, this time up to the helm.

Par let him go—Enio deserved a moment there alone—and in the meantime scanned the shipyards. Rows of naval vessels towered over their little boat, like old oaks over a sapling.

"Hey, Par." Enio stood smiling near the ship's wheel. He jiggled the ropes he'd strung there that allowed him to operate the sail with his weaving sigil. "Want to race up the rigging?"

"Forget it. You always win."

"Yeah." Enio laughed. "Anyway, the *Sea Dog* needs a shakedown. Let's take a ride."

"Can you invoke to work the sheets?"

Enio concentrated on a rope. Nothing happened. "Not yet. You have to help."

"But—"

"It'll be fine. We'll keep near the shore."

Par had been through this drill before, and maybe Enio could use a shakedown of his own. They released the bowlines, then trimmed the sails. The dockside guards didn't object: Lord Simeon's letter was enough to let them do as they pleased. With further tugs to the lines, the sail pivoted, and they left their berth. Enio stood at the helm with his head high and his cap's feather having a silent argument with the breeze. He was back in his element.

They glided out past the shipyard buoys and along the shore. Par kept a sly eye on his friend, but he seemed up to the effort. Time for a heart-to-heart.

"Hey Enio. I need to tell Lani—"

"I know." Enio steadied the wheel, a smile all over his face. "I'll tell her for you."

"No, I need to do it in person."

"But the Eminence said—"

"He said you're the captain. The captain chooses his crew, right?"

Enio's smile shrank. "The Asrai sounded pretty clear."

"I bet she'd make an exception."

"I'll ask her."

"What if I asked her myself?"

The smile disappeared. "It's too dangerous."

Par barked a chuckle. "With you to protect me?"

His friend didn't return the humor. "You don't get it. When the stags brought me to the Deep World, the air was thick with élan. Maybe that's why they only allow people there who can commune with it. What if only they can breathe it?"

"But when they brought you, they were trying to bring me too, until you steered out of their sea tunnel."

Enio raised his chin. He still seemed proud of that maneuver, though it had almost killed them both.

Par went on. "So they must have known I'd be fine."

"They'd *planned* it. They were ready for you. This time, not the same."

"They wouldn't just let me die."

"Don't bet your life on it. They've never cared much about the upper world or its people, remember?"

"The Asrai must. She invited us."

"She didn't invite *you*."

That was true, but Par pushed on. "Lani cares. She'd help."

"She might not be there. And she's not in charge. The Asrai is."

Par couldn't believe Lani would consider living in the Deep World if they were that hostile to normal people.

"We can't risk it," Enio added.

"But—"

"No." The tone was flat and clear. That was that.

"Fine," Par grumped. No use throwing words into the wind. "Take me back."

Enio eyed him a moment longer, sighed, and nodded.

The return trip was solemn. Enio gave a few subdued commands and worked the wheel. Par managed the ropes, chewing over other arguments and options. None seemed even worth trying.

When they reached the pier, the Abbot was waiting. The new guy, Rafael, stood beside him, still in spotless cuffs and collar.

Par lowered the gangplank and strode down. He'd decided on a last appeal to the Abbot.

The Abbot spoke first. "Rafael requests a visit to the *Sea Dog*."

Rafael added, "If you don't mind, my good men."

"You'll have to ask the captain," Par said with a shrug.

"As is proper." Rafael called to the deck. "Ahoy, Master Enio. Permission to board?"

Enio was inspecting the rigging where Par had furled the sails. He turned. "Who's asking?"

"Rafael. I'd hoped to be formally introduced to this fine vessel and its captain."

"All right. Permission granted."

Rafael strode up the plank.

Par remained on the docks to secure the ties. When he'd finished his last knot, he said, "Father Abbot, I know Enio better than anyone. If his health starts to go downhill again, I'll see it early and look after him. That lets Rafael focus on his own job. Wouldn't it be better if I went along?"

"I don't disagree with you, Par, but it's not up to me. To tell you the truth, I'm concerned about Enio and Rafael alone together."

"Why?

"Rafael is young, but he's also a dignitary."

Par understood. Enio and dignitaries? Gods.

"And the Asrai's emissary," the Abbot said, "was quite specific. Only those who can commune with the élan are allowed entry."

The emissary. Par winced again. Lani. "Did she say why?"

"She did not."

"It must be an oversight."

"Enio can ask while he's there, and you can visit on the next trip. Also, don't wheedle him to allow you on board. As the captain, he's responsible for his vessel. We know nothing of the Deep World's laws and taboos—or the penalty if he were to break one so clearly stated."

Par hadn't thought of that. As his spirits began another slide, angry shouts came from the *Sea Dog*. It was Enio, waving his arms at Rafael. "Get off! Get off!"

Rafael exited onto the gangplank.

"Problem?" called the Abbot. Par had no doubt.

Spit flew with Enio's words as he yelled over the rail. "He insulted my boat!"

The young diplomat remained composed. "I did no such thing."

"You said it'd seen its share of weather. What's that supposed to mean?"

Par couldn't argue with the observation: it had been through more than storms.

"I meant no insult." Rafael stepped onto the dock. "Its wear is a testament to its faithful service."

But Enio glowered. "So it's worn out? You think I'm worn out too?"

"Pardon me," the Abbot interrupted. "Rafael, may I speak with you a moment?"

"Of course, sir." He moved to the Abbot's side.

Still Enio glared after him. "We're not all fancy and spotless. But the *Sea Dog* is solid, strong..." He trailed off and looked toward the mast.

Then he began to climb the rigging.

"Hey!" Par said. "What are you doing?"

Enio reached the first spar, stepped onto it. "See?" He tugged on the canvas and walked along a yardarm. "Like I said. Good and strong and—"

He stumbled and flailed, his balance lost.

"Enio!" Par called.

His next step missed the beam completely and he slipped, began to fall, smacked hard into the yardarm and toppled off, plummeting into the water below.

Without hesitation, Par dove in and splashed to his friend. Rafael joined him. They dragged Enio back to the pier and the Abbot helped them onto the dock. Enio was breathing, but his forehead was bleeding. He was unconscious.

The Abbot invoked a healing. The bleeding stopped, the cut healed. Enio was still out cold.

"I don't understand how he could have fallen," Par said, dripping beside his friend. Enio had built this boat. He knew every inch of the timber and always won the climbing races.

But the Abbot wasn't done. His brow furrowed. "I'm going to check him. His mind, I mean." He eyed Par.

Enio had said no more examinations. But this was too serious. Par nodded.

The Abbot's glory flared as he laid his hands on Enio's temples.

Par waited, holding his breath. He'd never see the Abbot's face in such deep concentration.

Then Enio coughed. The Abbot removed his hands, and with a groan, Enio opened his eyes. He cleared his throat. "What happened?"

"You slipped," Par said, "and fell."

"Let me up."

They gave him room.

As Enio staggered to his feet, Par reached out, but Enio found his balance. "Don't. I'm fine."

"Allow me to dry you," the Abbot said. He invoked again on Enio, and a warm glow, like their own personal sun, reached out. In a moment, Enio was dry. Soon Par was too. The Abbot turned to Rafael.

"Thank you for the offer," Rafael said, brushing his frilly shirt, already dried. "But I didn't want to wait and wrinkle."

The Abbot gave a brief smile and turned back to Enio. "Now, tell me what you remember."

Enio scowled at Rafael. "He insulted the *Sea Dog*. He's not putting another foot—"

"Rafael," the Abbot cut in, "please excuse us. We will speak later."

The young man nodded. He bowed to Enio. "I apologize for any slight to you or your fine vessel." With that, he left the pier.

Once he was gone, the Abbot said, "Enio, I meant, before you fell. What do you remember?"

"Not much." Enio rubbed his face. "Everything sort of doubled. Then it got dark."

"Son, you are not well enough to sail without Rafael's help."

"Like hells."

"You can't even invoke," Par said. "What happens to the *Sea Dog* if you pass out in a storm?" Par was, of course, mainly worried about Enio's own welfare. But this seemed the better argument.

It turned out it was, though the fire in Enio's eyes stayed hot. "I guess I've got no choice. But I'm in charge."

"Of course," the Abbot said.

"Then, well… I have things to check." He strode back up the gangplank. "Coming, Par?"

"In a minute." Par lowered his voice to the Abbot. "He'll be all right, won't he?"

"He is far from all right." The man's face was tight with concern.

Par had meant well enough for the trip. "What do you mean?"

"He has not healed, Par."

"Yeah, not completely. A little more time—"

"The problem is deeper than I or the Reckoners can clearly see."

Even the Reckoners? They saw deeper into a person than anyone.

The Abbot rested his hand on Par's shoulder. "The trauma he experienced at the Immortus has nearly rent his soul in two, down to the very roots of life. Some wounds heal naturally on their own. Some require a bandage or a splint or sigil—but there are those that resist all known treatment. I fear that may be the case with Enio."

Par hadn't imagined Enio was that bad, and it chilled him to his own soul. "Then we have to make him stay." Par would tie him down if he had to.

"Under normal circumstances, I'd agree. Yet his best hope now may come from those skilled with the élan. No, Par, we must allow him to go to the Deep World. I will explain the situation to Rafael, so he may ask the Asrai for help. Beyond that, we still face a threat from the cults of the Lower Realms, and it's important to carry out this diplomatic mission. Everything considered, we need to proceed as planned."

"What if the Asrai can't..." Par began. He didn't need to finish.

The Abbot shook his head. "I don't know. I just don't know."

CHAPTER SEVEN

ENIO INSISTED ON getting right to the job of preparing the *Sea Dog* for the journey. Though Par knew he himself would be left behind, it was good to be working alongside his friend again, organizing the hold, hoisting things, cleaning, joking around. Like old times.

Almost.

As the captain, Enio assumed the management position. Par let him, not only because it was Enio's boat, but because his friend got winded when he tried to match Par in the labor. This let Enio do the job without doing the work, which didn't trouble Par.

But the memory lapses did.

"We need apples," Enio had said.

"Someone already delivered a barrel. You helped me roll it aboard."

"Oh."

And an hour later: "We need apples."

The first couple of times, it was funny and worth joking over. They both laughed.

After that, Par stopped his kidding. And he became distracted, searching for arguments to allow him to accompany his friend to the Deep World. He kept these thoughts to himself, not wanting to spoil his time with Enio. Still, no new appeals came to mind.

At sunset, when they'd made everything sea-ready, they returned to the Mercy House. They were too tired for a meal and had snacked while they worked, so they headed to their rooms.

Par paused before Enio's door. "Well," he said, and held out his hand, "have a safe trip."

Enio grasped it. "Sorry you can't come."

"Just be careful. Say hello to Lani for me, all right?"

"I will." Enio gave a sly smile. "Anything else I should say?"

"Tell her to come see me. And I might skip seeing you off in the morning. I don't think I could stand it, and you don't like it when I get mushy."

Enio nodded.

Someone approached. It was the Abbot. "That's enough chit-chat, you two. Get some sleep."

Par squeezed Enio's hand, their eyes saying what their words hadn't. Then Enio pulled away. "We'll be back before you know it." He gave a quick grin and disappeared into his room.

"Father Abbot," Par said as they walked, "did you tell Rafael about Enio's health?"

"I will brief him tonight."

"When you do, tell him not to tell Enio he knows."

"Why not, Par?"

"Enio doesn't like people knowing his insides. If that makes sense."

"I understand. I'll ask Rafael to be discreet."

With that, they parted. Par went to his own borrowed room. Instead of going straight to bed, he pulled a small chair to the window. He sat there, reviewing the situation and his options. He even began to write a letter to Lani but crumpled it before finishing. The words weren't good enough.

The night deepened, the bright part of the moon like a full sail towing its dark hull across the stars. At some point, Par nodded off. And he dreamt of riding on that moon, high above the *Sea Dog*, following in secret.

He jerked awake. That was it!

Par would stow away. Riding along without Enio's knowledge meant the Asrai couldn't hold Enio responsible. Par wouldn't risk them both being arrested or turned back.

He hurried from his chair and listened at the door. Not a creak nor peep. He crept through the dark halls of the Mercy House. The steward was asleep. Par made it outside and headed again to the shipyards.

A different guard walked the pier, his lantern lighting a round, scarred face. When he noticed Par, he blocked the way. "Business?"

"I've got a warrant." Par handed him Lord Simeon's letter, praying it was still valid.

The man held it up to the lantern.

Par fidgeted. "Long night?"

"Same as others. This says Par and Enio."

"Only Par this time."

The guard frowned, then handed it back. "Go ahead."

With the most casual, innocent smile he could muster, Par strode past. He made it to the *Sea Dog's* berth and climbed aboard, opened the door to the hold, and slipped down the stairs into darkness. As he felt his way among the crates, a sudden light shone behind him. He spun.

A yellow flame hovered above Rafael's hand. "Par? What are you doing here?"

Par didn't know what to say. "What are *you* doing here?"

Rafael glanced at the ceiling planks. "Oh," he sighed, "I thought I'd inspect the timbers, the rigging, maybe shore up a few things. While I meant no insult to your friend, this vessel has surely seen better days."

"If Enio finds out you're messing with the *Sea Dog*, he'll hang you from those sail arms."

"The yardarms?"

"Yeah."

"Then I have a suggestion."

"What?"

"It's obvious, old scout, you're planning to hide on board." Rafael's eyes glittered in the flame's light. "So let's make a deal. You don't tell Enio of my repairs, and I won't tell him of the third guest to the Deep World. You can reveal yourself in your own time."

Hide Rafael's tampering with the *Sea Dog*? Was there a worse secret to keep from his friend?

Of course, Par wasn't one to talk, sneaking on board.

"Problem?" Rafael said.

"I hate lying to him."

"We're only delaying the truth. Diplomacy often involves finding the balance between things of unequal value."

Whatever that meant, it sounded like lying.

"In fact, Par, it's to everyone's benefit you're aboard. You can be his caretaker. Or peacemaker, if needed, between me and your captain. Otherwise, if he becomes difficult, I'll have to resort to more troublesome means."

That didn't sound good. "Like what?"

"Do you think he's receptive to bribery?"

"Not really."

"How about a blunt object?"

Par raised his eyebrows.

But Rafael gave a little laugh. "I'm joking. I'm sure Enio is a barrel of fun."

He could certainly be a barrel of something. But Rafael's words had persuaded Par. "All right. I agree."

"Fine." Rafael moved to the steps. "I like you, Par. You're a smart fellow." He doused his flame and left the hold.

Par groped in the dark for a spot to sleep. He settled between two crates, wrapped his arms around himself and pondered this new wrinkle. They weren't lying to Enio by not telling him these things before they sailed, right? And Par's sneaking onboard protected Enio from responsibility if Par was discovered. Besides, what if Enio fell ill again? Par would be the best caretaker of anyone.

As Rafael said, this was for everyone's benefit.

And breathing élan in the Deep World? It must be safe. Enio must be wrong. Lani would have warned him otherwise.

Wouldn't she?

Chapter Eight

Par had slept up on deck many times, but the hold was different. It was like sleeping in a box. Worse, because with the mooring lines tied fast to the pier, the hull didn't float easy and free. That meant whenever a strong wave hit, the boat lurched, then yanked to a sudden stop, bumping Par awake.

At last, dim morning light seeped through the door at the top of the stairs. Par breakfasted on an apple and a little of the weak wine Enio kept down here. Soon the sounds of voices and footsteps drifted through the walls.

"I still half expected to see Par," Enio said. "He wasn't even in his room."

"Well,"—that was the Abbot—"we all understand why this pains him so. Perhaps he is nearby, watching in secret."

Par smiled. Half right.

"What course do I set?" Enio asked. "Did they give us a map?"

"The emissary didn't specify direction. Only that they'd meet you once you're underway."

That must mean the sea stags would carry off the boat again.

Par determined to stay hidden until then. Enio had finished his preparations, so had no reason to inspect the hold. Once far enough along, Par would emerge. Maybe yell *surprise!*

"And Rafael," the Abbot continued, "always remember: this vessel belongs to Enio. Unlike you, the Asrai invited him by name."

"I understand, High Sigil Master. He's the captain, and until we reach our destination I'm a deck swabby."

"Very well. Safe voyage and godspeed to you both."

Ropes snapped and sails fluttered. As the vessel swayed, Par braced himself against the hull. There was still time to bolt onto deck and abandon his plan. What if people without élan really couldn't breathe? What if he'd overreacted to Lani's aloofness, and her duties as an emissary meant she was too busy to deal with him? What if Rafael was perfectly capable of helping Enio, and no one needed Par hovering around like a nursemaid?

What if he was risking the goals of this trip by coming along?

He shook his head. Like Enio had said, Par tended to over-think things. He held his place.

The voices became harder to hear through the ship's groans and the sloshing of the waves. Par crept up the steps and pressed his ear against the door.

"I tied off the—" Rafael was saying.

"I saw you. Don't expect a medal."

"I require not your encomiums, Captain Enio."

"I got no flowers, either."

"What?"

"Get your geraniums from someone else."

"I… never mind."

Par grimaced. Not a promising start.

"What's next, Captain?"

"Keep out of my way. If you want to help, watch for the sea stags."

They traveled faster as the sails caught a good wind. The minutes rolled by. They'd have left the bay by now and entered the open sea.

Rafael shouted, "Long out to port, Captain. A green flash."

"That's the stags," Enio called back.

Par readied himself for the jolt to come when the stags grabbed the hull and sped them away.

Another minute passed. No jolt.

"Why are they keeping their distance?" Rafael said.

"How should I know?" Par detected worry in Enio's tone.

"Do you have to call them?" Rafael asked.

"They wouldn't be circling if they didn't see us."

"They've stopped circling."

"I'm not blind. Hey, sea stags! Hey!"

After more shuffling boots and creaking ropes, a strange shudder passed through the floorboards, different from the last time the stags latched on.

"What's happening?" Rafael said.

"I don't know. Hold on, I'm going to tack hard."

The vessel swayed and trembled. Par held tight.

"Crap!" Enio shouted.

"What's wrong?" Rafael shouted back.

"I don't—the ropes feel different. And the rudder." Enio's tone changed to anger. "What did you do?"

"I'm just standing here."

"You did something! What did you change?"

"Well, *fixed* is the proper word."

"*Fixed?*"

"No need to get frothy. Last night, I tightened some things. They were nearly falling off."

"You… you son of a—!"

The boat heaved and pitched. Par was jerked like a doll in the *Sea Dog's* teeth, and he had to grab a post to keep from falling back down the stairs. But whether something was wrong with the sea stags or the boat, or Par needed to stop Enio from disemboweling Rafael, he couldn't stay in the hold any longer. He pushed out.

Waves crashed over the rails and the deck. Rafael grabbed a rope, either adjusting it or preventing himself from being washed away. Enio stood at the helm fighting with the wheel.

Par shouted through the sea's roar and roll, "What's happening?" Had the stags somehow detected Par, and were venting their fury? If he surrendered, would they back off? He rushed to the rail. But they kept their distance and watched.

The sail and mast leaned hard. Par held desperately onto the side. A rising wall of water rushed around the *Sea Dog*. They were sinking—into a whirlpool.

"Crap!" yelled Enio again, clinging to the wheel.

Then, all around their vessel, massive white stones broke through the waves. The stones rose higher, lifted by ridges of red and grey.

No, not stones. Enormous teeth in an enormous mouth.

"We're going down!" Par shouted. "We're going down!"

His mates shouted too as their vessel sank into that monstrous maw, into a throat, and into a slick reeking darkness.

Chapter Nine

As the *Sea Dog* dropped, the boat tilted and pitched and nearly capsized. Par still clung to the rail, Rafael beside him. Enio remained up on the helm, huddled over the wheel. The great throat, so large the boat didn't scrape the sides, gulped them down.

But their shouts of panic eased as the plummet slowed to a forward slide through a slimy tunnel. The deck leveled out. They coasted to a stop.

At Par's first deep breath, he gagged. The smell was worse than a sack of dead fish a week in the sun. And while no sun shone here, luminous veins in the fleshy roof and walls were enough to light their surroundings and the foul liquid on which they floated. Besides the gut-wrenching odor, the humid air also carried distant thrums and gurgles.

"This does not appear to be a sea stag," Rafael said.

Thankful and amazed to be in one piece, Par didn't think so either. "At least it didn't chew."

Enio frowned down from the helm. "Par? Where'd you come from?"

Regardless of their new state of affairs, Par needed to get this over with. He climbed the dripping steps to the helm. Rafael followed.

His expression dark, Enio watched.

As they arrived, and before Par uttered a word of explanation, Enio hauled back and punched Rafael across the jaw.

Rafael staggered backwards. Enio stepped forward.

Par grabbed him from behind. "Enio, stop it!"

"What did you do?" barked Enio as he struggled. "What did you do to my *Sea Dog*?"

Wiping blood off his lip, Rafael steadied himself. "It's all right, Par. I had no right to tamper with this vessel without the captain's permission. Enio, I'm sorry."

"*Captain* Enio. And I don't care a spit if you're sorry. What did you *do*?"

Rafael rubbed his jaw. "I'll show you once everything's secure. Par, let him go."

Par couldn't hold Enio forever. He released his friend.

Enio kept hot eyes on Rafael. "Show me now."

"Now?" Par asked. "When we're about to be digested?"

"This is more craw than stomach." Rafael glanced around. "And if we're to improve our situation, the captain needs to know his ship."

"Improve our situation?" Par gave up. "Sure. It's not like we're going anywhere."

But Enio said, "Yes, we are. We're traveling. Moving through the sea, fast."

It seemed to Par they were stone still. "How can you tell?"

"I feel the élan whooshing by."

Rafael gazed at the glowing veins in the high cavern roof. "Remarkable. I sense it too, like ripples behind an arrow fish."

Enio twisted out his soggy cap. "When they brought me to the Deep World before, I saw creatures just as big. I think the Asrai sent it to bring us."

"They might have warned us first," Par said, flicking slime off his arm.

Rafael now faced Enio. "Well, if you're ready, Captain, I will show you my repairs."

They began with the helm, where the wheel post descended to the rudder. Rafael said he'd used a sigil to straighten a warp in the wood. Enio said nothing.

Then they moved along the rails, to cracked capstans and frayed lines, each repaired. Also to mid-decks, where buckled floorboards had been made flat. They finished in the hold, which had appeared watertight to Par. According to Rafael, it wouldn't have remained so for long.

Enio stroked the hull with his fingers. Over his shoulder, he growled, "Ask next time." Without another word, he headed back up to the deck.

"Of course, Captain." Rafael lowered his voice to Par. "For a diplomat, I've done a pretty crappy job so far."

"You're not kidding," Par said.

"Well, we might be stuck in this creature's craw, but I trust Enio has nothing more stuck in his. I'll try to do better in the future." He followed up the steps.

Did Rafael mean he'd be more honest? Or more sneaky? Of course, considering Par had hidden in the hold, he wasn't one to judge.

Once back on deck, it was apparent that Enio's hot temper toward Rafael had somewhat cooled. Par tried to keep it that way. "This reminds me of the story where the guy gets swallowed by a giant fish."

Enio worked a rope to pull in the sail. "And turns into a frog to escape?"

Par helped. "Out of every History you got wrong in classes, that's the one that stuck?"

"Saint Jarvus the Verdant," Rafael said, also pitching in to furl the canvas. "And the gods only gave him a frog's *head,* not a body. And the story is symbolic, anyway."

People in Par's country rarely called the Histories symbolic.

But Rafael wasn't from Eloria.

"Sorry," Rafael added, seeming to catch Par's concern. "I didn't mean to question your teachings."

Par forced a smile. "Don't they believe in the gods where you're from?"

"The people of the Borderlands believe in a little of everything." He turned to Enio. "What are your orders, Captain?"

"We wait."

After a moment of awkward silence, Rafael said, "Well, I'll check forward, in case there's something worth checking. If that's acceptable, Captain?"

"Go."

Rafael seemed to have re-earned his keep. Now it was time for Par to explain his own presence. He brushed off his hands. "Enio, I couldn't let you do this on your own."

"Is that so, Mister Stowaway? I could make you walk the plank."

Par eyed his friend.

Enio gave a slight grin. "I'll let it go this time."

"Thanks. And sorry. But if me being here upsets the Deep World, now the Asrai can't blame you."

"She can blame the captain."

"You didn't know I was here. Besides, I've got a fix for that."

"What?"

"Promote me. I'll be Captain. Then it's all on me."

His friend snorted. "I'll promote you to anchor first."

Par chuckled.

But Enio's humor faded. "We still can't tell how the Deep World will affect you, Par. So just… keep breathing, all right?"

"I'll do my best." Par also did his best to hide his lingering worries over it. If breathing was a problem, hopefully they'd send him back safely.

Rafael returned. "Everything is seaworthy. You have a fine vessel, Captain."

"I should." Enio buffed a spot on the wheel. "Built it myself."

"Indeed?"

"And I sail it myself."

"So I've heard, using a weaving sigil to work the ropes. I've never considered using the élan to operate a ship's tackle. Ingenious."

Enio seemed to swell a little with pride. Maybe Rafael was a better diplomat than Par had first guessed.

They settled on the deck. Since they might be here a while, Par brought up something he'd been wondering. "Rafael, aren't you kind of young to be the diplomat for this mission?"

He laughed. "Well, they couldn't find anyone else qualified that also communed with the élan."

"You said you were from the Borderlands?"

"Yes, and someday, we hope to become a nation of our own."

Par had never considered the Borderlands a nation. Just a big unclaimed territory that sometimes shifted sides. But it did have plenty of villages and towns.

Before Par questioned him further, Rafael added, "But that will take complex treaty work, not to mention new levels of trust, between Eloria and Arcana. Despite their budding friendship, they don't yet agree on much."

He turned again to Enio. "What are your next orders, Captain?"

"We set a watch," Enio said. "I'll go first."

A rough night in the hold and then a morning being swallowed by a sea monster could really take the wind out of a person, so Par didn't argue. He sat against a rail and stifled a yawn. "Let me know when you need a break, all right?"

"Yep."

Par closed his eyes. He briefly considered discussing more of their plans, or how to explain his presence to the Asrai. But before he thought of anything else to say, he'd dozed off.

✳

After what seemed to Par a brief and unsettled nap, Enio shook him awake. "We've stopped."

They were still inside whatever had swallowed them. Rafael snacked on a handful of almonds he'd gotten from the hold. He offered some to Par. But a sudden jolt shot through the *Sea Dog* and sent the nuts flying. Then a thunderous roar filled the air.

Enio dove to the wheel. "This is it!"

Whatever *it* was, it came with a shake and a rain of slime. Par grabbed the nearest support. With a violent shudder and a rush of air, the glistening cavern walls squeezed inwards. The *Sea Dog* rose.

Up the throat they went. The smell was twice as bad as anything before, and Par struggled not to vomit as he seemed to become vomit himself. But the tunnel leveled out. Light shone ahead. They gushed out and sloshed to a stop.

Par steadied himself and took in their new surroundings. Before them, milky green waters stretched to a bright, golden shore. An army of hundreds stood upon the sand. They wore helmets and armor that looked more like shell than metal. And some there seemed not quite human, with legs and feet Par could only describe as froggy. More creatures swam between the *Sea Dog* and the shoreline. Some were sea stags. Some, Par had no idea.

"Enio," he said, "when you told me about your trip here last time, you didn't mention armies."

"Last time, I didn't see any."

Beyond the armies and beaches rose lush, forested hillsides.

The sky was silver blue and clear, but there was something wrong with it. It took Par a moment to figure out what.

The sun was missing.

"So you can breathe?" Enio said.

Par had been so taken by the scenery he'd forgotten to check. He took a good breath. "I can!" Thank the gods! Enio had warned the air was thick with the élan. While Par couldn't sense élan, a thrilling freshness brought to his mind the bright flowers of endless spring meadows.

Another roar sounded behind them. Par spun to a sight that almost made his bowels drop. A head as large as a hillside loomed behind the *Sea Dog*. Six eyes stared over a snout of tree-sized whiskers and a mouth like an open cave.

Par staggered back.

But the creature's great mouth closed, its bulbous snout lifted, and with a final spray and grunt it eased into the waters and disappeared without a ripple.

Had this been the monster of Enio's dreams? Yet it had no black fangs, nor eyes of green fire. Perhaps that part of Enio's vision had been a dream after all. Still, all Par could say was, "Good gods."

Rafael joined him. "Not gods, my fine fellow. We're in the Deep World now."

Chapter Ten

A SUDDEN HORN BLAST turned Par back to shore.

The forward ranks of the armies parted. A man and woman strode forth. The woman was tall and clad not in armor but in a white gown decorated from neck to ankle with more pearls than Par had seen in his entire life—all a curious contrast to her pale green hair. The man wore black robes that seemed tattered yet somehow elegant. His scraggly hair looked for the world like rotten seaweed.

A younger woman in a simple straw-colored gown appeared behind them. Her amber hair fell over a necklace of shells and…

It was Lani! Par almost called out, but the formality of the gathering kept him quiet. She glanced his way, and her eyes widened in surprise.

The man raised his hands and a green glory encircled his tangled hair. A pathway of water between the boat and the shore foamed, and froze.

"I believe," Rafael said, "that's for us." He laid his dagger on the deck. "Leave your weapons behind."

Par hadn't brought any. Enio withdrew a knife and set it

down without objection. Par was quite sure that was more in deference to the Deep World than to Rafael: Enio had been here before and knew the rules.

Rafael dropped the *Sea Dog's* rope ladder over the rail and they climbed down. As they trod the solid strip of sea and stepped ashore, Rafael muttered, "The sand sparkles with gold dust. No wonder they keep this place a secret."

Par doubted that was the only reason, but it was impressive.

They stopped before the three welcomers. Par opened his mouth to greet Lani, but the tall woman began to speak in a language he didn't understand. Up close, her skin had a grey-greenish tint, and her cheekbones were sharp, like the ribs of a starving dog—or a very old one.

When she'd finished, the man said, "I am Ornot, chief advisor. You stand before the Asrai, ruler of the Deep. She welcomes you."

Taking a step forward, Rafael bowed. "We are honored. I am Rafael, here to speak on behalf of Eloria, Arcana, and the Borderlands."

"You commune with the élan?" asked Ornot.

Rafael cupped his hand, palm up, before his chest. The same green flame he'd invoked when Par had first met him sparked again to life.

The Asrai spoke, this time in words Par understood. "Welcome then, Rafael. And Enio, whom we've met." She turned to Par.

Par's palms were sweating. He was his younger self all over again, unable to invoke, lying about it, hiding it. But there was no hiding it here.

Before he figured out what to say, Lani said, "Asrai, I've told you about Par. He does not commune with the élan, but his heart is gentle and true."

Par stayed silent, touched by Lani's description of him.

The Asrai frowned. "Then it is fortunate that, to demonstrate our power, we sent the Bomtog to bring you. With only the stags as escort, your companion might not have survived our barriers."

"We acknowledge your might," Rafael said, "though we had expected only the sea stags, and were uninformed regarding your barriers."

Just when Par thought they had excused his arrival, Ornot added, "Your lack of knowledge did not stop you from spurning our laws. Those who come unsummoned, and without the élan in their hearts, we cast alone into the open seas."

Par nearly choked. Lani started to object. So did Enio. Rafael remained quiet.

The Asrai raised a thin hand. "Yet we are aware of Par's deeds at the Immortus. Are there other options, Advisor Ornot?"

"Perhaps, but his actions cannot go unanswered." The man leaned in and whispered into her ear.

"You're the diplomat," Par hissed to Rafael. "Do something diplomatic."

Rafael hissed back. "I am. I'm listening."

"But—"

"Par, we have to recover their trust, and that will happen during negotiations. Besides, you see that army. We need to let this play out."

The advice wasn't heartening, but stowing away had been Par's own decision. Hopefully, the Asrai's *other options* were not as severe. So he clenched his jaw and waited.

The Asrai finished her consultation. "There will be consequences for his actions. He will not, however, be cast into the sea."

Par breathed a little relief.

"We apologize for this lapse of judgement," Rafael said, "and remain honored by your invitation. We look forward to this opportunity to build the bridges of trust and friendship between—"

"You will come with us." She motioned to the army. Many of that number invoked together. Their emerald glories merged and flowed over the beach like a low fog.

"Wings," Enio said, a smile in his voice.

As the mist rolled around Par's ankles, his feet lost their grip on the ground. Those nearby and Par himself eased off the sands and into the air. He yelped and made a grab for Enio's arm. But Enio held it away and laughed.

They rose higher. The armies reformed ranks, spreading around Par and his group in the outline of wings. Then, like a magnificent ghostly bird, together they soared from the beaches and over the trees. Before them, forests, meadows and valleys, green and purple hills, and towering mossy cliffs painted the landscape; rivers and streams sparkled as if with a light of their own; and in every direction, a bright silver horizon shone like the seconds before dawn. Yet, without a sun the dawn never came.

Enio was beside him. "Told you, didn't I?"

Par had no words. His worries dropped away with the land. He was in an entire world beneath the sea.

Someone touched his other shoulder. It was Lani.

His spirits lifted like his body. "Lani, I—"

"Are you crazy?" she whispered. "What are you doing here?"

"Glad to see me?"

"No!"

That wasn't the answer he'd hoped for.

"Par, you're in a lot of trouble. I told the Asrai she could trust a delegation. How can I explain *this*?"

"Sorry." Par sighed. "How can I fix it?"

She shook her head. "Maybe you've already done enough."

Par didn't know what else to say.

They sped through the air, but the winds were soft. Lani's face softened too. She smiled a little. "I remember when two of you were a handful. How do I manage three?"

Though Par appreciated her effort to lighten the mood, he couldn't wait any longer to ask his next question.

"Lani, did you choose yet which world you want to live in?"

She looked away. "It's… complicated."

Did that mean no, she hadn't decided? Par waited for her to explain further.

She didn't.

Before he found the courage to ask again, their group made a sudden turn. They approached a run of high cliffs, even higher than they flew. They glided along the sides. Crystal towers grew upon their heights.

Enio called from behind, "That one up there. It's part of the palace where they took me before."

But the flying army swooped them all lower. Par glanced at Lani. She stared at a wide opening in the cliff-side stretching from summit to base and creating a deep ravine. They angled into it. The walls here were thick with vines and growing things; carpets of moss replaced the trees below. Par also sensed a change in the air. It grew heavier, like a swamp in summer. At the same time, it seemed to soothe and revive. There was no doubt about the life forces, the élan, at work here. And that renewed Par's hopes for Enio's healing.

As the ravine narrowed and the sky became a thin ribbon, the flying army dropped back. But Par and the others continued, gliding lower. The natural corridor ended before a boiling, steaming lake or lagoon. The lush cliff walls wrapped around it, so that only a high patch of sky remained. It reminded Par of a pool of nectar at the bottom of some gigantic stone tulip. Apparently, even the Deep World had deeps.

The group came to rest on a lip of rock well above the roiling waters. While Par got his land-legs back, the Asrai moved to a throne of sorts, carved into the rock wall and draped in flowering vines. She sat, closed her eyes, and breathed deeply. Advisor Ornot stood at her side.

"Pure élan," Enio said, his eyes also closed in bliss.

After a few more moments, Rafael cleared his throat. "Asrai, this is a historic moment. I speak for all when I say this begins a new era of understanding between our peoples."

The Asrai opened her eyes. "Perhaps one day. But not this day."

Rafael hesitated. As always, his face remained unreadable. "Your invitation mentioned an alliance against a threat from the Dark Tribes."

"Because of your victory over the Ortu," she said, "you deserve to know that the Dark Tribes are the source of your quakes."

Par had speculated as much to the Eminence. This confirmed it.

"Why do they attack?" Rafael asked.

"They fear the new friendship between Arcana and Eloria."

"We mean them no harm. Can you contact their leaders, arrange a meeting?"

"I asked you here in secret, because I do not want it to be known that I helped you."

"Why, Asrai?"

"In a fight against them, I do not believe that you will prevail."

Again Rafael hesitated. "What is the basis of your belief?"

She gave a deep chuckle, like burbling water. "Simple odds. Three magics of the Lower Realms outnumber two of the Higher."

"With your help, Asrai, those odds would be three against three."

"The Dark Tribes do not threaten the seas, and so equal odds do not persuade me to risk the safety of the Deep World. But we did not invite you here to then turn our backs. I mentioned an alliance. There are other magics as yet uninvolved."

Vex had once explained to Par the eight sources of magic. *Three above. Three below. Two the balance, then and fro.* Besides the élan, the three above included the golden lumina of the gods, and the silvery numena of the cosmos used by Arcanans. The three below were the Ortum and other such magics used by the Dark Tribes. But the two balances were a complete mystery.

"You mean the magics of the last two Sentinels at the Immortus?" Par asked.

The Advisor pointed. "Silence, interloper."

Sorry, Par mouthed.

But the Asrai nodded.

Rafael said, "We know next to nothing about those, Asrai."

"The people of the balance call themselves the Nowen. To understand them, you must learn of the Gardens of Gê."

"We know something of Gê," Rafael said, "and its destruction millennia ago."

"What you know of its history, you've learned from myth."

"And from the Vigil. That is, from their archives. And from the surviving member, Alexander Vex."

"Scarely better than myth." Her tone bordered on dismissive.

Rafael remained undisturbed. "By any account, Gê sounded quite beautiful."

"It was. And I say this," the Asrai added, "because, millennia ago, I was there."

CHAPTER ELEVEN

Lani had once described the Asrai as ancient. Par figured that meant older than even the Abbot. But from the time of Gê? How was that possible?

Ornot explained: "We live and breathe the élan. We are its root and wellspring, the Asrai more than most. Do not wonder at such long life."

Par wondered anyway, but the Asrai continued her story. "Gê indeed was beautiful. Its people worked together to keep it so, and many became skilled with the magics of more than one realm."

"Until Ridiax burned them up," Enio said.

Par grimaced at the crude description.

Rafael cleared his throat. "What Enio means, is until the mage Ridiax inadvertently opened the Immortus rift and caused the Devastation."

But the Asrai gave a slight smile. "Enio's interpretation is valid. Unlike the élan, lumina and numena are not magics of balance. Combining them is as dangerous as it is unnatural."

"What of the other magics?" Rafael asked. "Did only lumina and numena contribute to the disaster?"

Her voice spiked with anger. "Were they not enough?"

No one replied.

But her irritation was brief. She regained her composure. "Ridiax did not employ the lower magics: his intent, after all, was to elevate himself toward the Higher Realms. When we of the élan discouraged him from his pursuits, he did not listen. This brings us to the Nowen."

Par leaned in, all ears.

"The Nowen," she went on, "were as powerful as they were secretive. They have not been seen for centuries, but their last known city was high in the mountains that you call the southern Ults. It is there I send you."

"Send us?" Rafael said.

"Yes," she replied. "To find the last of the Nowen."

Par had been told to keep his mouth shut, but it wasn't easy. They had to leave? They'd just gotten here!

Rafael remained unruffled. "And when we find them, Asrai?"

"Persuade them to join your cause. Their allegiance would sway me to join as well."

"I worry that finding a people not seen for centuries may be difficult."

She sighed. "We cannot say. They lived in a valley called Nux. Two colossal curved stones, the Horns of Nux, mark the location. Like this." She brought her bony wrists together and cupped her hands. "Our last reports of Nux are themselves ancient, yet I do not send you on a fool's errand. Are you familiar with a mineral called moon marrow?"

Rafael looked at Par and Enio. They shook their heads.

She continued, "The Nowen used it to create many of their charms, such as the Thresholds. It is black as night, with red veins."

"The Thresholds?" Rafael said. "I thought the Vigil created those."

So had Par. At least, that's what Vex had implied.

"That is true, Rafael, but in the days following the Devastation, peoples of every magic formed the Vigil, Nowen included. The Nowen's magic is that of balance, but a different balance than ours. We sense the ebb and flow of life. The Nowen are sensitive to the ebb and flow of the lesser things. The comings and goings of the world."

"Three above," Rafael began, "three below. Two the balance, then and fro."

Par could have quoted that earlier, if they'd let him speak.

"Yes," she said. "Only the Nowen knew where to mine moon marrow, or how to fashion it. If you do not locate the Nowen, find that mineral. Bring it to me. I will use it to tip the balance of your war."

"How?" Rafael asked.

"It is an amplifier."

"Of what?"

"Magic. Life. Mind and emotion. I can use the moon marrow to turn the Dark Tribe's hatred against themselves."

Two ideas struck Par that might avoid this entire Nowen undertaking. He chewed his lip for a moment but had to try. "May I?"

Ornot glared and began to say something, but the Asrai motioned her advisor to remain quiet. "Speak," she said.

"If the last Immortus Sentinels are Nowen, they might join us, or they might know where the others can be found."

"Then you propose releasing them with the sigil used to release the other six?"

"Yes."

"If I understand the nature of the Sentinels," she said, "you'd first need a Nowen to cast that sigil."

"Oh, right." Par hadn't thought of that. Each other Sentinel had required magic of its own type to release its mage.

On, then, to his second idea. "Well, the wizard Vex once used something called a Blink Stone. I think it was the same mineral as the Thresholds. Is that what you need?"

"The moon marrow must be raw. Once bound to a purpose, it cannot be reused."

That was all Par had, all useless.

She focused again on Rafael. "Before we continue, do you truly represent the outer lands in these matters? Can you accept this proposition, or must you return to your people for guidance?"

Par expected Rafael to return now to Argent and discuss the situation with the Eminence. That would leave time to ask about treatment for Enio—and for Par to speak in private with Lani.

Instead, Rafael said, "I am commissioned to make any decisions necessary. We will do as you request."

Par shot him a dark glance, not convinced this was within his authority. He'd speak to Rafael later, especially about being volunteered with no discussion.

"Very good," the Asrai said.

"However," Rafael added, "the valley of Nux sounds quite distant."

"It is."

"Shall we again travel within the Bomtog?"

Par grit his teeth. This new plan was getting worse.

She rose from her stone chair and stepped to the brink of their rocky ledge, overlooking the lake below. Par and his group joined her. Wisps of steam rose from the bubbling waters. The surface almost seemed like molten metal.

"In your language," she said, "we call this place the Mother Spring." She ran her hand through the warm, rising air, as if petting a large beast. "If you've ever encountered an uncorrupt pool of peace and healing, it may commune with a place such as this."

Her hands outstretched, she began to invoke, muttering words Par did not quite catch. The mists below swirled into fog, then thickened into a bright cloud. A large shadow formed within. Par prepared to jump back in case she was summoning another strange creature of the deep.

But as the clouds thinned, Enio identified the shadowy outline first. He pointed. "The *Sea Dog*!"

He was right. The Asrai ceased her invocation. There floated the vessel.

The next words from Enio's mouth were, "Hey, is that boiling water hurting my hull?"

"Its timber is in no danger," Ornot said, "but here, at its source, the Mother Spring is supreme over living matter. It would take the flesh from your bones."

This place of healing suddenly felt less welcoming.

"You will board your vessel," the Asrai said. "The Mother Spring will deliver you where you need to go: a high lake in the Ults. From there, you must proceed on foot. We've provisioned you for the journey."

"And how do we return?" Rafael asked.

"Alehilani will accompany you."

Lani was coming with them? The plan brightened again. Did it also mean she was choosing the land over the sea? Maybe Par didn't need to persuade her after all.

But Lani seemed as surprised as anyone. "Forgive me, Asrai, but why me? I still haven't chosen between the two worlds. Will this force my decision?"

The Asrai motioned to Ornot.

He produced a blue shell from within his robes and handed it to Lani.

"While you wear this," the Asrai said, "it will postpone, for a time, the completion of your *chela élande*. As to why you: Rafael represents his lands to the Deep World, so I send you, Alehilani, child of the élan, to represent ours. You are also still at home on the dry lands, where others of us would be strained. When you have completed your task, call to me through the waters. I will hear, and ask the Mother Spring to bring you back."

"Yes, Asrai." Lani attached the shell among the others on her necklace.

The *Sea Dog* had floated across the lake and stopped just below them, the mast nearly as high as their feet. Enio paced the edge with no obvious way to get on board. At least he hadn't thought of jumping, or if he had, he'd remembered his last slip and understood the consequences of this boiling spring if that happened again.

But one more matter needed to be settled. While Enio was distracted, Par caught Rafael's sleeve and whispered, "Tell them about Enio."

Rafael nodded. He kept his voice low. "Asrai, Enio was injured during his struggles with the Ortu. The healers of our country still worry for his recovery."

"Yes. I have noticed the balance of his élan is quite erratic."

"Can you help him?"

"Perhaps." An emerald glory sprang around her head. She approached Enio from behind. "Child."

Enio turned.

She laid a hand on his brow.

Enio froze, wide-eyed.

Par started forward, but Rafael grabbed him. "Wait."

Enio began to tremble. His mouth opened in a silent scream.

"That's enough!" Par shouted.

"Please, Asrai," Lani called. "You're hurting him,"

Enio's eyes rolled up in his head. Blood trickled from his nose.

Par broke free of Rafael. He leapt at his friend and yanked him away.

Lani hurried to their side. For a moment, Enio's expression was empty, blank, as when he'd been bedridden at the Mercy

House. But his eyes came back into focus. He glanced around, sniffed, wiped his nose, looked at the blood smeared on his hand.

Protocol be damned; Par shouted at the Asrai, "What did you do to him?"

"Not to him, for him. I glimpsed the roots of his life."

"What's going on?" Enio said.

As Par turned back to his friend, he took a steadying breath. "Enio, the Abbot was worried you hadn't healed. He asked us to ask the Asrai to help."

Without so much as a shrug, Enio wiped his hand on his pants. "I'm good enough."

Par had expected Enio to be more upset about plotting his care and treatment behind his back. But Enio didn't get mad at all. And it made Par wonder: how much did Enio already suspect the seriousness of his condition?

"Asrai," Rafael said, "what did you find?"

"His life's essence unravels. It may heal. It may not."

Enio stood straighter. "I said I'm fine."

"What can we do?" Par asked, regardless of his friend's claims.

"This is a place of healing," the Asrai replied. "He may spend as much time here as he wishes, though whether it can cure him, I cannot say. However, if you bring me the moon marrow, I will use it to increase his chances."

"Then Enio stays here," Par said.

Again Enio began to object, but Rafael cut him off. "Asrai, how long does he have left?"

Par's stomach tightened at the blunt question, one he'd been afraid to ask.

The Asrai considered. "In body, he still seems fairly fit."

"Told you." Enio bent his arm and made a muscle.

"But leaf follows root," she added. "In his final stages, his mind will fade with his memory. He'll forget who you are, who he is. Yet he will linger, until he forgets even how to breathe."

The words were a knife in Par's heart. He spoke more gently to his friend. "You're already forgetting things."

"No, I'm not."

"You forgot who Lady Agatha was."

"No, I didn't."

"See? You forgot you forgot."

"Well, I…" Enio narrowed his eyes. "Don't try to trick me. I'm fine."

"You can't even invoke."

"Is this true?" asked the Asrai.

Enio's expression darkened. He held out a hand, as Rafael had done when invoking the green flame. But not even a *phut* this time. His nose bled a little more. He stopped and wiped it.

"Whatever you decide," the Asrai said, "you should leave now. I have received reports that your quakes are worsening."

"You're staying here until you're better." Par took his friend by the arm.

Enio pulled away. "She said I'm fit enough."

"Asrai, may I speak with Enio alone?"

"You may."

Par drew him aside. "Can you stop being a stubborn ass? You need healing. This place can do it."

"I'm just getting my second wind."

Par wasn't convinced.

Enio went on, and for once he didn't deny his condition. "She said the moon marrow can help me."

"We'll find it. You don't need to come."

"You think I'm going to just sit here, hoping for the best? Like you sat in Argent, waving bye-bye to the *Sea Dog*, hoping everything would just work out?"

There was no arguing with that.

Par tried anyway. "But you can't invoke."

"Neither can you."

Damn it. "Well," Par said, "then we both stay."

Enio raised his eyebrows. "Do you really want that fancy-pants Rafael handling this alone? I mean, just him and Lani?"

That pretty much clinched Enio's case.

"I don't like it," Par said, but saw no other arguments. "Fine. But I won't let you push yourself. Don't do anything crazy."

"Come on, Par. You know me."

"That's what I mean." Par turned again to the others. "All right. We're both going."

"No." Ornot frowned at Par. "Not you."

"What?"

"You came unbidden and unworthy, and are to be imprisoned."

As one, Par's companions objected, even Lani.

"Silence!" barked the Asrai, more strongly and loudly than Par had thought she could.

They stopped speaking.

She continued in her aged voice. "That is our law, and still less cruel than being cast into the sea. Complete your mission, and your reward will include this person's forgiveness and release."

"He'll be safe while we're gone?" Rafael asked.

"I will see to it," Ornot stated flatly.

"And my advisor, " said the Asrai, "is as strict with his word as he is with our laws. He will not allow Par to come to harm."

Despite the promise, Par's heart didn't much lighten. Again, like in Argent, everyone seemed determined to hold him back. To snatch away his hopes.

Lani gripped his arm. "Don't worry, Par, we won't abandon you."

He forced a smile and laid his hand on hers. "Good to hear. I'll miss you, anyway."

Enio nudged him. "What am I, chopped liver?"

Par grinned for real this time and nudged him back. "Yeah, you too."

"Asrai," Rafael said. "On behalf of the outer lands, and in cooperation with the Deep World, we are ready to begin this mission."

"Stand aside," Ornot directed Par.

Reluctantly, he did.

The Asrai invoked again. Vines along the walls reached out, toward each crew member—except Par. The greenery gently wrapped Lani, Enio, and Rafael as if in leafy cradles, and lifted them.

Enio waved as he rose. "I'll watch out for her."

"And who will watch out for you?" Par said.

Lani laughed. "Me. Who do you think?"

The vines lowered them to the deck of the *Sea Dog* and withdrew. But as Enio ran to the helm, the finality of what was happening hit Par. Everything was moving too fast. Did this plan really make sense? Though the Mother Spring might heal Enio, he was leaving its domain. Rafael had agreed to the Asrai's mission without consulting the Eminence. If Lani wound up staying on land, what then? How long would Par be imprisoned here, in the sea?

The Asrai now turned to the lake, invoking as she had when she'd summoned the *Sea Dog*. The waters below boiled with new fury. The swirling vapors licked up the hull. Lani stood close by the rail, Rafael beside her.

A worse thought struck Par: Whatever had made him stow away—worry, jealousy, selfishness—his friends were committing themselves to this task in part so that the Asrai would release him. If he knew Enio and Lani, they wouldn't return until they'd succeeded. And here he'd sit, safe and sound, while Enio got sicker, and Lani risked her future.

Was there nothing more he could do?

The mists rose higher, weaving like ghostly fingers into the rigging. Then, beyond the *Sea Dog* and somehow within the thickening clouds, images formed. First the sun appeared, the very thing missing from the Deep World. Its light shone down upon wintery hillsides surrounding a blue, glassy lake. That very light crept upon the *Sea Dog*, and as it did, the boat seemed, even without moving, to become more there than here. In another moment, when the Asrai finished her invocation, Par would be alone. He could still see Enio before the helm. And Lani and Rafael, together at the rail.

Par frowned. He'd never had time to really talk to her. He called out, "Lani!"

She didn't seem to hear. What if this was the last time he saw either of his friends?

His thoughts roiled like the mists. Finding the moon marrow was as much his mission as anyone's. Or even better, finding the Nowen. That would solve everything.

He turned his eyes to the mast and rigging. He'd often raced Enio up that very web of ropes. Enio had always won, but Par had never fallen; he'd proven he was no feeble there. Yet the boiling lake was deadly. Could he make the jump?

He couldn't decide. He couldn't move.

Then Rafael took Lani's hand.

Par's indecision broke. With a quick dodge around Ornot, Par leapt from the ledge. "Wait!"

"Stop!" shouted Ornot.

For an instant, Par felt something tug him back. But the force slipped, and he plummeted into mist and cloud, falling toward the netted rigging.

At least, he should have been. The new lands disappeared—along with the *Sea Dog*. Below him was only swirling vapor. And beyond that, spitting, steaming, molten green waters.

And then he hit.

Chapter Twelve

As Par hit the waters, he shouted and flailed, expecting that seething, boiling lake to burn and burn.

But no burning came. The clouds began to thin, and he stopped thrashing. He was up to his chest in comfortably warm water. Just within arm's reach, dull, rocky walls arched low over his head and stretched into a tunnel.

This wasn't the sunny blue lake he'd seen beyond the *Sea Dog*. But it also wasn't the Mother Spring. He'd never even gone underwater.

So where was he?

"Hello?" he tried. His voice echoed. There was a slight glow to the fading fog. As the vapors vanished completely, so did the light.

In full darkness now, he found the nearest wall, and paused there to catch his breath. "Hello?" he tried again. Same echo. Staying against the rock, he began down the pitch-black tunnel. He took a sip of the water and spit it out: not salty, but foul, like rotten eggs. And the air was thick, wet and warm, a bit like the Deep World, but stifling, almost suffocating. If he passed out, would anyone find him? The urgency to locate an exit spurred him to go faster.

The minutes passed. He felt a rough opening in the wall, like a narrow side corridor. He considered taking it, but it would be against a current, so he kept with the easier, wider way. Same with each new passage, and always wondering if he followed a way out or merely travelled a great loop. More minutes passed. Once, his feet lost the bottom and he dunked. He again found the stone wall, recovered his breath, and pushed unsteadily on in darkness.

More side passages. The current strengthened. So did his thirst, and his need for fresh air. He licked his lips, wiped his face—for all the good it did—and continued.

The rock beneath his feet sloped downward and he began to slide. He grabbed an outcrop and yanked himself to a stop. What if this passage dropped to some deep, godsforsaken cavern? How could he know? His plan to escape the Asrai and join his friends now seemed the worst decision of his life.

Or at least of the week.

Backtracking was impossible against this underground river, so he kept on, but the trek was slowly wearing him out. Fearful of being washed away, he found another handhold and hung on, dizzy, hot, and confused. "Hello!" he gasped into the blackness. "Help me!"

Only more echoes.

"Help—" He swallowed a splash of water. He coughed and gagged.

And fell away from the wall.

He was swept down the tunnel, slapping blindly for a hold. The slope steepened. He slid faster.

Turns and bumps. He dared not open his mouth to shout as the fast current carried him to his fate. A sudden bang against a corner knocked the wind from his lungs. He fought to keep his nose above the surface. For a moment, he thought he was passing out: mist swirled before his eyes.

But not mist. Dim light! The tunnel was brightening. Spray sparkled ahead.

Before he had time to rejoice, he tumbled through an opening. He was airborne.

Par shouted, caught a brief glimpse of trees and then plunged again into water. He went under without taking a breath. With his remaining strength, he clawed back to the surface and broke through with a panicked gasp.

Panting but unharmed, he floated there, catching his breath. Nearby splashed a waterfall, the one that had spit him from a cliff side. Dense trees and fat-leafed bushes surrounded his small, scummy green lake. Sharp caws and chitters filled the canopy. And in a clear blue sky shone the sun: wherever the Mother Spring had transported him, he was no longer in the Deep World.

He made his way through slithery weeds toward the nearest bank. After a last crawl onto a pebbled shore, he collapsed.

The birds continued their caws or curses. The air was filled with a mix of sweetness and rot and musk. As strength seeped back into his body, Par rolled over to get a drink. But the green waters seemed too green to risk. So he pulled himself to his feet. The lake must drain from here, and maybe would be cleaner down the line. And he needed to figure out where he was.

Brushing off scum and sand, he stumbled along the shore. He found an outflowing creek and followed it, pushing through underbrush and gigantic leaves, some as big as a blanket. His head bumped into a drooping stem. The frond turned out to be covered with tiny colorful frogs. They chirped in annoyed unison and leapt, some bouncing off him. He waved his arms and yelped, but they hopped away, seeming to care as little for his company as he did for theirs.

As he walked on, a spot on his hand where a frog had hit began to itch.

Not much he could do about it except scratch. He followed the creek deeper into the trees. The jungle here was so thick he couldn't see beyond ten paces. He'd expected the sounds from his waterfall to decrease. But they didn't. Through the branches, he caught sight of the long cliff where he'd come out, and other falling streams along the same edifice. But it seemed best to keep heading away from them. Otherwise, who knew how long he'd wander in these trees.

Of course, who knew either way?

The skin on his hand turned from itching to burning. He rubbed it.

Then somewhere ahead, *crash!*

Par froze.

Shouts followed, and laughter.

"You're crazy, Jake!"

"But I told ya."

"How'd you know?"

"Smelled the conks."

"You're better than a rum dog."

Par squeezed his wrist as the burning spread. But he crept closer.

Through the trees, he saw three large, burly men. One held an axe.

Another examined a fallen tree. "Yep, she was a rotter."

"Like my last wife."

"The rotters always fall for Jake." Everyone laughed again.

One said, "Good job, fellas. One less snag to worry about. We got our haul, so I'm callin' it."

"Drinks on you, Jont?"

"Drinks on me."

Par stumbled forward. "Wait!" Fire shot up his arm.

They turned.

"I'm lost," Par winced. He leaned against a tree, dizzy and sick.

"You all right, son?" someone said.

But Par slumped to the ground, collapsed face-first into the musky forest floor, and sank into a deep, empty darkness.

PART TWO

LOST AND FOUND

CHAPTER THIRTEEN

AS THE MISTS around the *Sea Dog* thickened, the sounds faded away. Enio could still see Par, wide-eyed, watching from the ledge.

And just as the clouds became a solid wall of white, Par jumped.

Enio shouted, but his words came out muffled. He stumbled forward to catch his friend. Par should be right there.

Nothing.

A cold breeze parted the mists. Enio ran toward the rails. The last of the vapors dissolved.

The *Sea Dog* floated on a lake very different from the Mother Spring. They were outside, on crystal waters under a sunny sky. Rocky hills, raw with frost, rose around the shores.

Shielding his eyes, Enio searched the lake. "Par!" His voice carried now, echoing from the hillsides. Steam puffed from his mouth and his lips tingled in the chilly air.

Lani joined him. "We've left the Deep World."

"I know but—Par jumped."

Rafael was there too. "Not that I saw. Are you sure?"

"I saw what I saw," Enio said. But then again, everything had been a blur. "Or I think I did."

"If so," Rafael's said with his usual confidence, "the fact that he's not with us means they stopped him with another vine or something."

"But—"

"But," Rafael went on, "on the outside chance you're right and he missed us, the people of the élan are superb healers." He studied their surroundings. "We can help him best by focusing on the task at hand."

The guy must be a hard nut to dismiss the agony of boiling water on flesh—whether or not it was healable. Enio just hoped that, as Rafael said, Par had been yanked back.

Rafael turned to Lani. "My lady, I assure you, Par is fine. My present concern is that we were never formally introduced. I am Rafael, diplomatic envoy from Jod, representing Eloria and Arcana."

She nodded once to Enio, as if to convince him, and herself, that Par was safe and sound. Then she spoke to Rafael. "I'm Lani, representative, apparently, of the Deep World."

"I am honored, and I am charmed." He lifted her hand and pressed his lips to her knuckles.

Enio rolled his eyes, but something along the shore caught his attention. He pointed. "There's a pier."

"That crumbling ruin?" Rafael said. "Doesn't look like much, but I see no better option. Can you take us there, Captain Enio?"

"Sure. Unfurl the sails."

Instead, Rafael approached an open crate near the cabin. "These looks like the provisions the Asrai mentioned. Let's wrap up first. You especially, Enio."

"Why me especially?"

"You're, as they say, thin as a grin. That's dangerous in this climate."

"I'm not afraid of a little cold." He sniffed and wiped his runny nose, clear now of any blood.

They gathered around and Rafael handed out clothing. There were boots and gloves and furs. The hood bent the feather on Enio's cap, but he tucked it under as best he could.

Once they were snug in their new garments, they positioned the sails and drifted to the pier. It was indeed a ruin, but enough foundation remained for Enio to tie to the surviving moorings. Nearby, a thin, half-frozen creek trickled down the frosty hillside. Broken stone steps bordered its banks.

Enio returned to lower the sails. Rafael had laid out packs. When Enio had made sure the *Sea Dog* was secure, he examined a few short pointed poles Rafael had found. "Spears?"

"No," Rafael said with a chuckle. "Those are hiking poles. But speaking of weapons, the ones we left behind are here." He passed Enio back his dagger. Enio tucked it in his belt.

Lani stood gazing at the lake, rubbing the blue shell on her necklace.

"Anything wrong?" Rafael asked her.

"Just the opposite," she said. "The Asrai was right about this charm. It's holding back my *chela élande.*"

"I chose not to ask during the meeting, but what is a *chela élande?*"

Enio paused from trying to heft on a pack. "Fancy-pants doesn't know? Well, let me explain: when nymphs reach a certain age, they get bound to a place. Like a lake nymph. But not the men. They take on new forms instead. Like sea stags."

"Well done," Lani said.

Enio resumed his struggles.

"But because I'm half-nymph," she added, "it seems I may have more of a choice, as long as I don't wait too long to decide."

"Quite fascinating," Rafael said.

Enio made it to his knees, then tipped over.

Rafael reached to help.

"I can do it." Enio grunted himself up.

"Everyone ready?" Rafael asked, watching Enio. "Good. Let's start with those stone steps."

Poles in hand, they left the *Sea Dog* and began to climb the hillside. The steps became too broken and buried to be usable, but the ground alongside was frozen, and it crunched securely under their boots. Enio soon found himself breathing hard. At first, Lani and Rafael outpaced him. After a few glances back, they adjusted their tempo, and the group stayed together.

At last they crested the hill, and the view that opened before them almost made Enio forget the tough climb. Blue-shadowed valleys stretched among white, majestic mountains. Thin clouds drifted like ships of cotton between the stark peaks and ridges. Enio had never been in the Ults. The distances were impossible to judge.

"No trees," Rafael said. "We're higher than I expected." He invoked with a golden glory, narrowed his eyes and peered out over the sweeping landscape. "Ah. See where that shelf slopes toward a high cleft? Near the top there's a rock formation like the one the Asrai described."

Enio could barely make out a shelf, much less a rock formation. Rafael must be using Long Eye, another sigil Enio had always wanted. But best not to spend energy trading any now. Through his panting he managed to say, "The Asrai's crazy if she expects us to climb mountains."

"It's not a mountain," Rafael said. "It's a shelf. If we pace ourselves and don't go much higher than that, we'll be fine. We'll aim for that valley," he pointed at a blurry scar of shadow near a run of hills, "and head up from there."

"And if *you* think that's going to be easy," Enio said, finally catching his breath, "you're off your rudder."

"It's true we won't know the difficulty until we get closer. As they say in Choga: lift the lid to smell the soup."

Enio leaned toward Lani. "You know what else they say? Don't catch what monkeys throw."

She chuckled. "Shh."

Rafael smiled at her. "I've traveled mountains before. They're unpredictable, never to be taken for granted. But they can also be quite… lovely."

"Lovely?" Enio gestured to the expanse. "It's dead and barren, so I bet the élan is weak. Lani, if there's not enough for your sigils, maybe you should stay with the *Sea Dog*?"

But she shook her head. "There's always life, and where there's life, there's élan. And don't think I'm letting you two go off without me. The Asrai sent me for a reason."

"Point taken," Rafael said and turned to Enio. "But perhaps you are right that someone should stay behind."

Lani immediately took Rafael's side. "It's your boat, Enio. And it's important. We'll need it to return."

Did they think Enio wasn't up for this? He stood straighter. "The *Sea Dog* can take care of itself. So can I." And there was no way in the purple hells he'd leave her alone with this guy. He'd promised Par to watch out for her.

"Very well." Rafael started off along the hill's crest. "Onward, then. Forthwith and posthaste. We are not a glacier."

The brief halt had given Enio time to recover from the climb. He lowered his voice to Lani. "Should he be in front?"

"Why not?"

"He seems, I don't know—city soft."

"Then let's find him one."

"A what?"

"A city. The Nowen's."

Enio doubted anything in this wintery wasteland would be that easy.

They continued along the top of the hill through shallow, crispy, untouched snow. It was almost pleasant for a time, with the sunny blue sky and brisk, fresh air. Then a sudden gust hit. Enio couldn't even yell out. It was as if the frigid wind had claws. He scowled, pulled his hood tighter, and pushed on. No one else complained, so neither did he.

After at least another grueling hour, the crest ended in a lengthy slope toward lower ridges and hills. Rafael led them down. They traveled in careful slants, this way, then that. Enio now found good use for the poles—several times, they saved him from a tumble.

Finally, at the bottom of a long run of ice and rock, Rafael stopped beside a house-sized boulder. Enio's lungs were raw, and the shadows here blocked the slight comfort of sunshine. Despite his thick coverings, Enio shivered, even inside his stomach.

"Well, that's one hill behind us," Rafael said. "Next, we'll head into that ravine."

As far as Enio could tell, they seemed no closer to the valley Rafael had earlier pointed out. "Isn't it getting late?" Enio asked. His exhales steamed thicker than before, but he was careful to keep his voice strong. "Maybe we should stop here."

He felt their eyes studying him. His didn't meet them. "I think it's going to snow," he added after a glance skyward. In fact, he had no idea. But his legs had begun to tremble during their descent, and not from the cold.

Rafael looked about. "The clouds seem wispy rather than snow-heavy, and the day is still young. With a little alacrity, I bet we can reach the shelf's base before dark. Besides, we might find better shelter on the way."

"Are you sure, Rafael?" Lani said, eyeing Enio. "Aren't we getting near our limit?"

Their words puffed in little clouds, but no one was breathing as hard as Enio.

Rafael nodded. "Oh, of course. Out of wind, Enio?"

"I'm full of wind. I'm worried about the weather, that's all.

If we get buried in a snowdrift, it's his fault." He motioned with his chin at Rafael.

"Fair enough." Rafael paused. He pulled out his dagger. "We'll keep going, but I think I'll mark our route, in case we need a little help to get back." He scratched an arrow in the side of the boulder.

Enio didn't think this simple route required any help, but he let Rafael have his fun, if it meant another few minutes of relief.

"Enio," Lani said, "are you sure you're all right? If you need to stop a while—"

"Me? Nope."

"None of us are used to these conditions. Don't be embarrassed if you need a break."

But he forced a grin. "I don't get embarrassed."

She gave a little laugh. "That's my Enio. All right, then, let's go."

Once they'd started off again, his smile disappeared. He gritted his teeth and followed.

The going turned from simply awful to painfully awful. To distract himself, Enio focused on happy memories. But that strategy backfired. Sometimes a bright memory drained of its color, then of movement, then slipped into darkness. Once that happened, it wouldn't come back, the way a dream gets harder to remember until it's lost completely. A quiet panic took root. Was he freezing to death? Or was he losing his mind, as the Asrai had warned?

Of the options, he preferred the first, since losing his mind was terrifying. Maybe too much remembering made it worse. So he fell into the endless, numbing rhythm of placing one foot after another after another. Walking and walking and not thinking. Just walking.

Chapter Fourteen

Enio trailed behind Lani and Rafael in an endless bitter slog. They hiked a frozen black ravine, then a snow-caked valley, then a field of icy boulders, on and on. But Rafael's directions turned out to be correct. Late in the long day, they reached the base of the shelf. It angled up the mountain like a road, one side against the steep, rocky slope, the other often slanting toward the drop-off. Keeping near the safety of the wall, they started up, their boots kicking through low powdery snow. At least it wasn't icy and slippery. At least not yet.

The temperature plummeted when the sun disappeared. Enio's entire face went numb; his feet throbbed with each step; his pace slowed everyone, and he knew it. But he pushed on, determined not to turn back and ruin their mission. Yet finally he had to stop.

Lani and Rafael gathered around him.

"It's too… dangerous." Enio gasped. "We have to wait for dawn."

"There's at least an hour until total darkness," Rafael said, looking around. "And this isn't a suitable campsite. I can make light and—"

"Rafael," Lani said, "Enio's right."

Rafael glanced at her, at Enio, and nodded. "Yes, well, I suppose we might cram ourselves into some crack in the rocks."

Enio couldn't deny the truth: they were stopping because of him.

They searched along the ice-crusted stone wall and found a sort of deep depression.

"This will have to do," Rafael said. As he made another arrow on the rock, Enio sat against the back, gradually steading his breathing.

Lani dropped beside him. "I'm exhausted. You too?"

"Just about."

"Do you need anything?"

Even Enio's thoughts were almost too cold to flow. "Got a sigil to dig us a cave?"

"There's an idea." She eyed the upper lip of their dent. "Or freeze down the snow into another wall."

That sounded good too.

Rafael was gathering small stones into a pile. "That might destabilize something. We'd better not."

"I suppose you're right," Lani said.

Enio sighed.

"But," Rafael added, "we can take the chill off." He invoked with the emerald glory of the élan. The stone pile glowed red.

"Stonefire?" Lani said. "I'm impressed, Rafael."

"Well, it's rather basic, from what I understand of nymph sigils."

"Still, few humans can manage it."

"I could," Enio said, more himself with the blooming heat. "If I had that sigil."

Lani warmed her hands over the stones. "That's a good point. And if we get separated, you might need it."

"But he can't use his sigils," Rafael said casually.

Enio started. "What? Of course I can. It's Par who can't. People call him a feeble, and he says some hate him and—"

"Remember?" Lani touched his hand. "Back with the Asrai, when you tried?"

He shook his head and tried to invoke the flame sigil.

Nothing.

"Don't worry," she added. "We're tired." But her eyes were full of concern.

"I'm just cold," he said and shrugged. But he'd never had trouble before.

Wait. Yes, he had. Their meeting with the Asrai returned clear and sharp. At least his more current memories weren't disappearing as fast as the older ones. That must be good, right?

They rummaged through their packs and found edibles. Lani identified the odd vegetables and sea fruits from the Deep World, noting which benefitted from heating. Enio just wanted to sleep, but she made him try a few bites. It was tasty, warming, and soon he was eating like a wolf. Rafael said something snarky about manners, but Enio ignored him.

It was dark once they'd had their fill. Rafael began to stack their packs before them to create more shelter.

"Hold up." Enio stood, somewhat restored after the meal. "I have to go and… you know… before it's so cold I can't."

Rafael paused his task. "You shouldn't go alone."

"I've been going alone my whole life."

"There might be danger. Bears, even."

Enio huffed.

"And if you slipped," Lani said, "we'd never find you."

"I won't—"

"You know," Rafael cut him off, "I need a moment myself. We'll be right back, Lani."

There didn't seem any way to stop the guy, so Enio headed out. They followed their old tracks several steps down the shelf. Rafael found a bare spot against the rock wall. Enio turned away and kept his distance.

"You shouldn't do that over there," Rafael said. "Find a rocky spot and—"

"Shut up, already."

"But it's easier. You can lean on the wall. Besides, if you stumble, or if anything melts or slips or—"

"Don't tell me how to pee."

"I'm only saying—"

"For Oä's sake, you never *stop* saying."

They were silent after that. Rafael finished. "Well, I'll give you some privacy. Call if you need help." He headed back toward camp.

If the bears didn't get Rafael, Enio might strangle him with his own hands.

When he'd also finished, he remained there a few moments. On top of everything, now he had a headache. Since he couldn't invoke, he couldn't soothe it like a normal person, but he resolved not to whine and worry everyone. Besides, he had another friend who couldn't invoke. Enio never heard him complaining about headaches. Was this how his friend, what's his name, dealt with things like that?

Enio had to admit, it wasn't any fun.

He shivered and turned to camp. As he approached, whispers made him stop. He listened.

"I was afraid it would come to this," Rafael said. "He has to go back. I left him arrows."

That was why Rafael had been making those damn scratches?

"He might not make it alone," Lani replied. "And anyway, he won't leave us."

"I suppose you're right. But he shouldn't have come. He's feeble."

Enio waited a moment for Lani to defend him.

Silence.

He peered beyond the shelf and across the dark valley. In the gloom, the distant hills took on an eerie cast, like enormous, crouching beasts. By all rights, he should go back.

Who was he kidding? He'd never make it.

He took a deep breath and shuffled to the glowing rocks.

Lani looked up. "No bears, then?"

"Nothing to worry about," Enio said, probably his biggest lie of the day. He could no longer fully trust his mind. If they didn't get to where they were going soon, would they have to turn back because of him? He rubbed his face. Damn this cold anyway.

But he knew their biggest risk, their biggest danger, wasn't the cold or bears or quakes or mountains.

It was him.

Chapter Fifteen

Even near the warmth of the glowing rocks, Enio barely slept. His companions had no trouble.

At first light, before anyone else woke, he decided to go outside again. Though his legs were a sackful of cramps, he stretched as best he could, eased himself to his feet and slipped around the packs and poles. At least the wind hadn't started yet. He kept away from the drop-off, stepping to the bare spot Rafael had recommended.

That guy was right. It was easier.

When Enio finished, he turned back, but lost his footing and stumbled against the wall.

Something above him gave a loud crack. A few small clumps of snow tumbled onto his head.

He shook it off, scanned the cliffside a moment, and shuffled back to the others. Rafael was watching him through half-closed lids. Lani still slept.

As Enio edged around the packs, an even louder crack broke the morning peace, then faded into silence.

But the others were now wide awake. Rafael eyed him. "What did you do?"

"Nothing!" Enio hesitated. "Well, outside, I slipped and bumped—"

CRACK!

Rafael leapt up, grabbed him, and pulled him against the back wall. The sound of rumbling grew until thunder shook the mountain. Sheets of snow rolled down before them.

They huddled together until the white deluge slowed and stopped. A waist-high mound of snow blocked them in.

Rafael crawled forward. "We have to get out of here, fast."

"Our packs," Lani said. "They're buried."

Side by side, everyone dug. They found two poles and one pack: the rest had been swept away. Piles of uneven snow covered the way they'd come. Occasional clods still dribbled from above.

"This is insane," Enio said. "We can't do this."

Their young diplomat was undaunted. "Yes, we can. The trail higher was spared the worst."

"But—"

Lani chimed in. "He's right, Enio. We have to keep going."

Up looked as dangerous as down. Enio supposed, in that sense, it didn't matter which way they went.

"I'll carry this." Rafael hefted the surviving pack. "You two use the poles."

"I don't need a pole," Enio protested.

"I think you do. It helps with balance and the consequences of... missteps."

Enio sighed but took one.

"Rafael," Lani said, "if you're carrying the pack, you need a pole more than me."

"No, I—"

"Nymph, remember? Nature girl and all that. I'll be fine."

"You sure?"

"I'm sure."

"Perhaps to get started, then. Thank you." He unstrapped a coil of rope from his pack. "Let's tether ourselves together. Just in case."

They did, with Enio at the back. He didn't wonder at his position until they were underway. But had they put him there to more easily pull him along? Or catch him if he slipped?

Maybe so he wouldn't wander off like a witless child.

He felt smaller than ever.

It didn't help matters when Rafael called back, "Can we pick up the pace? The less we're on this incline, the better."

Enio tried. The snow now reached his knees. Though it was powdery and not difficult to push through, his legs were stiff, and even with the pole he sometimes stumbled. The others were much more sure-footed.

When at last they paused for a rest, his heart was racing and his lungs ached.

Lani eyed him. "You don't look well," she said. "Here, let me give you a little healing."

Enio was too exhausted to object. She used her élan. A blissful warmth flowed through his chest. She used it a second time, and it reached down his legs. But a person can harness only so much sigil magic each day. What if Lani needed some for herself?

Before she gave him a third, he raised a hand and forced a smile. "Thanks, but that's enough. I feel much better."

She started to say something, but Rafael spoke instead. "We're near the halfway point."

"How can you tell?" Enio asked, turning from Lani.

"When I first saw the shelf," Rafael said, "I remember it steepened there, like it's doing now."

Shortly after they resumed their march, the sky clouded over and the wind picked up. Snow fell on the other side of the valley, the hills shredding the clouds like tattered sails. Thankfully, it wasn't snowing here yet. But Enio's legs became heavier and heavier.

More endless walking and stumbling. More rests. Then, after beginning again, Enio's legs simply stopped working. He fell face-first into the snow.

The rope pulled the others to a stop. They turned.

"I'm giving you another healing," Lani said.

Enio didn't argue. He didn't even meet her eyes.

As she touched him, warmth ran through his body. He tried to stand and slumped back down. His weakness was going to kill them all. They were right: he should not have come.

"Let me," Rafael said.

Enio sat still and let him.

Rafael used the golden glory of lumina. When he finished, Enio could get up. But before they started off, he said to them, "Look, you need to get to the top before the weather gets worse, and I'm just an anchor. I can go back to the *Sea Dog*. It'll be easy. It's mostly downhill."

"Not alone," Lani said.

"But I—"

"We stay together." Rafael glanced around. "Give us your best effort, old wart."

Any progress after that was agony. In the afternoon, thin snow began to fall. They pushed on. Enio had always heard of the Lower Realms being dark and sometimes fiery. But he couldn't imagine a worse hellscape than this.

Late in the day, when Enio's need for rest seemed constant, Rafael pointed out a crack in the rock wall. "I doubt we'll find better."

They approached. Rafael leaned in farther. "It's big enough. We've still got daylight, but I imagine this is as far as we'll make it today."

"I think you're right," Lani said.

Again Enio knew they'd only stopped now because of him. His shame grew. He remained silent.

The cave roof hung low; they had to bend. But it was better than a dent, and anywhere to sit was enough for him. He slumped against a wall.

Rafael slipped off his pack. As he dug through it, Lani examined their little dwelling. "Nothing's lived here for a while." She gathered scattered rocks, stacked them in a pile, and set them glowing red with stonefire.

Then she eyed Enio. "What about another healing?"

But he shook his head. "The heat is plenty."

Besides, he'd caused the loss of packs, poles, and nearly their lives. He was already burden enough.

Since he didn't seem to be needed for anything, he pulled off his gloves and held his throbbing fingers close to the hot stones, but not so close that they hurt worse. He kept any pain off his face.

Rafael laid a bundle nearby. "We've still got food, so there's that. Let's get comfortable." He spread his fur cloak on the ground. Lani did the same.

Though their cave had already warmed nicely, removing any wrappings didn't appeal to Enio, but he didn't want to seem weaker than he already was. So with cramping hands he shed his fur, laid it out, and eased once more against the wall.

Lani untied the food bundle and picked out some finger-like green potatoes. "I'll heat these."

Enio mainly looked forward to the oblivion of sleep. He closed his eyes.

"Been a hard day," Rafael said. "While those are heating, why don't I lighten the mood?"

Enio opened an eye. Rafael settled beside Lani, cleared his throat and, in a soft but lively voice, began to sing.

> *Old Captain Chum, with a will nigh unbendable,*
> *Consistently sailed with a wonderful chemical.*
> *Rum, he said, was highly medicinal,*
> *A cure for diseases imagined and physical.*

Enio sighed. So much for sleep.

> *Oh how incredible, oh how commendable.*
> *His crew praised their captain as smart and dependable.*
> *But his barrels of rum he kept locked, inaccessible.*
> *Too costly, said Chum, for a casual festival.*

Lani grinned ear to ear. Enio had to admit, the tune wasn't bad. And he wouldn't mind a mug of rum one bit. But did Rafael have to show off with all the big words?

Apparently, he did. He continued, more dramatically.

> *But one fateful night, with the moon full and sensual,*
> *Old Chum went to seek out a midnight digestible.*
> *Skipping the grub, he thought rum the more preferable.*
> *A flagon—or three—would indeed be delectable.*

> *Neglecting discretion, he drank 'til insensible,*
> *And more tragic still, this man none judged expendable,*
> *His perch on the barrel now no longer tenable,*
> *Slipped he and drowned, a death most regrettable.*

Lani made a comical gasp. Enio wrinkled his nose.

> *Oh how lamentable, oh how fermentable.*
> *The crew mourned his death in a way most respectable.*
> *Yet each carried on with a heart irrepressible.*
> *Yes, their captain was gone...*
> *...but the rum was impeccable.*

Rafael bowed where he sat. "Thank you."

Lani laughed and prodded Enio. "A diplomat, a child of the élan, and a musician. Is there anything he can't do?"

"Maybe shut up?" Enio murmured. Fell in the rum? Disgusting. But the singing had been flawless, like everything fancy-pants did.

"Sorry, old wart," Rafael said. "But I was first tenor in the lamasery."

Enio opened his other eye. "In the what?"

"It's like an abbey. It's where I was raised."

"You grew up with llamas?"

"No, it's... Never mind."

The llamas sounded like the best part, so Enio frowned.

"Where was this?" Lani asked.

"The Borderlands."

"I've been there," Enio tossed in, trying to show he had something to contribute. "I've been all over."

"Really?" Rafael said. "What did you think of Jod?"

"Well, not to Jod..."

Lani handed Enio a leaf-wrapped potato. "Let it cool." Then one to Rafael. "Jod is by the sea, right?"

"That's the one. Largest city in the Borderlands. And oldest. Wonderful, ancient architecture."

"Sounds a nice place to grow up."

"I didn't grow up there. I spent my early years in the lamasery. It was by the sea, but not near Jod." He shrugged. "I was an orphan."

"I'm sorry." Lani said.

"Thank you, but I don't remember my parents. In fact, since the lamasery had mostly nuns, you might say I had a dozen mothers." Rafael laughed.

Enio had only had one mother, and not for long. This guy had an entire battalion? No wonder he was good at everything.

Lani said, "May I ask how you ended up there, Rafael?"

"Rescued by sea stags during a storm. Our ship capsized."

Enio could relate. "They rescued me once too, and—"

"That was my first encounter with the élan," Rafael went on. "They nursed me back to health, then delivered me to the nuns." He gazed at Lani. "Though a child, the vitality of the nature magics never left me. When I was old enough to study sigils—Elorian—I found I could also use the élan."

"So can Enio," Lani added. She smiled at him.

He perked back up. "Me and Par took classes at the abbey. They say the monks are the best teachers of lumina. Lani taught me élan."

"Lani is quite special," Rafael said, still gazing in her direction.

Enio unwrapped part of the potato. "I figured out numena too. On my own." That one-upped even Rafael.

"Numena, you say?" Rafael lay aside his food and brushed off his hands. "I forgot to mention, whenever the weather allowed, I slept on the rooftop. My blanket was the moonlight, and the sea my lullaby. I was alone, yet with so many stars, somehow beyond loneliness. It stirred something within me."

A glory, not gold or green, but silver, sparked around Rafael's head. He reached out. A silver flame rose from the rocks, danced a moment, and dissolved.

Numena, too? Son of a—

"The Borderlands has always been a mix of magics," Rafael said. "One of the other orphans traded me an Arcanan sigil. After a while, I found I could manage it. It's called fire-fly."

Enio changed the subject. "I'm good with knives."

No one responded.

"A girl I knew, a courier for Arcana, taught me."

"Your girlfriends carry knives?" Rafael winked at Lani. "I wonder why."

Lani snorted.

Enio's face warmed, and not from the rocks.

She changed the topic again. "What else did you learn from the nuns, Rafael?"

"My outlook, I suppose. With their studies, their philosophies—I like to believe they taught me well. In fact, they said I read too much. I tended to avoid the other children."

"We have that in common," she said, peeling the leaf from her vegetable. "Growing up in the woodlands, I didn't meet many other nymphs, much less humans."

"I understand." He gently squeezed her wrist.

Enio narrowed his eyes.

"For myself, I can't blame anyone." Rafael removed his hand and returned to his meal. "They say I was a bit dark."

"Our jolly entertainer?" She chuckled. "Dark?"

"Grim. Serious. I realized early that life is short. You might be walking along, minding your business. A cart comes by, a rock takes a bad bounce. Wham, you're gone. You know?"

"Mister sunshine," murmured Enio. He bit into his food, leaf and all.

"Oh, I've changed, I hope. I decided to make a difference while I'm here. With help from the lamasery, I enrolled in a school in Jod. Studied history, diplomacy. My élan made me the right choice for this mission."

As Rafael droned on, Enio took another bite, but found he had no appetite. He lay back and closed his eyes, not caring to listen further.

After a pause and a low whisper from Lani, Rafael said, "So… Enio. What was it like growing up in Eloria?"

"It was crap." Enio rolled to the side.

"You must remember some good things. Try."

"Yes," Lani said. "Try."

They were testing him. A few images came to mind. "My river. My canoe."

"And Par," she said.

The name stirred a memory, but one too hard to reach. "Sure." He curled up.

After another pause, Lani added, "You didn't finish your potato. Shall I cut it up for you?"

"You can have it. I'm going to sleep now." At least he could still do *that* without help.

Chapter Sixteen

Enio's dreams were river dreams. He rowed through the night in his old canoe. Then the paddle slipped from his hands. He searched the waters, but only his dark reflection stared back.

He looked for the shore and couldn't find it, so he let the current take him. The night chilled, and he began to shiver. He floated into weeds, their motionless shapes stretching in every direction. The water thinned to mud and the canoe slowed and stopped. All he could do was sit there, lost, shivering, his only company the whisper of weeds and water against the hull.

Then the whispers changed.

"We need to ration." That was Rafael, almost too low to hear. Enio opened his eyes a slit. Night still hung beyond the cave. Lani and Rafael sat huddled over the glowing rocks. Lani began to turn. Enio closed his eyes again.

When she asked, "How do you think he's managing?" he heard the answer in her question before Rafael even replied.

"Not well. We can keep healing him physically, but not his mind, which is obviously slipping fast. Soon he'll need everything we've got. And if it's a choice…" Rafael hesitated. "Lani, we must heal ourselves first."

She sighed. "That's a decision I never want to make."

Enio grimaced.

She added, "We can't go back?"

"Not anymore. Our only chance is to press onward. But after Enio's misstep, the snowpack has become unstable. We need to move as fast as we can. If it comes to it, we'll carry him."

Carry me?

"Let's make him comfortable," Lani said. "Can you rewarm the rocks? I've exhausted my élan for today."

Exhausted it on him.

"I think so." A wave of heat moved through the cave. "That's as much as I can do tonight. Sleep well, Lani."

"You too, Rafael."

But Enio had become too agitated to sleep. Because of him, they'd lost most of their provisions, and any hope of going back. To make matters worse, sometimes he could barely walk, not to mention his memory was rotting like wormy wood. He was putting everyone in danger, dragging them down. He'd tried to tell them he was just an anchor, and now an anchor keeping a storm-battered ship from safety. If they sank, it'd be his fault.

He lay in silence, working through the situation. Like everything else, even the details of their mission had become fuzzy, but one thing remained clear: at first light, they needed to get off this part of the mountain as quickly as possible, and before he put them in greater peril than he already had.

But the entire way, Lani and that fancy guy—what was his name? Rafael. The entire way, they'd waste their sigils healing him.

And they'd keep losing time, and risking avalanches and ice-falls, while he lagged more and more.

Or they'd wait while he rested.

Or carried him.

The more Enio reviewed things, the angrier he got. He cursed in silence. He cursed himself. The mission's pieces became confused and fragmented.

Then, for a moment, they realigned, like an evil constellation. He saw what he needed to do.

Enio pulled himself up. Lani and Rafael, no doubt exhausted, didn't stir. Swallowing a bitter resignation, like facing a childhood night with an empty belly, he wrapped himself in his furs and crept from the cave. Immediately, a frigid gust blew back his hood and snatched the feathered cap off his head. He reached for it too late. The night had taken it. It was gone.

He pulled his wraps tighter and blinked away the fat snowflakes collecting on his eyelashes. By getting a head start, he could speed everyone's journey. He drew out his dagger and made an arrow along the rock wall, a route for the others. They'd see he'd come this way, and follow it fast and safely until they caught up.

He plowed into the cold wind, slow but careful, saving his little energy. His thoughts numbed with his nose and cheeks. He grasped at old memories, though he'd found that remembering made them disappear faster. But he needed them now, before they were gone forever.

For years, Enio had lived in a broken shack with a broken father. But it hadn't been all pits and apple cores. He'd had his river. His canoe. Not much else, until Par showed up. He'd helped Enio see a better world. Now Enio understood more magics than anyone. Well, except Rafael. Enio didn't envy other things or people—not even Rafael, who was maddeningly perfect—but he envied Par. Par had a way with people. He made friends easy. Probably because he didn't mind the mushy stuff.

Enio stayed close to the wall, scratching with the dagger whenever he found a good spot. The other faces in his life drifted away, deeper into the snowy night. But not Par's. It had taken

Enio years to call Par his friend. Before that, Enio had lost anything or anyone he had gotten close to. Admitting Par was his friend had been too risky.

But some things were worth the risk.

Now, Enio had to make sure Lani got back to… uh…

Par.

Yes, that was the name. Those two were meant to be together, even if she was the one person Par seemed unable to tell his feelings.

The wind shifted, ushering Enio forward. Instead of resisting, he let it push him on. He hadn't taken a hiking pole. The others needed it more. And he could admit now that his plan hadn't been getting a head start for them to catch up. He'd never last that long. But at least things were simple again. Clear. No more complicated goals. While he'd never just sit down and wait for the end, he wouldn't turn back either. All he had to do was keep walking. Maybe he should've left a will. Par should have the *Sea Dog*.

But Par would know that.

He scraped his knife along the wall, hardly needing to keep his eyes open. He hardly could, anyway. And his damned fur wrapping had become like a sail, each wind gust pushing him around. When a sustained blast threw him toward the drop-off, he panicked and fumbled with the ties. At the last instant, the fur flew off and soared into the night like a frightened ghost.

Gasping, Enio scrambled back to the rock wall. He felt less cold than he probably should. More numb. And when he started off again, the going seemed easier. He wasn't an anchor any longer. He was like that ghost, untied and free.

So he kept on. Whenever he stumbled and fell, he pulled himself back up, though each time that took longer. He figured he'd seen the last of the sun, and once, while he tried to catch his breath, he realized he was whimpering. "No!" he shouted and cut it off. No one would know, except him, but he didn't want to die crying, even if the snow hid the frozen tears.

On and on, one dragging step after another, keeping near the wall, always the wall. Then he tripped and bumped his head against an outcrop. Pain flared behind his eyes and he dropped to his knees with barely a shout. A little warmth ran down his face. Kind of nice, really. The wind continued to howl, daring him to get up again. His arms moved a little, but not his legs.

Was he done?

He made another feeble attempt to rise. This time he simply fell over, into the soft snow. After that, not a muscle, not a finger stirred. With a long shudder, he closed his eyes and let himself relax. Oddly, dying hurt less than he'd always expected. He floated in a strange place between agony and warmth, fear and calm.

When the others—their names were gone now—saw his arrows, they'd know he'd passed this way. That it was safe. They'd make good time. And they were better off without him. Par wouldn't like Enio leaving that pretty woman alone with that other guy. But there was no denying that fancy-pants was strong and smart and capable. Better than Enio. He'd keep her safe until Par saw her again. Enio didn't need to be around for that reunion.

Enio wasn't angry anymore. He'd done his best.

A blissful sleepiness pressed him into the snow. No more lumina, or numena, or élan. Just him, an empty shell with a hollow head. Little left, except maybe a few regrets. He hadn't sailed the sea as far as he'd wanted. But he'd gotten to the Deep World. How many sailors could say that? Or say that and lived?

He wished he'd seen more, traveled to places no one dared. Under the sun, or the stars, no plan, no destination. But now he would rest. With his remaining moments, he'd remember the good things. The good people.

As he tried, his memories went dark, like a landscape after sunset, drained of color and life.

Just one last face. The name was gone. But it was Enio's friend. More than a friend. But Enio had no better word.

The wind shouted in his ear. It tried to rock his unmoving body.

He made an effort to open his eyes, but those were sealed forever under a crust of ice. Damn distractions, anyway. Were his final moments going to be all pushing and shouting? Who did you complain to around here?

If he'd been able to laugh at that, he might have. A smile touched his frozen lips as his last thoughts slipped away.

CHAPTER SEVENTEEN

A LONG, BLANK PERIOD took Par's mind, followed by his
nose, from the musky forest where he'd collapsed into
the fairer smells of fresh bread and cinnamon.

He groaned himself fully awake.

Sunlight carried bird song through an open window. He lay
on a simple bed of blankets and woven reeds. A frog rested on
his chest.

His mind was still fuzzy, but he recalled his previous assault
by a mob of such creatures. So he didn't dare move.

It stared back, unblinking, its eyes still and dull and…

Wooden.

It was fake, just a carving.

Somebody around here sure had a sense of humor.

Across the small room stood a humble door. He palmed the
little carving, eased out of bed, and stepped first to the window.
He was in the upper story of a forest cottage.

As he stared, confused, the chaos of his last memories finally
returned: his imprisonment by the Asrai; the mission to the Ults

to find the Nowen and stop the Dark Tribes; his leap to the *Sea Dog* as his friends disappeared into the Mother Spring's mists.

Yet the view out the window was nothing like the snowy Ults. Throughout the moss-heavy forest he saw people, climbing steps and makeshift ladders among cottages and treehouses, standing on porches and walkways watching the world as Par did now. Beyond the trees was a large lake. Boats and canoes drifted over its calm surface, many more fastened to docks and piers. The village continued into the woodlands on the lake's far side. Further off rose rough cliffs with the sparkling waterfalls that had brought him here.

Wherever *here* was.

The door to his room creaked. In peeked a young girl.

Despite his uncertain situation, Par managed a smile. "Well, hello." His words came out raspy. His mouth was as dry as a desert wind.

Her eyes widened. With a petite gasp, she hurried away.

Par checked himself over—thank goodness he was dressed. His skin was a little splotchy, but otherwise he felt normal. He went to the door. Hushed voices came from down a narrow hallway. Wherever he was, he had someone to thank. He headed toward them.

"He's comin', Miri."

Par followed the deep, familiar voice down the stairs and arrived on the ground floor of the cottage. A husky bearded man, one Par remembered from the forest, sat at the table. The little girl rested in his lap.

"I see you're feelin' better," the man said. He nodded to the chair opposite. There was a pitcher and mugs between them. "How's he look, Miri?" He squeezed the girl. She giggled.

Par took the seat. He smiled again and held out the toy frog. "Yours?" His voice came rough. He cleared his throat.

She nodded and pressed into her father's chest.

"It's a bit of a luck charm," the man said. "To keep away the dew frogs. Or at least, to help you feel better when it don't."

As Par's eyes locked on the pitcher, he licked his lips. His throat hurt.

The man set the girl down, like a bear placing a tea cup. "I think there's a raisin cake in the cupboard. Bring it, please darlin'?"

She hit the ground running.

"How long…" Par began. He swallowed hard.

"Two days."

"Two!" Par began to stand—too fast. Lightheaded, he sank back again.

"Easy," said the man. He lifted the pitcher with a meaty hand and filled Par's mug. "Here. Start with the water. It's better in the mouth than the eyes."

Par took the mug in both hands and sipped. Then he gulped and gulped. Just water, but the best he'd ever had.

"Careful not to choke." The man refilled the mug. "I'm Jont, brother of Moal. Welcome to my home."

Wiping his chin, Par sipped more slowly. "Thank you, Jont. I'm Par. You brought me here?"

"After you passed out. Your last words were about bein' lost."

"Where am I?"

"You're in Kathnu by Toadwalk. Where were you tryin' to get?"

"We… I was…" How could Par even begin to explain? As he tried to organize his thoughts, an unlikely yet insistent possibility brightened his mind. "Jont, are you a Nowen?"

The man seemed to consider. "Am I a Nowen…"

Par waited.

The man continued. "Am I a-knowin' what?"

"Are you a Nowen?"

"A-knowin' what?"

"Just…" Par stopped. It had been a long shot. "Sorry. Someone I was looking for."

"I'll ask around."

"Thank you, Jont."

"No trouble. By your accent, I'd guess you're from down the Greenin'."

Par started. "You know the Greening River?"

Miri arrived with a small bundle.

"Thank you, dear." The man unwrapped the cake and broke off a generous chunk. He handed it to her. "Go next door and share with Taffa."

"Wait," Par said, and held out the frog.

She shook her head. In a mousy voice, she said, "Better?"

"Very much, thank you."

She giggled again and ran out.

"Seems you're supposed to keep it." Jont passed Par a hunk of the raisin cake. "Now you asked about the Greenin'. It lies south, beyond the highlands."

Par pocketed the carving. As he nibbled his sweet, earthy breakfast, a map of Eloria flashed through his head. "Hold on. Am I in Choga?"

The man chortled. "Of course. You *are* lost, aren't ya?"

Par could barely believe it. The Mother Spring had taken his friends to the southern Ults, but brought him to the northern province of Choga? Was there any place farther from where he needed to be?

He chewed his lip, wondering what to do now. "You're right about my accent. I was born in St. Livius."

"Not many of your folk come up here. Not very fashionable, or easy to get to. And the forests are dangerous if you don't know the plants."

"Or the dew frogs." Par rubbed his arm. But now what? Well, if he couldn't help his friends in person, could he at least get a message to the Abbot and the Eminence? They needed to know the Dark Tribes were indeed causing the quakes. And they needed to know about the mission Rafael had accepted, not to mention what the Asrai had said about Enio's health.

"Jont," he said, "can I send a message bird to Argent? A navigaunt?"

"To the capital?"

"Yes. To the Eminence."

The man frowned. "Did you hit your head too?"

"I'm fine. It's important."

"Never heard of anyone messagin' the Eminence." Jont stroked his beard. "I suppose we might send a navigaunt to the Master Merchant's Guild there, but whether the message would go beyond that, I can't say."

"Then I'll go myself." But to reach the Greening, Par would have to cross over the highlands. That had to be a long, slow journey. "Can someone take me down the seacoast to Argent?"

Jont shook his head. "Our vessels aren't licensed for passenger transport."

"I don't suppose someone might skip that license part?"

"Penalties are harsh for such violations."

"Does it help that I know the Eminence? He'd dismiss any penalties."

The man cocked an eyebrow. "So our lost jungle child is personal friends with the ruler of all Eloria."

Par didn't blame the look. "I wouldn't believe me either. And yeah, I suppose it's not fair to ask anyone to sneak me aboard again."

"Again?"

"Last year, I hitched a ride on a Chogan barge."

"Did you?" Jont leaned forward. "Whose?"

"I, uh, don't want to get him in trouble."

"Nobody in Choga is blabbin' to the Hierarchy."

There seemed no harm in revealing it now. And he owed Jont an honest answer. "His name was Agron."

"Agron?"

"You've heard of him?"

"I might. What do you remember of him?"

"Well, he had kids and two wives. On his barge he pretended he only had one, what with the Rule. I was with my friend Enio and—"

"Enio? Brother of Iorgas, brother of Terod, brother of Loam?"

"Yes!" Enio had introduced them to Agron with names like that. He'd said trust and relationships were everything to the Choga. "I was called a brother of Enio. By the time we'd left, we'd become brothers of Agron too." Par made a face. "Well, after they made me drink fermented mud-maggot juice."

Jont broke into a belly laugh.

At the memory of that surprise initiation, Par laughed too.

"You were highly honored, brother of Enio, to be welcomed into Agron's family."

"Does this help get me a ride to Argent?"

"This is important, is it?"

"It's life and death, Jont. Enio is very sick." That seemed the most important of everything for Jont to hear.

The man was silent for a moment. Then he said, "The sailors on the sea route must make their ports. It might take you weeks."

Par began to slide into a new despair, but Jont added, "However, if Enio brother of Par is in hard distress, we must do better." He pushed back his chair. "Are you able to walk?"

"I am." Par stood to make sure.

"Then follow me." The man headed for the door.

"Where are we going?" Par hurried after him.

"To the Greenin'."

"Over the highlands?"

"Shortcut," Jont said, stepping outside. "Best not to speak of it further."

Par could only follow, anxious to see what the man meant by a shortcut to the Greening River. And though even a river trip might take several days to Argent, that was better than the weeks Jont had quoted for a barge along the coast.

But either way, Jont had said he'd been unconscious for two days. In that time, what had happened to his friends? Had they already found the Nowen or the moon marrow? Were they at least safe? He could hope, but there was no way for him to know.

Chapter Eighteen

Enio sank away from the bothersome chaos of his fading senses. There were no dreams—just some strange blurry stars deep within the nothingness. They seemed familiar, like he'd sailed under them before. And while the last of his worries and memories faded with his thoughts, those timeless stars remained.

He could have drifted there forever. Maybe he did.

But the stars changed. They came together in a single, painful prick of light.

He had opened his eyes.

The sun shone brightly. He was wrapped in blankets. From nearby, gruff words reached his ears. He strained his head to see three figures in heavy robes huddled around a sooty iron pot. Reddish steam rose from the pit beneath.

"Think he'll make it?" one said. His words came heavy and slow, like molasses from a cup.

"He should," said another, livelier. "Why, you claiming his bones?"

My bones? Enio swallowed and coughed.

They turned.

"Where…?" He coughed again.

The one who had last spoken approached. He drew back a hood to reveal a ruddy face and dark eyes. "You're in our camp. I'm Keb. We found you half frozen near the eastern ridge."

Enio rose up a little, but rope bound his wrists. He was in a craggy pass. A pair of small tents sat nearby. In the distance, beyond the jagged granite walls, loomed two soaring rock formations, like opposing cupped hands or horns, almost touching at their summit.

"So," Keb said, "where were you going?"

Enio's mind was blank. "I… I'm not sure."

"Well, you're safe. Give yourself some time."

"Why are my hands tied?"

"While we were warming you, you took a swing at Hector. You were pretty out of it."

"Sorry. I'm all right now." Except that he couldn't remember a damn thing.

Keb eyed him a moment, then reached into his cloak and withdrew a short knife. "Hold still."

Enio did.

With a quick, easy slice, the man cut the bonds. "Come over to the hotpot. Need a hand?"

"I think I can manage." Rubbing the blood back into his wrists, Enio joined them. The hole beneath the pot glowed red, but no flames or embers were visible through the steam. Two others sat near Keb. Grey whiskers and a hooked nose grew from the man with the heavy voice. Cloak and shadow hid the silent one.

"Hungry?" Keb said.

"Starving." Enio rubbed his stomach.

Keb ladled him a bowl of thick brown something. Enio tried a spoonful. Bitter, but hot. He ate more.

The man offered him a mug.

Enio drank. Warm beer. Just as bitter. Just as satisfying.

He wiped his mouth. "Thanks. What are you guys doing out here?"

"Hector and me," Keb nodded toward the man with the hooked nose, "we're on patrol. What do they call you?"

"Enio." The name came automatically, like a reflex, but nothing else came with it. "I don't think I'm from around here."

Keb took a deep gulp from his own mug. "Join the club."

Enio liked these guys. He remembered nothing about an eastern ridge, but they'd invited him to their fire and given him a warm meal. He gestured to the third figure. "Who's that?"

"That's Morty," Keb said. "He doesn't talk much. Takes after Hector."

"Hi, Morty." Enio held out his hand.

The figure's robed arm lifted. The hood fell away.

It was the hand, and face, of a skeleton.

Dropping his drink, Enio scrambled backwards.

After a brief rattle, the skeleton collapsed, settling into a mound of bones under a crumpled robe.

Keb laughed.

As Enio gawked wide-eyed, Hector spoke again, his words as weighty as before. "Can we show the deceased a little respect?"

"Respect?" Keb said, chuckling. "You're the one who dug him up." He noticed Enio cowering to the side. "Sorry, friend, didn't mean to startle you."

Enio stared at the shell-white skull peering from the pile of robes. A memory of other robed men and rising skeletons flashed through his mind. Then, like vapors from the cooking pit, it was gone.

"Oh, and Hector," Keb said, "you lose."

"Wasn't fair. Morty was untimely disturbed."

"Not by me. That was the bet."

Keb helped Enio back to his seat. "Hector bet he could raise a skeleton to last the night, even without a boost of Ortu sorcery."

Ortu? That, too, rang a very faint, uneasy bell. "You're tribesmen of Ortu?"

"Not us. Hector's a necromancer. I'm a diviner. And you?"

Enio rubbed his face, trying to remember. "Ortu—maybe."

Keb patted his shoulder. "See Hector? Told you I sensed a touch of Ortu in him."

"You're the diviner, not me."

"What say we lend this kid Morty's robe?"

Not thrilled about the previous owner, Enio winced. But the robe looked more functional than his blankets.

As Hector sorted through the bones, Enio asked, "You said we're on the eastern ridge? Of what?"

"They call it the Valley of Nux," Keb said. "I call it depressing. We should be back before evening."

"To your village?"

"No villages around here. Just ruins. Back to the Horde."

"Horde?"

Keb smiled. "Does your bag of questions have a bottom, Enio?"

"Sorry."

"No worries. The Horde is our army. There's plenty of Ortu mixed in, so you can hitch with them if you want."

"Great," Enio said with fake enthusiasm, unsure if that was good news or not.

Hector stashed Morty's bones in his pack. Enio's new robe turned out to be twice too big, but Keb used a sigil to scrunch it so it didn't drag. His glory shone a glittering bronze. Bronze glories, diviners, and necromancers? None of that had even a whiff of the familiar. But Enio figured he shouldn't ask too many stupid questions too close together.

Instead, he helped Keb and Hector break camp. They were

high up, on the icy brim of a deep, long valley. Keb led them through the pass, opposite the horns that towered beyond the ragged cliffs. Regardless of Enio's full belly, warm robe, and renewed strength, his memories refused to return.

He wasn't comfortable making small talk with Hector and his pack of rattling bones. So as they made their way down, he tried Keb instead.

"Keb, you said there are ruins?"

"A few stones steps, broken pillars, and those giant rock-things." He gestured back to the horns. "Good luck if you were sneaking around looking for treasure. We didn't find any."

"Don't think I was."

"Might be you were trying to catch up with the Horde? Most joined earlier, but we've seen stragglers. Remember anything else?"

"The sea." Enio again surprised himself at the quick answer, though it seemed an island memory in its own empty sea.

"The Southern Sea?"

"Not really sure. Where is that?"

"South of the Ults. The Horde's going there."

"Why?"

"To meet the Gorga."

"What's a Gorga?"

Keb stopped them. He eyed Enio. "Have you heard yet of the Rise?"

"Still got frost on the brain, I guess."

"That may not be your frosty brains. Happened not long ago. Details are still going around." Keb explained that deep in some place called the Devastation, an entity of Ortu had risen from the Lower Realms. "People from Arcana and Eloria defeated it, uniting to fight for the first time in memory."

"Ortu? So we lost?" Enio was, admittedly, having trouble keeping up.

Keb's answer complicated things further. "No, Enio. The entity's defeat was fortunate. It was summoned by selfish men, and that much power under so few always turns bad."

Enio nodded.

"But as part of the fight, Eloria and Arcana—the Highers, as they deem themselves—realized they could resolve their differences and work together. Now, as their friendship grows, so does their might, and the threat to us."

"Why?"

"They call us the Lowers, since we draw our magics from realms they see as inferior, even dark and evil." He huffed. "They even refer to those realms when they curse, like *purple hells*. Now they believe they have the strength to be rid of us forever."

"So says the Gorga," Hector mumbled.

"The Gorga," Keb continued, "unites us, as the Highers have united. And though we are fewer, we've got Morty."

"Morty?" Enio's face must have shown his doubts about their bag of bones.

Keb explained further. "A diviner, such as myself, can call up echoes of the dead: old patterns of thoughts and memories, the waves after the pebble has sunk. Hector, as a necromancer, can raise their very bones. Together, we can bind both together for a time, like we did Morty. When those of Ortu imbue it with lost life energies, then Morty can last. And he can fight."

Morty with a sword? Enio shivered at *that* image.

"And not Morty alone," Keb continued. "We're few now, but with the world's dead, we'll far outnumber the living."

"Like from graveyards?" Enio could barely grasp the nightmare. A person's dead family, or friends, rising to fight against them?

Family and friends? Did he have any of those?

Hector said, "We have laws against raising a revenant without a relative's permission."

"Yes," Keb added. "But untold multitudes lie in sea graves, along every coast, under every shipping lane, all unclaimed and beyond such permissions."

Enio suspected that even if his memory were intact, he wouldn't know of anything like this.

Keb resumed their walk. "So it is to the sea we march. Under the Gorga's leadership, we will raise an army as none have ever seen. You'll do your part too, Enio, when your memory returns."

"If you say so."

"Well, it's your decision," Keb said. "Join us, or continue wherever else you might have been going."

The sweeping valley and the snowy peaks drew Enio's eyes. He would probably not get a better offer today. "Where is this Horde?"

"Most have already reached the coast. Our group was tasked with visiting this valley first. We were to look for a rare black mineral. Moon something or other."

"Moon marrow," Hector said.

Again something stirred deep within Enio's head, and sank away.

Chapter Nineteen

Enio continued with Keb and Hector through the rocky passes. The land below, the immense valley they'd called Nux, was still mostly cloaked in morning shadow. The pace remained relaxed, maybe for Enio's sake. If so, he was grateful and didn't bother them with more questions. Instead, he did his best to learn Keb's occasional walking songs, which had too many odd words to remember. But their rescue had left Enio feeling, if not strong, at least capable. His hope was that his memory would catch up.

As the morning wore on, they made their way down. There was less snow on the trail now. The sun pushed back the remaining shadows, leaving a thin reddish haze farther up the valley. Keb said that was smoke from the camps.

After a noonday rest, they made it to the bare valley floor, and were soon following wagon tracks heading south. Later in the afternoon, they spotted a distant throng of tents, and at last reached its edges. Keb led them confidently among the people. Though he'd referred to this as an army, there were no uniforms or sparring or marching—just rough-dressed men and women attending their horses and donkeys and cooking pots. The tents were of every kind, some decorated with festive cloth or colorful ribbons. Enio even caught sight of children playing near a wagon. And music was never far: flute sounds drifted from a tent; a group of young men took turns dancing before a drum; a woman hummed a tune to her infant.

Enio also noticed their strange glories as someone invoked to mend a boot or heal a wound. Some were bronze, like Keb had used to fix the cloak. Blackish purple also seemed familiar, though Enio couldn't quite tell why he felt that. The dirty red ones were completely new.

"Recognize anything?" Keb asked with a friendly glance.

"Not really."

"Well, no need to strain yourself. We'll be at our campsite shortly."

As Keb had promised, it wasn't long before they stopped before a tall, roomy tent.

"This is us," he said. "I'll be back." Instead of going inside, he disappeared among the neighbors.

Hector slipped off his pack and focused on a shallow hole near the tent's entrance. He invoked with that same grim red, and the ground coughed up wisps of steam. Enio peeked in and grimaced. It looked like bloody mud.

He wrinkled his nose. "What is that?"

Keb returned with a kettle. "I call it the Necromancer Special, since they have a talent of drawing from hidden places. Hector conjured heat out of the earth. Not unlike how he healed your freeze."

"He put heat in me?"

Hector took the kettle and placed it over the hole. "I conjured out the cold."

Enio wasn't sure of the difference, but he was thankful either way.

Hector added, "Keb helped."

"A little," Keb said. "To find the life in your frozen corpse."

"Corpse? Was I—?"

But Keb laughed. "Not quite. If it had come to that, we'd have given you a proper burial. But we're glad you pulled through."

"Not as glad as me."

"Then again," Keb said, removing food bowls from his own pack, "your bones would be smaller than Morty's, easier for Hector to carry. So…"

Enio was pretty sure Keb was kidding.

He was. He grinned at Enio. "Just pulling your leg—I mean, your femur. Hey Hector, that won't take much warming. The next tent had extra, already hot."

Pungent vapors floated from the kettle's spout. Hector lifted it and poured a broth with little hunks into a bowl. He handed it to Enio and poured some for Keb and himself.

"Thanks." Enio tasted it. Rodent or rabbit soup, he guessed. He flicked out a tiny bone, maybe a rat claw.

As they ate, a horn blew.

Both Keb and Hector paused their spoons.

"What is it?" Enio asked.

Keb looked towards the sound. "Finish quick and we'll see."

They gulped down their food. Keb returned the kettle to the neighbors, then led farther into camp, to a circle of tents around a larger steaming red pit. A crowd had gathered. An old woman with long grey hair stood before them all. She held a gnarled staff with dangling bones. She raised it. "Bring them out."

Two figures were escorted from a tent. They wore furs, thick and plush, different from the tattered and everyday cloaks of most others in the camp. One, a young woman, had long golden hair and a friendly face. For reasons Enio didn't quite understand, he found the looks of the young guy at her side annoying.

"These two," said the grey-haired woman, "were found wandering in the hills. They are not tribesmen." She pointed her staff at them. Its bones—thankfully too small to be skulls—jangled and clacked on their strings. "Speak. Who are you?"

Though his hands were tied behind his back, the young man managed a bow. "I am Rafael, diplomatic representative from the Borderlands."

"Spies!" someone shouted.

"No," Rafael replied. "We had no idea you were here."

"What is your business?" the old woman asked.

"Initially, to search for the Nowen. Are you they?"

"Never heard of them."

"Is this the Valley of Nux?"

"Of course," she croaked.

Enio's curiosity increased. The prisoners seemed as lost as him. He eased through the crowd for a closer look.

"Well," Rafael continued, "our search was an uncertain venture. Now we—"

"And your companion? Who is she?"

"I'm Lani," the woman said, "from the Deep World, sent by the Asrai."

"More gibberish."

Rafael spoke again. "I would meet your leader."

"I am Yantra," said the old woman. "You will speak to me."

A voice from the crowd objected. "No, Yantra. You're a necromancer. The diviners outnumber—"

And another. "Neither speak for the Ortu."

She raised her staff. "I rank highest of all present. Tell your kindred that Yantra has captured strangers. Summon whom you will. In the meantime, I will question them."

That quieted the people. Again Enio wondered what kind of army this was supposed to be. It didn't seem very organized. He stepped to the front edge of the circle.

"Now," she said, "You will answer my questions."

"Happy to." Rafael's gaze wandered to the crowd. "What would you—" His eyes shot wide. "Enio!"

Enio jolted.

"You!" Yantra pointed at him. "Come here."

"Go ahead," Keb whispered from behind. "Yantra is fair."

Enio stepped forward.

"You recognize our captives?" she asked.

Enio examined them again. The one who called herself Lani showed obvious relief. He couldn't help but like her.

But he didn't know her.

He shook his head. "Never seen them before."

Confusion flashed in Lani's eyes.

Rafael furrowed his brows. "Perhaps I was mistaken."

"Your name is Enio?" Yantra said.

Enio nodded uncertainly.

Keb stepped beside him. "We found him near death, Yantra. His memory, for the most part, has not returned."

"What tribe?"

"Ortu, we think."

She scanned the crowd. "Does any tribe here claim him?"

No one spoke.

She turned back to Enio. "Where do you come from?"

He frowned. "I don't remember."

"Yantra," Keb said, "I don't believe he is an enemy."

"Yet you know nothing about him."

Keb eyed Enio. "Well, that is so."

"We will bind him," she said, "until we discover more."

"Sorry, son," Keb muttered.

Two husky men grabbed Enio's arms. "Hey!" He yelped and struggled with no real hope of overcoming their strength. Still, he was shocked at how quickly his muscles ran out of fight.

When they had bound his hands and placed him beside Rafael, Yantra came before him. "Your business, like all free people, is your own. If you are not a spy, you need not pretend you are forgetful."

"Pretend?" Enio kicked at the dirt. "I'm not pretending. I can't remember. It's driving me nuts."

"Then you are not of Ortu?"

"I don't know!" Enio was tired of being asked questions he couldn't answer.

"He speaks the truth," Rafael said. "But he came with us."

"For what purpose?"

"That is a longer story." Rafael hesitated. "Perhaps it should wait until your leaders gather."

"Or perhaps," she said, "it involves Eloria and Arcana."

Rafael's lips tightened.

Yantra smiled. "We are well aware of your plans to make war."

"War? Yantra, our plans are only to defend against *your* attacks."

"It is you who attack, always and everywhere. Cursing us, chasing us. It is we who must defend ourselves."

"As I said before, Yantra, I'm a diplomat. We can discuss—"

"Will your words halt the hatred of your people?"

"They—" He paused. "I admit, there are many who shun you and your magics. And yes, it will take more than talk to change their perspective. But you need not fear them."

"You can speak for those lands?"

"By authority of the Eminence of Eloria and the rulers of Arcana, I can."

Yantra eyed him for a moment. She looked around. "We will wait for the other leaders. But we will get to the truth." She again focused on Enio, her staff's dry bones hanging before his face, and narrowed her eyes. "One way or another."

CHAPTER TWENTY

H IS MIND HEAVY on the fate of his friends, Par followed
Jont out the door of the forest cottage. The ground
beyond the porch was muddy at best, and downright
swampy otherwise. Jont took them over zig-zagging boards, past
neighboring cottages, and across short wooden bridges until they
arrived at the lake Par had seen from his window.

The piers seemed as random as the forest paths: some ran forward, others sideways or slantways. The lake stretched east as far
as he could make out, probably leading to the sea. But Jont had
brought him near the western end. There, a massive granite hill
pushed from the trees and into the water like a giant beast come
to drink. In the rockface loomed a house-sized wooden gate that
fell even below the waterline. The hinges alone were taller than a
boat mast. Fanciful carvings covered its surface, out of place with
anything Par had yet seen in Toadwalk.

Without a word, Jont continued along the shore in that
direction. They reached a small, somber cabin nestled against the
granite hill.

"Par," said the man, his voice low, "this secret we keep from the other provinces, and exercise under the rules of the Elorian Merchant Guild. However, the Channel Master has been known to bend those rules in an emergency."

"Channel Master?"

"He's old and has forgotten most of his sigils—whether by age or illness, no one knows. But he still remembers one, and it's the one we need."

Jont turned to knock but stopped. "He can be a bit, uh, moody. Don't stare at his beads."

Par nodded at whatever that meant.

Jont rapped.

They waited.

Nothing.

He knocked again. "Channel Master?"

"What?" said a rough, impatient voice.

"May I speak with you? It's Jont."

The door cracked open, and a grizzled face peeked out. The man wasn't much taller than Par and seemed a dwarf before Jont. His eyes squinted; Par couldn't tell if they were even open. Long, straggling white hair, like dying grass on a cemetery hill, weaved across an age-spotted head and fell to sharp shoulders. Some of those strands were strung with colorful beads. There were green ones, yellow ones. A red one hung above his forehead. And a brown one—no, that was another age spot.

"Something wrong with my hair?" grumped the man.

"Uh, no," Par said. He shifted his eyes to the granite hill, then the lake, then the sky.

"Forgive us," said Jont. "I found this young man lost and wounded in the forest."

"I'm not a healer." He made to shut the door.

Jont blocked it with his foot. "We need your services, Channel Master. This is Par, brother of—"

"Of everyone and their uncle, I know. Does he have an appointment? I don't recall any appointments until Thursday."

"It's a special rush, Master Eggwise. Enio brother of Par is near death. The Greenin' is the quickest route to help him."

Par hadn't said Enio was near death. To be honest, he didn't know. But the possibility sent a chill down his spine. He didn't correct it.

The man's squint squinted more. "Well, that means special rush prices, of course."

"I will owe you."

"Jont, if I had a copper for every… very well. Follow me."

Eggwise led them inside. The cabin was little more than a shack, with a cluttered desk beside an unmade cot beneath a grimy window. It all smelled like onions. The strange little man found a ledger among his papers, opened it and made a note. "Sign."

Jont did, without reading.

Par stood at his side, trying to see the terms.

Eggwise snapped it closed. "Let's go."

"I'll pay you back everything," Par whispered to Jont.

"I do not bind you to it, brother of Agron."

Farther back, in the wall of the granite itself, was set another door, this one of iron. Eggwise pulled it open with an ear-grating squeal. Glowing lanterns lined a tunnel. He lifted one from a hook and led forward.

After a few turns, the passage opened into a yawning cavern. A little light slanted in between the boards of the great gate Par had seen from outside. A sizable barge could fit in here, masts and all. The deeper end lay in total darkness.

Stone steps descended to a landing fenced by roped pylons. A thin canoe waited on the black water.

"Does this lead to the Greening?" Par said.

No one replied. Eggwise continued down.

Before Par followed, Jont gripped his shoulder. "Sweet sailin's and fair landin's, son."

Par took the hand in both of his. "Thank you, Jont. I won't forget this." He grinned. "Say goodbye to Miri."

"I surely will. I believe she has a crush on you."

As Par broke into laughter, so did Jont. But the cavern turned their echoes into cackles.

With a final nod, Jont disappeared the way they'd come.

"In or out," Eggwise said. He already sat in the back of the canoe. His lantern hung beside him from a shoulder-high hook.

"I'm coming." Par hurried down the steps. He gripped a pylon rope to help him in, but a small black bat hanging near the end squealed and fluttered off it.

"Crap!" He ducked down. But it had disappeared into the darkness.

"While we're young," said Eggwise.

Par checked the ropes again, then eased himself onto the front seat. The canoe wobbled precariously.

"Rules," Eggwise said the moment Par was settled. "First, don't invoke any sigils without asking."

That was the least of Par's concerns. The canoe seemed too unsteady for him to turn, but he nodded so Eggwise could see.

"Second, whatever I say, you do. No questions. Hear me?"

Now Par sighed. Agron's family, along with Jont, had formed his impression of Chogans. Hard-working and friendly. Private, but good people. Still, there were all sorts, and Eggwise was the cranky sort. With any luck, their time together would be short.

Nevertheless, the man's attitude irked him as petty. "If number two states people can't ask questions," Par said, impatient and a little annoyed, "how do they ask when they can invoke a sigil for number one?"

The little boat made an abrupt tilt. Par yelped and grabbed the ropes again to keep himself from the murky waters.

As they steadied, Eggwise went on, "Number three: don't be a smart ass. I meant no questioning my directions."

Jont sure wasn't kidding about the moods.

"Ready?" the man added.

After his tumble from the waterfall, Par had no love of dark, damp caves, especially with this guy for company. At least this time Par was in a boat. He nodded.

They sat there, unmoving.

"Uh, Mr. Eggwise?" Par said carefully. "When do we leave?"

"Just Eggwise. We leave when you let go of the rope."

"Oh." Par did. He found a short paddle at his feet. "Do I use this?"

"That's what it's there for. Take us in deeper. Go where I say."

Par nudged them away from the pier, then turned the boat into the cavern's dark end. The lantern became their only light. There was no current, and except for the paddle's plunk and echo, there was also no sound. He found it all unnerving.

"So," Par said, trying to lift the gloom with a little conversation. He lowered his voice at its unwelcome volume. "This leads to the Greening?"

"What did Jont tell you?"

"Nothing, really."

"Good. Then, yes, it leads to the Greening." Eggwise paused. "More or less."

"More or less?"

"They tried digging there, once. Cave-ins ended that. Too far anyway."

"Then where are we going?"

"To the Greening."

"But you just said—"

"I heard what I said. Let's just get this over with. It's supposed to be my day off."

Words didn't seem any improvement over silence. Par let the man be.

They continued, the roof often so high it might as well be the dome of night. Sometimes they passed smaller passages, and other times Eggwise chose between equally large routes.

"Stop," he said at last.

Par withdrew the paddle. "What's wrong?"

"Hush."

The paddle dripped, its plinkity-plink the only noise. Par strained to make out the area beyond their globe of lantern light. They'd entered another large cavern.

As Par's anxiety smoldered, Eggwise jangled the lantern. Par glanced back to find him closing the metal hood, plunging them in total blackout.

"Sit tight," Eggwise said. "I'm taking over." With his own paddle, he rowed the canoe forward, then made a quick turn. The motion repeated, forward and right, forward and left, in strange, tight zigs and zags.

Par gripped the sides and waited, seeing nothing except the little bright blobs of light that sometimes echo in your eyes after stepping into darkness. One after another, even those faded like cooling embers. Yet a thread-thin glimmer lingered after the rest. It shifted weirdly in front of him, a tall scratch in the darkness.

Before he pointed it out, the glimmer smeared across his vision and a wave of nausea crashed over him. His head spun. He gagged.

Eggwise reopened the lantern. All was still, but the roof was much lower, covered with stalactites nearly touching his head. And clinging to those stony swords were bats. Lots of bats.

Par cringed and covered his hair.

Eggwise barked out, "What did you do?"

The bats squeaked in unison.

"Me?" Par spoke in a low hiss. "Nothing. Was I supposed to row or—"

"A sigil!" The man stomped the canoe floor. A bat screeched past. "You invoked a sigil!"

Par ducked again. "I did not!"

"You're lying."

"No, Eggwise. I can't use sigils."

"That's not the point!"

"Then what is?"

"It's… don't confuse me."

"I'm not trying to confuse you. Since I was born, I've had a condition."

"Oh." Eggwise paused a moment. His anger eased. "Well, Jont should have told me. I'll. Use. Small. Words."

Par rolled his eyes. "I'm not *that* feeble. Even if I had invoked, the glory would've shone like a sunrise."

"Yes, well." Eggwise cleared his throat. "No need to panic. Sometimes it gets a little twitchy."

"What does?"

"Doesn't matter. We need to backtrack."

"What about these bats?" But the thousand winged bodies seemed to have returned to their thousand bat dreams.

"They won't bother you if you don't bother them. Personally, I'd worry most over the cave curses."

"Cave curses?" Par peered at the shadows within the shadows. "What cave curses?"

"The cave curses people get for constant questions."

Par caught the hint.

Eggwise turned the canoe. Each way looked the same. Dark.

"I can paddle," Par said.

"Not this time."

Leaving the bats behind, they moved in silence through the gloom. Eggwise's attitude ruled out any more questions.

But after several minutes, it was Eggwise who restarted the conversation.

"With any luck," he said, "we'll be out soon."

Par took advantage of the opening. "You know where we are?"

"No idea. I'm the Channel Master, not a mole."

"I've never heard of a Channel Master, Eggwise. I'm not from around here."

"Lost in the forest, Jont said?"

Par was inclined to skip the part about the Asrai and the Deep World, but he didn't want to lie either.

"Well, you might not believe me."

"Try me."

"Are you familiar with nymphs?"

"Been a while since I've met one."

"You've met them?"

"They're more common in the forests here than in the other provinces. Chogans leave them alone."

"I was with some, far away. Then, believe it or not, I fell into an enchanted pool and wound up here."

"An enchanted pool?"

"They called it the Mother Spring."

Eggwise stopped paddling. After a long pause he said, "I will get you to the Greening, if that's what you wish."

"Yes, please."

"Once you tell me, really, what's going on with you."

"What do you mean?"

"You know what I mean."

Crap. Par wasn't getting out of here without the man's help. But was there any reason to keep the rest of the story secret? Even if there were, who'd believe this old crank if he blabbed it? On the other hand, if something happened to Par before he got to Argent, maybe it was better someone else knew at least the essentials.

"All right." Par eased around to face Eggwise. "But it may not make much sense."

"Try me."

Par took a breath. "There was a meeting with the ruler of the Deep World, the Asrai, because, after we defeated the Ortu at the Immortus—that's where Enio got hurt—the tribes of the Lower Realms got worried about Eloria and Arcana teaming up against them and began attacking us with earthquakes. We'd hoped for the Asrai's help, but she won't, unless we get the Nowen to help too, or we find her some moon marrow in the Ults. So she sent my friends through the Mother Spring because it would take them where they needed to go. She kept me back to be imprisoned because I joined the delegation to the Deep World without being invited." Par took another breath. "But I jumped into the spring anyway and ended up here."

The man just stared.

"Told you," Par said. "You think I'm off my rudder."

But the man leaned forward. "Were those her words? That this Mother Spring would take them where they needed to go?"

Par nodded.

"And then it brought you here?"

"Yes."

"Then perhaps this is where *you* needed to go."

Par hadn't considered that. "To Choga? Why?"

Eggwise sat back, and for the first time, broke into a rough-toothed smile. "Because, Par, you found your Nowen."

Chapter Twenty-One

Eggwise, a Nowen?

Or more likely, Par was lost in the earth's bowels with a crazy man.

It didn't help Par's worries when Eggwise gave an eerie chuckle and resumed rowing. "I must say, Par, your story raises more questions than it answers."

Par agreed, but for now, he let his own questions hang in the gloom. After giving that wild explanation of his arrival, he wouldn't blame Eggwise if he thought Par the crazy one. Even dangerous-crazy, and Eggwise was humoring him until they found the way out.

Which, in fact, was fine with Par.

They continued through shadowy dripping caves, some draped with indifferent bats, others full of crystals glistening in the walls like petrified roots. Why did the man keep the lantern half dimmed? At least they coasted slowly enough to avoid crashing into anything.

Then once more, Eggwise covered the lamp completely. "Let's try this again. Stay still."

As Par's eyes adjusted, he saw another shimmer ahead. "Do you see that?" he whispered.

"What is it you think you see?"

"Like a glow, or the way air trembles around a fire."

"Hmm," was the man's complete reply. They moved toward the strange, wavering line running from the water to the low roof. Par might still question whether this existed in his eyes alone, except that Eggwise must see it too since he took them straight at it.

As they got closer, it widened the way a doorway does when approaching it from an angle.

"Is it safe?" Par asked.

"Just don't do whatever you did last time."

"I didn't do anything last time."

"Good. Don't do it again. And close your eyes."

"I can't see as it is."

"Rules."

Par sighed, gripped the sides more tightly and closed his eyes. The canoe glided forward. Eggwise zigged. He zagged. Suddenly, like before, Par's head reeled and his stomach twisted. He was near vomiting when light burst beyond his eyelids. He snapped them open.

The dark caves had vanished. Instead, their canoe floated beneath sun-dappled willow trees. They were outside, on a river. And unlike Kathnu by Toadwalk, there was no granite hill or lake or boats or piers or cottages—or people.

Par's stomach gave a final, uncontrollable squeeze. He lost his breakfast over the side.

"Just breathe," Eggwise said. "Happens to everyone the first time."

After wiping his mouth and getting himself together, Par began to recognize things about the surroundings: the insect sounds, a crawtad scurrying along the muddy shore, the earthy-sour smell. In another moment, he was certain. "This is the Greening River."

"It is." Eggwise guided them toward the banks.

They had somehow completely bypassed days of travel over Choga's bordering highlands. But though Par had traveled the Greening with Enio, from St. Livius to the Silver Sea, he didn't remember this stretch. They must be well north of his hometown. "How'd we get here?" Par eyed the man. "And are you really a Nowen?"

"Yes. And that's how we got here."

"But the Asrai said the Nowen hadn't been seen for centuries."

"Perhaps the Asrai doesn't know everything."

If the Asrai was wrong about the Nowen, what did that mean for the mission to the Ults? But Par needed more proof. "What's a Nowen doing so far from home?"

"Far? I've lived in Choga all my life."

"I thought the Nowen lived in the Ults?"

"They did, long ago."

"What happened to them?"

"That will take some explaining. Since you know about Nowen, are you familiar with the Devastation and the Vigil?"

"Yes!" Par said. That confirmed Eggwise wasn't making everything up. Few had knowledge of the Vigil.

They reached the shore. Eggwise remained sitting. "After the Devastation, many Nowen joined the Vigil to help the survivors. Others made lives elsewhere. My ancestors chose Choga."

Par hopped out to a sandy spot. "I grew up downriver. Why have I never heard of the Nowen?"

"We've kept ourselves quiet. The Chogans we confided in never betrayed us. What would your Hierarchy have done if they'd found out?"

That was a good point. In the past, Eloria had not been known for tolerating those of different magics. Or no magic, like Par.

"Then why tell *me*, Eggwise?"

"I have my reasons."

Whatever those reasons might be, Par's excitement grew that maybe he could bring the Asrai an entire army of Nowen. "How many of you live in Choga?"

"These days, I'm it."

"You're it?" That threw a wet blanket all over Par's enthusiasm.

"I'm no more thrilled about it than you are. Help me out."

Par took the man's elbow and ushered him ashore, then pulled up the canoe. At least a single Nowen was a start.

Eggwise stood to the side and stretched his back. "But even when there were more of us," he twisted and grunted, "it's easy for Nowen to hide our invocations. Our glories don't stand out like the others."

"How are yours?"

"A transparent shimmer."

"Like you invoked in the caves?"

"I didn't invoke in the caves. I took us through a fold."

"A what?"

With a last, long groan, Eggwise finished his exercises. "Folds are like hidden passages, cracks in the world. Long ones, short ones, as common as chimney smoke and most are as useless. A few, however, can take you a great distance."

Par's face no doubt showed how many questions he had. "Then when Jont said you were, uh…"

"Feeble?" Eggwise smiled. "That deception keeps me safe. Long ago, Nowen set up folds in those caves. Ever since, we've made a living by taking Chogan merchant vessels through them. We use the main fold for the barges—we call it the Channel—though there are a few obscure, smaller ones, like we just used, handy for landing farther downstream if you need to avoid certain inspections. And all under the guise that we, the Channel Masters, use a private family sigil for each trip, perfectly legal and long ago approved. But Jont was almost right: the truth is, I can no longer use any sigils at all."

Still stunned by this revelation, all Par could manage was, "Well, that's nothing to be ashamed of, as you get older."

"It's not because I'm *older*," grumped the man. "Another thing about the Nowen is that we require a partner to work a sigil."

Par's scrambled thoughts finally began to steady. "Eggwise, can that fold take us to the Deep World?"

"Folds go where they go. That one goes here."

"Then can you help me catch a barge to Argent?"

"Argent?"

"I need to tell the Eminence and the Abbot—I mean, the High Sigil Master—what the Asrai wants and where she's sent my friends. Even one Nowen might be enough for the Asrai to bring Lani and Enio back from their mission."

The man gazed south along the river, seeming to consider. A pair of squawking ducks flew overhead and continued upstream. He turned, following them with his eyes. "Yes. Argent. Let's try that."

Par nodded gratefully, hoping this didn't cost Jont any extra in the bargain. When Par made it to Argent, he'd ask for help paying.

"Eggwise," he asked, "you said you're the last Nowen around. Are you sure?"

"I haven't seen any in quite some time. The last one died six, no, seven springs ago." He sighed. "I miss her. And her fruit pies."

"Could there be others you don't know about?"

"Possibly." Eggwise remained with his back to Par.

"Or others who learned to use Nowen sigils? The way my friend Enio learned numena ones."

"I've never known anyone to use Nowen sigils who wasn't born to them. Still, life has a way of surprising us."

If anyone could figure out Nowen magic, it was Enio. Par would introduce him to Eggwise one day. But seeing his friends again now depended on getting Eggwise to the Asrai. And the first step was getting to Argent.

Eggwise began to walk north up the shoreline.

"Wait," Par said. "Argent is south."

"You don't say." The man continued north.

Again Par wondered whether this old guy was losing it. Best to be tactful. "Yeah. It's hard to tell which way is which when the sun his high, but south—"

"Remember what I told you?"

"What?"

"Don't be a smart ass. You don't think I know where south is?"

Yep. Same old Eggwise.

The man added, "I'm looking for the entrance to a different fold."

"Back to Toadwalk?"

"Of course not."

"Then where?"

"Where do you think?" He continued walking without a pause. "To Argent."

Chapter Twenty-Two

When Eggwise mentioned there was a fold to Argent, Par thought he'd won a lottery. Instead of a long trip down the Greening, maybe they'd get to the city this very day.

Fantastic.

Mostly fantastic.

In truth, a river journey had sparked a guilty hope: they'd pass Par's hometown. He hadn't been there in over a year. The memory brought a surge of homesickness. But in truth, taking the time now to visit would be selfish.

"The fold we seek," Eggwise said as they strode along the river, "was placed long ago by the first Nowen in Choga. My parents once took me through it. They said it was only for emergencies. For example, if a Nowen needed a quick escape to the Silver Sea." He chuckled. "Or if my uncle, rest his soul, ran out of his favorite wine."

Par dismissed his clawing nostalgia. "Why out here, in the middle of nowhere?"

"Folds are fragile. Other magic can disturb even the anchored ones. It's best to set them in lonely places."

"What will it look like?"

"Like before, a shimmer, or a thin distortion as in a cracked mirror. Sometimes there are other signs: a cold spot or a whirl of leaves. Wait, I see a little one." He pointed to a grove of maples. "There, by that tree. The bigger folds, the one we just traveled, for instance, often attract small, natural ones, the way ripples form around a current."

"I only see trees," Par said.

"Let's get closer."

They approached the grove. Eggwise stopped before an old maple with a fat trunk. "Look here."

Par leaned in. Indeed, there was something odd about it, where the bark running up the trunk didn't quite match, and the groove between the ridges seemed brighter or sharper than the rest. "That?"

"Yes!" Excitement, stronger than Par had yet heard from the man, filled the word. Eggwise cleared his throat. "All right, shuffle left and keep your eye on it."

Par did. The brightness became a shimmer. It widened as he moved, as had the one in the gloomy cave.

"Now, when it looks big enough, stick in your head."

"My head?"

"It's safe. As you approach, the fold may seem to thin or slide away. Shift a bit until it returns. You'll lose it if you go straight too fast."

Eggwise was right: if Par approached straight on, it slipped from view, like reaching for a fountain's rainbow. But he remained vigilant and it reappeared, widening again. He tried to touch it. His eyes told him it should be at his fingertips. Yet his hand continued forward, into or somehow past the bark, as if the tree were farther off.

He hesitated, took a breath, and pushed his face into the distortion.

The world blurred and twisted. Walls of color washed over him, then a wave of dizziness. He panicked and yanked out.

"See?" Eggwise said. "Nothing to it."

Par tried to steady his breathing, and his heartbeat. "Nothing?"

"Disorienting, perhaps. In all things unfamiliar, fear is strongest at the edges."

There was no denying the fear: the world had seemed to be melting. But at least he hadn't vomited this time.

Eggwise nudged him aside and faced the shimmer. He shifted one way, then another. Suddenly he stepped into it as casually as if he were turning a street corner, and was gone.

"Eggwise?" Par said. He shouted, "Eggwise?"

"Over here," the man called back.

Par looked around the tree.

Past the grove, in the middle of an overgrown field, stood the waving figure of Eggwise.

"You try," he yelled. "Keep moving, slow and steady. Watch the zigs."

The zigs? Par turned back to the tree. He began the awkward walking dance to keep it in focus, and with a last deep breath stepped inside.

Ahead lay a definite, though crooked, path. Shapes on the misty walls, maybe of trees and fields, rippled and ran like chalk graffiti in the rain. Par took one careful step. The images tilted. Their colors ran up, down, sideways. The corridor ahead drifted from left to right. He dared another step. The path zigged back left. He lost his balance and his hand shot out to a wall, but he found only cloud. With a yelp he fell into, and through, a ghostly mass of rushing colors. Then he was crashing through leaves and bushes and thorns, to at last be rudely stopped by solid ground.

He lay there, moaning quietly, while his head stopped spinning.

"Par?" said Eggwise, his voice coming closer. "Are you all right?"

Par tried to move. A thorn stabbed him. "Ow."

The brambles above parted. Eggwise's concerned face peered down, his hair beads hanging like berries. "I'm guessing you zagged instead of zigged."

"I'm guessing that too."

"Always keep moving, but never rush." Eggwise helped him up. "And don't leave a fold before the end. You never know where you might land."

Par took that to heart. He brushed himself off and removed the last of a couple small thorns.

"Now, if you're fully plucked, let's get going. Why don't you tell me about this unwell friend of yours? What ails him?" Eggwise resumed the journey north.

"Might be a long story," Par said, catching up, still a bit unsteady.

"Might be a long walk."

By now, Par trusted Eggwise—somewhat. But how much of that was justified? The man had given his own trust, revealing he was a Nowen, showing Par these incredible folds. And he already knew of the Vigil. It seemed reasonable, and fair, to return the sentiment.

So as they walked beside the river and Par recovered his wits, he told how Cronus had possessed the Eminence, and of Enio's sacrifice at the Immortus, allowing Cronus into his mind to drive back the Ortu creature, for which he still suffered. Par also told about the Vigil's demise at the Citadel, since the Eminence planned to make that public. But Par kept the Vigil's outposts and the Thresholds to himself, believing the Eminence was keeping those secret for now. Still, Eggwise seemed to grasp certain parts of the story Par had kept vague, as if he already had knowledge about them.

On their way, Eggwise found another fold. He dismissed it as too small to be useful.

"What if," Par asked, still amazed at their existence, "someone stepped into a fold by accident?"

"You saw how tricky the entrance is."

"But still."

"I suspect that person would be quite surprised."

Par couldn't argue with that.

For a while, their conversation dropped off: Eggwise was no doubt digesting Par's story. At last, as they approached a small rise, Eggwise said, "We're near a big one."

"Where?"

"The other side of the hill. You can't see it yet."

"But you can?"

"I'm a Nowen, remember?"

"Right," Par said.

The man looked back and winked. "Actually, I recognize the landscape."

They topped the hill. Beyond, a narrow creek ran through a field of rocks and boulders before emptying into the Greening. Eggwise led down. After a few false turns and some backtracking he stopped between two boulders as alike as two stone cows. A faint shimmer twinkled there, but in the wrong place to be a reflection of the sun.

"This is it," Eggwise said. "Come on." With that, he maneuvered into the fold.

Par followed. As before, blurry painted walls stretched before him. Eggwise led at a steady, careful pace through the strange corridor of rushing landscapes, and around bends more cloud than corner.

As Par got used to the going, he made better time—whatever that meant inside a fold. Eggwise had said to always keep moving. What if Par needed a rest? But in a matter of minutes—though to Par, long and tense ones—they reached the end, an opening of sharp color and light. They stepped out onto an endless expanse of flat granite. A cool, salty breeze hit Par's face and tossed his hair. There were no trees in sight, just a few scattered weeds and stubborn plants growing from cracks.

"Where are we?" he asked.

"Can't you tell?"

The stony ground continued in every direction except one, where it simply ended several paces off. After a few steps that way, Par gasped. They had arrived atop high seaside cliffs. Beyond the thousand-foot drop at his feet, rising from the waters, floated the island city of Argent. And Par stood, amazed, not only at the view but at the fact that the trip should have taken days by barge or canoe instead of scarcely longer than planning the journey over a map.

On this side of the bay, between a break in the cliffs, lay the mainland town. The causeway connecting it to the island seemed extra busy. But now the question hit: how would he and Eggwise get down? Par had never been on these cliffs, a place mostly for lookouts and thrill-seekers. The climb was famous for steep and narrow steps.

"Couldn't they have put the fold closer to sea level?" he asked.

"Remember what I said? Folds that run near people—near magic—risk breaking up."

A thin voice interrupted, apparently from nowhere: "Name yourself!"

Par spun. But he and Eggwise were alone.

"Did you hear that?" Par said.

The voice spoke again. "Par? Is that you?"

Again Par turned. "Who's speaking?"

Eggwise stepped forward. "I believe it's your shirt."

"Par?" repeated the voice.

A faint vibration touched Par's chest, where his Lustering medal hung. He drew it out. "Uh, hello?"

"Ah!" came a clear voice from the medal. "Hold on. I'll explain in a moment."

Par looked at Eggwise. The man shrugged.

Three steps away, a sharp, rectangular doorway opened in the air, very unlike the shimmer of a fold. In fact, Par had seen it before. A Threshold! A white-haired man in blue robes stood beyond its frame. It was Alexander Vex, the wizard.

"Vex!" Par said with no small relief. His troubles were over.

Vex spotted Eggwise. "Who is that with you?"

"His name is Eggwise. There's a lot to tell."

"You trust him?"

"Yes," Par added. Then again, he'd just met the guy, and had already avoided telling him of the Thresholds.

The wizard thrust his hand through. "Very well. Hurry. Argent is being evacuated."

Chapter Twenty-Three

Vex brought Par, with Eggwise in tow, through the Threshold into a dim chamber. A ghostly orb, several paces wide, floated in the air. Golden sparks twinkled across its surface. Par recognized the place: the Vigil outpost, deep within the cliffs under Argent's High Temple. That was the monitor, each spark reporting the use of magic in the lands nearby.

Eggwise stepped toward it. "What do we have here?"

"Sir," Vex said, "please don't touch that."

Par's relief at arriving in Argent had suffered a blow. "Vex, you said the city is being evacuated. Why?"

"The quakes grow worse." The wizard ushered Par aside and lowered his voice. "What were you two doing on the mainland cliffs?"

"Eggwise took me there."

"Why?"

"I better start at the beginning. I stowed away on the *Sea Dog* when it sailed for the Deep World."

"We heard," Vex said.

"You did?"

"From the Asrai. There's been another communication."

"Oh." Par sighed. "She must be furious with me."

"She barely mentioned you. Overall, she seemed impressed by our delegation, especially Rafael. She said his relations with their own representative, your friend Alehilani, seemed quite promising."

The word *relations* struck an uncomfortable chord. But why hadn't the Asrai spoken of Par's crime and imprisonment? Had she forgiven him? "What else did she say?"

"She confirmed the Dark Tribes are causing the quakes. In fact, Cornelius asked me here to use the monitor and pinpoint their source. No luck, sadly. Perhaps it is out of range."

"Did she tell you of the mission?"

"What mission?"

"To find the Nowen."

"Nowen?"

Par told Vex what the Asrai had said regarding Nowen and raw moon marrow. He added how he'd leapt for the *Sea Dog* but wound up in Choga. Then he hesitated. Should he reveal that Eggwise claimed to be a Nowen? The man had spent a lifetime keeping that secret. So Par would wait to see if Eggwise revealed it on his own. He'd also leave the part about the folds for Eggwise. He finished with Enio's illness and decline, and how the moon marrow might help him.

"I'm very sorry to hear Enio has not healed." Vex scratched his chin. "The Asrai did not speak to us of moon marrow or Nowen. I've revisited the Citadel—as I suspected, the Luminary's ring allows me to pass the seals when properly used—and read more of its tomes, but found no mention of such curious things. She's proposed a meeting between the Eminence, the rulers of Arcana, and a leader of the Dark Tribes she referred to as Gorga."

Except for that new name, Par swore Rafael had asked for just such a meeting. But the Asrai had wanted to remain uninvolved.

"Maybe the mission has already succeeded, and that changed her plans?" While Par hoped so, his heart wouldn't believe it. Not until he saw his friends again.

Before Vex responded, Eggwise cleared his throat.

They looked over. "Yes?" Vex said.

"I think it's obvious your Asrai is hiding something."

Par was wondering the same thing. "Vex, when does she want to meet?"

"She awaits our reply. Your Eminence plans to accept."

A tremor ran through the floor. Par startled and steadied himself against the wall. The tremor passed.

"We've questioned some of the Lowers about the quakes," Vex added, "but learned nothing."

"Lowers?"

"People who use the magic of the Lower Realms. They're difficult to find. They live on the fringes or pretend to be feeble."

Eggwise's interest had turned from the monitor to the Threshold, now just a dull arch in the wall. He knelt at the base, running a finger along its single black step.

"Excuse me, sir," Vex said. "Don't touch that either."

Eggwise withdrew his hand. "Sorry. But it's quite interesting."

The mention of interesting magics reminded Par to ask, "Vex, how did you make my pendant speak?"

"Ah. Keep this a secret for now," Vex said, his gaze lingering briefly on Eggwise, who seemed otherwise occupied with the Threshold's base.

Par nodded.

"Your pendant, it turns out, is charmed."

"My pendant?" Par again examined the small, flat piece of hammered gold hanging from his neck chain. Just a common Lustering medal, with the flame sigil engraved on one side. "I got this from my parents. They got it from the abbey."

"Your Hierarchy distributes them, but did not create them. The Vigil did."

"The Hierarchy worked with the Vigil?" Par thought the Vigil had kept themselves hidden and anonymous.

"No. The Vigil delivered the pendants to your Hierarchy covertly and indirectly."

"Why?"

"While the monitors appear to detect magic, that's not quite true. Your pendants do, along with other keepsakes such as the rings and necklaces of Ascendency in Arcana. These form a web of nosey nannies, gossiping with each other and any monitor within range which, in turn, communicate with each other through the Citadel, allowing any monitor to show magic activity in range of any others. At least once I take down the Citadel seals. I am still working on that."

The Vigil had spied on the lands for centuries, but Par never imagined the citizens were part of that machinery. The revelation tied his tongue.

Vex went on. "Just now, as I was using the monitor, I noticed a strange rippling unlike any I'd ever seen. From the Citadel tomes, I learned what I've just told you about the pendants and how to converse through them. So I tried it on that location. To you, it turns out. I then opened the Threshold there."

He stepped closer to the monitor's translucent orb. Eggwise paused in his examination of the Threshold to watch. Par had to smile at how Vex was so easily distracted by magical explanations, especially when he was the one giving them. If only Par could turn off his worries that way.

Vex gestured a few times, rotating the globe. He placed his finger on a dot of light and spoke. "Like this."

Par's pendant repeated the words. *Like this.*

Par let it go as if it had become hot. It dangled again from his neck. "The Vigil—these monitors—can listen to anyone's pendant?"

"Any that are in range."

This was downright creepy. "So they could eavesdrop on entire nations?"

"According to the Vigil tomes, they did not use the ability lightly."

Eggwise finally said something. "A secretive group of mages with unchecked powers of surveillance? I'm sure they never abused *that*."

Par had to agree with the sarcasm.

Vex cleared his throat. "Yes, well. The Vigil has been gone for years. The people will soon be informed. But by your Eminence, not by you or me." He frowned at Eggwise. "Sir, what was that strange rippling magic I detected? Some sigil of yours?"

"Oh," Eggwise said, "not a sigil. You saw a fold."

"Fold?"

Eggwise chuckled. "Not in your tomes, eh?"

Again Par eyed the man. Here was one of the Nowen they'd gone to find. That gave hope of finding more, and of the Asrai joining their fight against the Dark Tribes. If Enio needed moon marrow, who better to find some than another Nowen?

Par couldn't keep this secret any longer. "Eggwise, you have to tell him."

"I don't see why."

"Tell me what," Vex said.

There was no point easing into it. "Eggwise is a Nowen."

Vex peered at the man. "Indeed?"

Eggwise brushed a blue hair bead from his forehead. "It's impolite to stare."

"If that is so...." Vex's eyes widened. "I've just realized. One of the remaining Sentinels must be a Nowen, and I still have the sigil to release it, but the sigil requires a Nowen to use. Sir, I'll grant you that sigil, and—"

"Nowen invoke sigils in pairs," Par said. "We'd need two."

"Two?"

"Two Nowen. It's how they work."

"Remarkable." Vex studied Eggwise again. "Then perhaps both Sentinels are Nowen. In any case, this news cannot wait. We must inform the Eminence. Come with me."

Eggwise crossed his arms. "I'm not going anywhere."

The excitement in Vex's face drained into a frown. "Then I will bring the Eminence here. And I must warn you—the corridors beyond are guarded."

"He's a friend," Par said, pushing down his guilt for betraying the man's secret.

"Par, we know nothing of the Nowen, or of this individual. We must be careful. Now, come with me."

"I'll wait with him." It seemed the least Par could do.

"I'm not sure that's a good idea," Vex said.

"Are we then *both* in your custody?" Eggwise countered.

Vex glanced at Par, then sighed. "Very well. I'll be back soon." He strode out the door.

"Now that you've given me away," Eggwise said, "what do you think they'll do with me?"

"They'll ask for your help."

"Ask or demand?"

Unsure, Par hesitated. "Well, you'll help them, right?"

"Help them what?"

"Get the moon marrow. Or find other Nowen."

"And if I don't?"

"Why wouldn't you?"

"That's my business. But again, do you think if I declined, they'd let me walk away? Are they any more interested in my free will than were the Vigil? And if I resist their questions, do you doubt they'd steal their answers from my mind?"

The Confessors could do just that. Par respected the Eminence and the Abbot, but he wasn't as familiar with the other higher-ups, like Master Simeon, the Keeper of the Gates, in charge of war strategy. What might he do?

It hit Par again. Eloria had its own ways, enforcing the Rule and the proper invocation of the gods. Anyone who didn't *fit* was labeled a criminal, or an abomination, like Par. The policies had recently changed, but it took longer to change hearts, and there were still those in Eloria who felt disgust, even hatred, toward anyone incapable of invoking. They'd judge Eggwise as one of those. As they judged Par.

"You're right," Par said. "And I'm sorry, Eggwise. I shouldn't have told Vex you're a Nowen. But we have to help with these quakes and—"

"And your friends," the man said softly.

Par stopped. The threat by the Dark Tribes was a big thing, bigger than him. And the quakes might soon turn deadly. But he couldn't deny he had motives of his own.

"That too," Par admitted. "But your secret wasn't for me to tell."

"I accept your apology." Eggwise turned back to the Threshold's black step. "Look, Par, the work of the ancient Nowen, my ancestors."

A rumble ran through the floor. A drizzle of dust shook loose from the ceiling.

"Get down." Eggwise crunched near the Threshold. Par joined him.

The room jolted. Par covered his head, praying the cliffs above them weren't collapsing.

To his great relief, the quake faded. Guards shouted to each other. One peeked in. "Everyone all right?"

"Yeah." Par brushed off his shoulders. "But we're not safe here."

"My orders are—"

A small piece of plaster dropped from overhead and shattered across the floor.

The guard squinted at the ceiling. "Uh, I'll catch the wizard." He hurried off.

"Well," Eggwise said, "I have no desire to have my head opened by either falling rocks, or by your Eminence." The man pursed his lips. "War and politics aside, you want to help your friends, yes?"

"Of course." Par also eyed the ceiling, uncertain what to do next.

Another tremor shook the walls. The monitor blinked dark, and lit once more. Dust sparkles drifting through the ghostly globe.

Par began to stand. "That guard is taking too long. We should leave."

"I agree," Eggwise said, but instead lay his hand on the Threshold. "This way."

"Vex has the keystone. Besides, it only allows passage once a day. He used it bringing us here."

"Regardless, Par, if we could leave through it, where would you go?"

"We don't have time for games!"

"Humor me. What would you do?"

Par blurted the obvious. "I'd show the Asrai I found a Nowen and try to find my friends."

"I have as much interest in the Asrai as in Argent's Hierarchy." With his finger, Eggwise traced a sigil on the step. "Par, there's something I need to tell you. I've been trying to pick the right moment."

"What's that?"

"You're not feeble."

Despite the situation, Par smiled a little. "I know. I have a thick soul, that's all."

"No, Par. The reason you can't invoke isn't because there's something wrong with you."

"Vex said I was born with a condition."

"Not in the way you think."

"What do you mean?"

"This may be difficult to accept." Eggwise watched Par with an unusual intensity. "But believe it or not, you, my boy, were born a Nowen."

Chapter Twenty-Four

The words stuck in Par's ears, too immense to fit. "What? Say that again?"

"You're a Nowen, Par."

"You mean," Par said, trying to make some sense of this, "an honorary one. Like I'm a brother of the Choga."

Eggwise shook his head. "It's the reason you've never invoked a sigil. You were born a Nowen, grew up a Nowen, and are one now."

Was this some kind of joke? With the quakes, and Vex summoning the Eminence, this wasn't the time for weird humor. "Cut it out, Eggwise. I can't be a Nowen. I was born in Eloria, like my parents."

"Yes, nuts usually fall close to their trees." Eggwise sat on the Threshold step and patted the space beside him. "But sometimes an acorn takes a bounce. Didn't you say your friend Enio uses other magics?"

Par remained standing. "He does now, but he was born to lumina. I've never been able to invoke like normal people. Vex and the Abbot said it's because my soul is too thick."

"What could they know of a Nowen soul?"

Par hesitated. That was true. "But… why do you think I'm a Nowen?"

"I began to suspect in the caves, when the fold threw us off course. Something interfered, and it wasn't me. But what clinched it is that you can see the folds yourself."

"Only after you point them out."

"They can be subtle. But only our kind can see them. Trust me, Par, you are a Nowen."

Par was running out of arguments. "It's not possible." He started to pace. "I would have known. Someone would have told me."

"Well," Eggwise said, "growing up, I imagine you only encountered sigils compatible with lumina. You had no chance of learning anything else. And of course you needed a second Nowen to invoke a Nowen sigil."

Par's heart beat faster. Could this be true? All along, he hadn't been feeble? Or thick?

When another tremor passed, he barely noticed: his life's very foundations were shaking. Before his legs gave out, he settled on the step next to Eggwise. Dare he believe it? Thoughts rushed him, a new world coming into focus. New possibilities. New hope.

This changed everything.

He turned eagerly to the man. "Eggwise, if you're right, then we are two Nowen, together. What if we can release the last two Sentinels, like Vex suggested? Those are ancient, powerful Nowen mages. They might have moon marrow. The Asrai will join our side." *And she'll return Lani and Enio.*

"You've got that sigil too?"

"I do!"

Eggwise gave a patient smile. "And you're suddenly able to invoke Nowen sigils?"

"Well…" Par frowned. Not a chance in the purple hells. He had no clue how to invoke like a Nowen.

"Chin up, Par. As in all such things, you'll need training. Practice. Besides, those mages likely wouldn't help us anyway. Even in their time, Nowen retreated from your world, remaining hidden and uninvolved. Same as today. As far as these new problems, the Dark Tribes, the Asrai—it's just not our business."

"Not your—" Par's words caught in his throat. He understood why Arcana and Eloria had been at war so long: their distrust, even hatred, had been guided—and misguided—by fears created by the Vigil. But for someone to turn their back because they didn't care? How was that any better?

Eggwise stood and brushed off his hands. "But enough what-ifs. Let's return to the here and now. Look closer at the step."

Par's thoughts whirled with this new revelation, and with frustration at Eggwise. Stunned for the moment, he examined the black stone of the Threshold and its strange carvings. "What about it?"

"See that corner sigil? The one shaped like a dancer?"

Par had examined these sigils before but had never noticed the resemblance. He nodded.

"Touch it."

He did. Thin, shallow, cold. A bit dusty.

Eggwise laid his hand on a similar sigil that mirrored Par's. The man cleared his throat. "Threshold, open."

To Par's absolute astonishment, the space through the arch shimmered like a fold.

"But how—" Par began.

"The Nowen created the Thresholds. Stands to reason a Threshold would respond to us."

Par didn't see how that stood to any reason. But it seemed pointless to argue.

"I can take us to Meridon, Par. The city of the Nowen."

"In the valley of Nux?"

"The Nowen haven't lived in Nux for millennia."

"But that's where the Asrai sent—"

Another tremor coursed through the room. More plaster fell from the ceiling. Gravel shivered across the floor, some disappearing into a long, thin, growing fissure.

After ducking down and waiting for the quake to pass, Eggwise said, "The guards will soon return. This is not your fight, Par. You are a Nowen. In Meridon, you will learn your sigils. You won't have to fear your future anymore."

"I never said I feared it." Par brushed debris from his hair.

"I understand the lie you've lived better than you think. You've been afraid of being found out."

Par couldn't deny it. "I was, but the Eminence declared new policies. No one can persecute me now."

"Don't kid yourself. But that's not the root. You're afraid of being disowned, discarded, forsaken. Of being left alone."

The words hit deep. If Par had been asked his greatest fear, he might have said the Reckoners, or drowning, or being buried alive. But in his bones, for as long as he remembered, he'd lived in fear of those close to him discovering his curse, his unworthiness before the gods, and driving him away, or abandoning him. To live alone.

Grow old alone.

Die alone.

He'd lived his whole life around that fear. That selfish fear.

Eggwise continued, "No one is immune to these feelings. Perhaps it affects you more than most. But your answers, the life you're born to live, wait beyond that Threshold."

Par gazed at the shimmering doorway. "But my friends are on this side. I can't just leave."

"Your friends are not within reach. Meridon is. Face it, Par. It's time to try a new path."

Was Eggwise right? Whether or not Par was a Nowen, he'd come to Argent to tell of the Asrai's plans. He'd told Vex. What else could Par do here? What else did anyone need him for?

Or want him for. Last time he walked the streets of Argent, someone tried to drop a flowerpot on his head. But in Meridon, he wouldn't be different anymore. As he was from Enio. And from Lani.

He was torn between something he wanted and something he needed. But which was which?

A shout echoed down the hall.

Eggwise stepped up to the Threshold. "Decide now, Par. Stay here, feeble in their eyes, taking their charity, their pity. Living the life everyone expects of you. Or come with me. Live the life you're born to. In Meridon, you'll never be afraid of being different. Of being outcast. Of being alone."

Vex shouted from the room's doorway. "The Threshold! How—"

A fantastic jolt shook the room. The crack in the floor split wide and Vex fell back. Mortar rained from the ceiling. Dust filled the air.

Par coughed and gagged. The room was veiled with a thick haze, like his brain. Everything he thought he knew about himself, his life, his future, had become clouded.

But the Threshold shimmered clear and sharp.

Eggwise reached out. "Come, Par."

Par took the hand.

The floor shuddered again.

Vex's voice barked from somewhere across the room. "Par!"

"Go back, Vex!" Par shouted. I'm leaving with Eggwise! I'm going to be a Nowen!"

With that, Par stepped through the Threshold.

PART THREE

THE GORGA

Chapter Twenty-Five

ENIO SAT SHACKLED on the ground, surrounded by tents and a mob of strangers. The two sitting beside him named themselves Rafael and Lani. Rafael continued to argue with Yantra, an old woman, about quakes and armies and missions to lost cities. She in turn argued with others. The words flew round and round.

"They're spies," bellowed a bull-like man with a black bone through his nose. "I say we dig out the truth."

Yantra shook her head. "It might corrupt their memories."

"Try the sickly one. He's not gonna last."

"Now wait—" Rafael began.

But Yantra interrupted. "Not unless we've no choice. The Gorga will want their minds intact."

Bone-nose suggested another approach that sounded suspiciously like torture. Yantra again pointed out the risks, and their arguments went in a circle.

"Is the Gorga in charge?" Lani whispered.

Enio thought Keb had said so. But Rafael whispered back,

"Let's find out." He spoke up. "I request an audience with your leader, with the Gorga."

"When we reach the rest of the Horde," Yantra said, "you will surely have your audience."

Enio had no part in this conversation; a growing weariness now fought his mind and body and he was doing his best to shake it off. No telling what this crowd might do to him if he fell asleep.

As Yantra's attention shifted to a private conference, Lani leaned over. "Enio, how are you managing?"

"Good enough."

Rafael turned too. "You still don't recognize us?"

Enio groped through his memories, but it was like fishing in an empty pond. "They found me about frozen. They thought it affected my head."

"Cold doesn't wipe memories," Rafael said.

Lani lay a shackled hand on Enio's arm. "Not long ago, you had an injury deep to your spirit. We fear it's getting worse."

"I'm just tired." Her friendly eyes grabbed his attention. "I don't remember you, but I feel like, I don't know. Like I trust you."

She smiled. "We first met last year. You were lost with Par in the forests of the Urdel."

Enio was tempted to ask more about his past, but details would be wasted on him: he'd only forget them again. Still, the name jarred something. He concentrated. There were no images, but feelings of familiarity lingered. "We trust him too, right?"

"We do."

"Where is he now?"

Her smile faded. "Far away. I hope he's all right."

Rafael said, "I believe the Asrai will keep him safe. No need to worry."

She sighed and looked down.

"Ah." Rafael nodded. "You and Par are… close."

Her jaw seemed to tighten. "It's complicated. The Asrai asked me to remain in the Deep World as a bridge to the outer lands."

"A diplomat?"

"Of a kind."

"Is that what you want?"

She gave a slight shrug. "It's an important job. And living with others like me—you don't know how tempting that is. But once I decide, that's that. I'll go through the *chela élande* I told you about. My changes."

"Big decision, then."

"Very. And I don't feel ready to make it."

"Is Par involved?"

"It has nothing to do with him." She hesitated. "Or maybe it has everything to do with him."

Just then, a blast of air smacked into Enio's face. Everything blurred. The blur became a light. An arm reached from its center. Enio gasped and fell against Lani.

"Guards!" yelled Yantra.

Enio blinked his vision clear. Spears pointed at his chest. Rafael had disappeared.

Yantra pushed closer. "Where did he go?"

"I have no idea," Lani said, her wide eyes searching the camp, spears directed at her too.

Bone-nose, now invoking with a bronze glory, said, "I do not sense deception."

Yantra focused on Enio. "What can you tell me about this?"

"Me?" Enio shook his head. "Nothing."

"He holds back," said the man.

Her glory blazed red. "I've no time for lies."

The reddish light hit Enio's eyes. He squeezed them shut, yet a dull red reached past his eyelids, into his very thoughts.

A voice. *Tell me!*

Enio recoiled into the shadows of his mind. *Tell you what?*

What happened to Rafael?

Without even trying, Enio's memory pieced together what he thought he'd seen. An arm reached out of the air, grasped Rafael, pulled him into the light. For an instant, there was a second face. Then the entire scene dissolved.

Whose face was that? The voice shoved deeper.

I don't know!

Don't resist.

I'm not!

Where do you come from?

I can't remember!

Why are you here?

Enio was sliding into blackness. He reached to the dim red light for rescue. *Help me!*

The light shot forward, enveloping him.

Enio cried out and opened his eyes.

Lani was beside him. "Leave him alone!"

Yantra had already backed away. "His memories sink into an abyss. He sinks with them. But I sense no deception."

Sinking. He'd felt that for days. Scraping his way up. Sliding down further.

But this time was different. Something below had pulled.

"Search the camp," Yantra said, "and chain these two in a tent." She eyed Enio and Lani. "If you escape, I suggest you do it together, for the one left behind will die most horribly."

A spear-point prodded Enio's chest.

Enio froze, muddled and confused. But he understood the point of a spear.

✳

Par had used Thresholds before. He knew the rules. In each instance, he'd stepped from one location to another, an entire country to another, to wherever the person holding the keystone envisioned. But not this time. From all appearances, he'd stepped from the quaking Argent outpost into a fold. Not a smeary, cloudy fold, but a grand arched hallway, as smooth and white as marble.

Eggwise stood beside him. "Now, Threshold, to Meridon."

The passage swung. Par reached for Eggwise to steady himself, but the corridor settled, ending ahead in a dim opening.

Par glanced back. A featureless wall had replaced the room they'd left.

"That last quake…" Par said. "Is Argent all right?"

As the question left his mouth, that blank wall shimmered and reopened, and there, as if Par had taken flight, appeared the entire island of Argent. Dust rose from every quarter. Monstrous waves crashed against the southern cliffs. And atop the highest point, the triple-spired High Temple, the pride of Argent, had only two spires left.

Gods. Par struggled for words. "Can we help?"

"I don't see how," Eggwise said. "Now hurry. We must continue to Meridon."

But this backwards view had opened in response to Par's last words. Could he direct it again? One place jumped to mind. "Show me the Valley of Nux."

The portal blurred.

"No, Par!" Eggwise shouted. "We must move forward!"

But the portal behind sharpened to show a rugged valley dotted with tents.

"Closer!" Par commanded.

The view dove to where he could see wagons and horses, then individual men and women.

Eggwise gripped Par's shoulder. "This passage will not last!"

Par twisted free. The camp appeared loose and random, except for a large group gathered around a vaporous red pit. Others walked that way. He had a feeling about it. He pointed. "There!"

The doorway slid toward the crowd. Three people sat on the ground, seemingly the focus of attention. Par's heart leapt. It was Lani, Enio, and Rafael.

The corridor trembled.

Eggwise shouted, "The fold is collapsing!"

The doorway came to rest beside his friends.

As Par thrust out his hand, the view jolted, fading into cloud. He could barely make out anyone now. Enio had been close to Lani. Par reached that way. He grabbed someone. He pulled.

Eggwise grabbed Par and yanked him backwards.

A horrible sensation of falling twisted his every internal organ. He landed hard in a dim chamber. Stone pillars carved with frowning faces, half in shadow, loomed above him.

Squeals and shouts filled the air. He groaned and tried to move. Someone lay on top of him.

But it wasn't Eggwise.

And it wasn't Enio or Lani.

He'd snagged Rafael.

Chapter Twenty-Six

Par pulled himself from under Rafael. The shouts he'd heard came from children dropping their books, scattering from pews, scrambling around the pillars.

He struggled to his feet on a stage of sorts. A sculptured arch loomed behind him. The Threshold, if that's what it was, no longer showed any passageway—merely another wall. Black curtains hung beside it, pulled into clumps.

"Nux!" Par yelled at it, trying again to reach Enio and Lani. "Valley of Nux!"

No change.

A voice rang through the chamber. "Hold!"

Two new figures had entered, their robes patterned like colorful quilts. The woman in front had black hair gathered into a melon-sized bun. Alongside her walked an elderly man with thick white dreadlocks. He held a fat sword in both his hands. It drooped.

These two approached down an aisle, then up brief steps onto the stage. They stopped several paces away. The woman studied Par and his group. "You younger ones are not our students, I'm sure of it. Who are you?"

Eggwise stepped forward, his hands raised in surrender. "No need for hostilities, madam. I've come from Argent with news for the High Assembly."

She scowled for a moment. "Stand away from the Gate."

As they obeyed, Par whispered to Rafael, "Why are you shackled? What about Enio and Lani?"

"They're safe for now," Rafael whispered back. "We were captured by the Horde: the army of the Dark Tribes."

Par didn't think that sounded any kind of safe.

"Want to tell me what's going on?" Rafael added.

"I rescued you."

Rafael eyed the sword. "Not my first guess."

"Quiet!" barked the woman. She spoke to her companion. "Guard them."

Sweating now, the man pointed his sword at Eggwise. The woman addressed the arch. "Open to High Assembly."

A sunny room with tall windows appeared beyond, stately but empty.

"Probably on another holiday," the older man said. "Try Regent what's his name—Zinger? Zippy?"

Par caught a faint child's giggle from near the gate, behind the curtains. No one else seemed to notice.

"Zizik," the woman corrected. She spoke again to the arch. "Meridon South."

Cottages appeared. The view slid past them, down a well-groomed country lane and then to fields and farmlands. Green hills rose in the distance, some home to great columned buildings.

Then, near a vineyard, they spotted a man in simple brown work clothes and a straw hat. He was examining a hanging clump of grapes.

"There," said the woman.

The view stopped beside him.

"Regent Zizik?" she said.

He looked up, his face glowing with sweat. "Oh, hello, madam. How is your day?"

"Interrupted. We have visitors. They request to see you."

"To tour the winery?"

"No. They asked for the High Assembly. They came through the Gate."

"Is that so?" The man removed his hat and hung it on a post. He wiped his damp, bald head and stepped through the arch, joining them in the room. The view through the Gate evaporated.

Zizik gave a smile. It didn't seem very sincere. "And whom do I have the pleasure?" he asked.

It was Eggwise who answered. "I am Eggwise, Nowen of Choga, arriving through the Vigil's Argent Threshold. You are Regent of the High Assembly these days?"

"I am. Let us hail." Zizik held out his hand.

Eggwise took it. A shimmering glory, colorless like heat, surrounded his head and that of Zizik.

"Nowen?" murmured Rafael.

"I'll explain later," Par said.

The glory around the men's heads rippled a moment longer and faded.

Zizik released his hand. "You speak true, Eggwise."

"I bring with me Par. He has just discovered he is a Nowen. I present him for the choice."

Par eyed Eggwise. Present him? Choice?

Rafael spoke, seeming now to take everything in stride. "And I, sir, am Rafael, diplomatic representative of Eloria, Arcana, and the Borderlands."

Zizik raised an eyebrow. "A Nowen diplomat?"

"I'm not a Nowen."

The eyebrow fell. Zizik switched his interest to Par. "Just discovered, you say? Can you hail?"

Eggwise replied instead. "He has lived outside our circles. He hasn't yet been taught our hail, or any other sigil."

"Then why do you believe he is a Nowen?"

"He can see the folds."

"That is not definitive."

"Yet the Threshold opened for us."

Again Zizik gave a patronizing smile. "The lesser Thresholds are not a recognized test. They were built for use by outsiders."

"Nevertheless, I'm sure his nature will be confirmed. Now I want to discuss my own—"

"Please." Par interrupted, losing patience. He pointed to the arch. "Help my friends. They're still prisoners."

"Our Gate," said Zizik, "is available only to our own people, with the Assembly approving all passage beyond Meridon."

"But—" Par and Eggwise said in unison.

Zizik raised a hand. "However, regardless of how you arrived, we must allow every Nowen their choice."

As Zizik had raised his hand, an amulet peeked from the man's shirt. The mineral was black with red veins.

Moon marrow.

Eggwise cleared his throat. "I feel confident, Regent Zizik, that after a bit of instruction, he will prove himself a Nowen. But as I was trying to say, I need to speak with you about—"

"Then you, Eggwise, shall instruct him."

"I what?" Eggwise said, taken aback.

"He will?" Par's eyes flew from the amulet to Eggwise.

"It is the most reasonable solution. I cannot enroll this boy in the Anthenaeum since he is not a verified Nowen. I gather you have another issue to discuss with me, Eggwise, but you made your choice long ago and are here uninvited."

Eggwise grumbled.

Zizik continued, "I will, however, grant you a temporary stay while you prove Par is a Nowen and worthy of his choice. Or you may refuse and leave now."

"But the quakes," Par said, exasperated. "My friends, the Asrai—"

"Sir," Rafael addressed Zizik, "may I have a moment with my companion?"

"Take all the moments you need."

Rafael drew Par aside. "Calm down. Now, what's this about you being a Nowen?"

The young diplomat needed to be fully informed to be helpful. So Par steadied himself and quickly explained where he'd been since the Mother Spring.

As he finished, Rafael frowned. "If you ask me, Eggwise seems to have another agenda beyond bringing you here."

Par hadn't considered that, and indeed Eggwise seemed intent on engaging Zizik in some personal matter. And what was this business about a choice? "You think he's been lying to me?"

"Or perhaps using you as a means to his own ends. For now, let me handle things."

"Do we have time for diplomacy? Lani and Enio—"

"—are safe, as I said. The Dark Tribes intend to bring them to the Gorga, their leader, who I gather is still some distance away. That gives us time and opportunity. Let's use it."

Vex had mentioned that name too. "Use it how?"

"I'll explain everything to this Regent Zizik, and in my own way. Remember, we still need their cooperation to get the Asrai on our side. I'm trained for this. I know what I'm doing. Be patient and give me a chance, all right?"

Par had no better plan. He nodded, then lowered his voice further. "That amulet Zizik is wearing—I think it's moon marrow."

Rafael kept his eyes on Par. "Well, one more reason for diplomacy. Nowen or not, you're a smart guy, Par."

"Stop saying that."

Rafael, with his shackles clinking, shuffled a step toward Zizik. "Sir, the lands of Eloria and Arcana are in danger."

"That is not news," Zizik said. "The outer lands have forever been unbalanced." He again addressed the woman. "Let's unbind our guest. We are not without manners."

She nodded and moved to Zizik's side. Rafael held out his hands. Instead of unfastening the shackles, Zizik and the woman invoked with their odd wiggly glories. Rafael's bonds, hand and ankle, dropped away and clanked to the floor—yet they hadn't been touched, and they hadn't opened. They just fell off, as if for an instant, Rafael's limbs weren't there to hold them up.

Rafael rubbed his wrists. "You know of the attacks?"

"Attacks?" Zizik shook his head.

"It is imperative we discuss them."

Zizik seemed to consider. "I confess, I find the political circus beyond our borders entertaining. Very well, Rafael, you and I will speak while Eggwise instructs Par."

This seemed to satisfy everyone—except Par: Lani and Enio remained center stage in his anxieties. He felt like he was abandoning them, the very people that, as Eggwise had pointed out during their walk, Par feared might one day abandon him.

Yet he'd come here to discover his Nowen nature. Not only had he found their city and met their leader, but he'd found moon marrow. Raw or not, there must be more. These people didn't yet seem very cooperative, but if Par proved he was a Nowen, it might open doors. Literally, like the big one through the Gate. And he might convince these Nowen to help with the Asrai's demands.

Rafael had said to be patient. That attitude seemed to be paying off. So Par resolved to give diplomacy its chance.

But not a long one.

Chapter Twenty-Seven

Zizik addressed the woman and her companion. "Thank you, educators, for your help." He pointed to the sword. "Please put that back before you hurt yourselves, and collect your students. I expect they've left a trail throughout the Anthenaeum."

"Oh dear," the woman said, "the students." She and the elderly sword carrier hurried away.

"Anthenaeum?" Par asked Eggwise.

"Place of learning."

"Eggwise," Zizik said, "I must attend a few things regarding your arrival and your training of Par. Please wait here." He followed the others out.

Eggwise repositioned a bead, making his hair no more orderly. "Well, Par, I suppose we're going to be together a while longer."

"This is a school?"

"And a museum. They use the Gate for lessons about the outer world."

Now that the Nowen had removed Rafael's shackles, he was

shedding his cold-climate furs. "Wherever we are, my backside has gone from sledding to sweating."

The giggle came again from behind the black curtains. This time, Eggwise and Rafael seemed to hear it too.

Par put a finger to his lips before they said anything.

They nodded.

"You know,"—Par spoke more loudly—"being strangers, we don't know what monsters might lurk in the shadows. Big ones, with green horns and giant purple noses, waiting to eat us."

A snort erupted behind the drapes.

"And with such big noses, they must have smelled us already." Par added a mysterious tone to his voice. "And any second now, they'll jump… out!"

He threw aside the curtain.

A small lad crouched there, wide-eyed, hands over his mouth.

Par bent down. "You're not going to eat us, are you?"

The boy shook his head.

Digging in his pocket, Par produced the small carved frog he'd gotten in Choga.

The boy's hands slid from his mouth. "What's that?"

"A special frog someone gave me."

"From outside?" He leaned closer.

"Yes. And I hope, Sir Monster, you'd rather have a toy than a meal?"

"I'm not a monster," the boy said, never taking his eyes off the frog. "I'm Jeffrey."

"Hello, Jeffrey. We have a deal? No eating us?"

Jeffrey nodded like a woodpecker.

Par handed it over. "And it's lucky."

"It is?" The boy examined it as if it sparkled.

"You saw. It saved me from Sir Monster."

Jeffrey laughed.

"Now," Par added, "shouldn't you be with your teachers?"

The child glanced toward the exit. Then he lifted a string from around his neck. A simple setting held an oval black stone with red veins.

Moon marrow?

Jeffrey offered it.

"For me?" Par forced himself not to snatch the stone like a cat pouncing a mouse. He glanced at Eggwise.

The man shrugged.

"Thank you, Jeffrey." Par took it.

The boy scurried away, and out the door.

"You're good with kids," Rafael said, watching Jeffrey go.

The black stone now glittered in Par's hand. "Thanks. Used to be one myself."

"Let me see that," Eggwise said.

Par passed it over.

The man turned the stone, tapped and squeezed it. "As I suspected. A good fake, but just a toy." He gave it back.

Of course, getting moon marrow couldn't have been that easy. Par draped the string around his neck, alongside his Lustering pendant, and hoped this wasn't an omen of things to come: fake marrow for a fake Nowen.

Zizik returned wearing a colorful robe like the teachers. He carried a worn book. "Sorry for my earlier appearance—I was unprepared for guests. Eggwise, a moment?" The two huddled over an open page.

Rafael murmured to Par, "Zizik changed clothes. He's trying to impress us."

"He called our politics a circus," Par whispered back.

"Pretense and posturing." Rafael rubbed his hands. "Diplomatic opportunity."

Zizik handed the book to Eggwise and turned again to Par and Rafael. "The important thing is that this young man demonstrates a Nowen sigil. It doesn't matter which. Now, Rafael, let us chat privately. We'll reconvene at sundown."

Par's eyes met Rafael's as if to say good luck.

Rafael winked.

"Come along, Par." Eggwise led him out of the chamber.

With a last glance back, still uncertain whether Rafael's confidence was justified, Par said to Eggwise, "At least Zizik seems friendly."

"You think so?"

"He smiles a lot."

"So do crocodiles."

They entered a columned hallway. Oversized statues lined the walls, some holding real books or scales or other symbols of learning and government. The one nearest held the very sword the teacher had carried, returned to its place.

"Your lessons begin here," Eggwise said. He stood before a statue of a woman gesturing as skilled speakers do. "These seemed a lot taller during my own training and choice. I was younger than you."

"Why didn't you tell me about this choice thing before we got here?"

"I implied it."

Par wasn't so sure. "What am I choosing?"

"Whether to live in Meridon."

That was indeed the choice Eggwise had proposed before leaving Argent: continue in his old life, different from others, unable to invoke; or live in Meridon, no longer an outcast. But that choice was irrelevant if he wasn't a Nowen. Even if he were, the quakes might destroy Argent before he secured the Nowen's help. "How long is this going to take?"

"That's up to you. I suppose until you manage your first sigil. We'll start on that soon."

"And then Zizik will listen to my request for help?"

"Let's cross that Threshold when we come to it." Eggwise stepped to a portrait of a man with long wavy hair. "This is a big place. Soak up what you can."

Par glanced at the painting, then down the hall to dozens more waiting pictures. He groaned.

Eggwise eyed him. "Not a fan of art?"

"It's not that."

"You're in a hurry, I know. Well, let's keep moving."

Now ignoring the statues and paintings, Eggwise strode onward. He came to the diorama of a large domed structure. Its noble proportions rivaled, even surpassed, anything Pad had seen in the capitals of Eloria or Arcana.

"What's that?" Par asked, leaning in.

"The Nowen center of government, before the Devastation."

"The Devastation destroyed it?"

"No, the Nowen avoided the Devastation. You're walking through the building now."

They soon entered a two-storied chamber of broken stone tablets, decorative pots, old tools, primitive clothing, even bracelets and necklaces. All had plaques with forgettable names and dates, and Par began to wonder just what he was learning. He tried a question. "Is any of this stuff magic?"

"Not unless you consider art for art's sake magic. Except..." The man had spotted something. He motioned Par to an exhibit. Nestled among fancy trinkets lay a thin silver chain holding an oval pendant of black material with red veins.

"Moon marrow," Par stated.

"The genuine article. To the Nowen, it's more valuable than diamonds and often worn as jewelry by the elite." Eggwise glanced quickly around, then lifted it from its display. "I don't think anyone will mind us borrowing this, but let's keep it to ourselves. Its properties may speed your training."

"Is that raw? I mean, unprocessed?"

"It wouldn't be much help otherwise."

Finally! Their tour no longer seemed a complete waste of time. "Where does that stuff come from?"

"From places only a fold can reach." Eggwise pocketed it.

"Do you think Zizik would give me some, for the Asrai?"

"Not in a million years."

Par was afraid of that. His impatience ebbed back up. "When do we start my training?"

"We have: cultural context." Eggwise paused in his tracks. "But our book is vague on how much is required. We've made an effort, so let's find an exit."

They joined another hallway that led them outside, onto a sunny patio with marble tables and chairs. Steps ran from there down through tiers of gardens to a spreading green lawn bounded finally by a thick tree line. Everything appeared well tended, except for the structure they'd left. It was the large domed palace from the diorama but chipped and discolored with age. Vines climbed high on the walls.

"Your Anthenaeum has seen better days," Par said.

"Better centuries, in fact."

The weather here was spring-like. That brought a new realization. "Eggwise, I thought Meridon was in the Ults?"

"Used to be. After the Devastation, the Nowen moved it."

Had Par heard right? "Did you say *moved*?"

"Yes. Meridon is now within the largest artificial fold ever created. Follow me." Eggwise led down the steps and through the gardens.

Too stunned to speak, Par followed. The lawns, hills, fields, buildings—all inside a fold? There was still a sky and a sun, unlike within the other folds he'd traveled. Yet the sky outside the sun's path seemed faded and milky. Not quite cloud, not quite sky.

Like the walls of a fold.

They proceeded across the lawn, then into the trees. Eggwise led him along a cobbled path, but that was soon swallowed by dirt and brush. The farther in they went, the taller and more ancient the trees.

Then somewhere ahead came the burble of water. They arrived at a river lined with grassy banks and wildflowers. A simple log cabin stood nearby. The setting was peaceful, beautiful. Lani would love the place.

"This is one of the best spots for training," Eggwise said. "Not much to blow up."

"Blow up?" Par snapped back.

"I'm joking."

Par wasn't laughing.

Eggwise added, "It's just a quiet spot. I thought it might help you focus and relax."

Relax? That was a word Par hadn't considered for days. Lani and Enio were being marched to the ruler of the Dark Tribes. Vex said the Asrai hadn't even mentioned their mission, yet that last quake in Argent had been catastrophic. If Par hoped to gain the Nowen's help, or leave here with moon marrow, there wasn't time to relax.

Right here, right now, he needed to prove he was a Nowen.

Chapter Twenty-Eight

Near the river lay a mossy log. Eggwise brushed a spot, sat, and thumbed through the book he'd gotten from Zizik.

Par waited, wondering—hoping that he might be an actual Nowen. For his own sake, and for everyone's.

Eggwise flipped another page.

"What do I do?" Par asked. "How do I start?"

"I was invited back to Meridon once, long ago, to witness a distant relative's Ceremony of Choice." Eggwise squinted at the book. "Never prepared an initiate myself."

That didn't sound promising. "Should we get someone who has?"

Eggwise looked up.

"Or," Par said, not wanting to insult the man's age or capabilities, "somebody who's seen them done, uh, recently?"

"The best swordsmen have the most scars."

"You have scars?"

Eggwise stood and motioned Par to sit. "It's a metaphor. Let's give this a whack."

Finally! Par took the man's place on the log.

Using his finger, Eggwise traced the text on the page. "Here we go. The traditional ceremony begins with speeches and robes and other fluff and bother. We'll skip all that. I'm obliged, however, to read the preamble." He cleared his throat. "Know ye now the Nowen, the people of the now and of the here, of where and nowhere. The Nowen, sail and anchor, salt and sea, morrow to morrow. Three above. Three below. Two the balance, then and fro. The No—"

"Hey," Par said. "Vex found that last phrase in the Vigil tomes."

"Good for him. Where was I?"

"But *then and fro*? What does that even mean?"

Eggwise thought for a moment. "It's as old and obscure as the rest. Perhaps someone was trying to force a rhyme with *three below*."

"Oh."

Again Eggwise eyed the book, then closed it. "Enough of that. The next stage is a little history. I apologize in advance."

"I like history."

"That makes one of us. Stop me if it's old news."

Par nodded.

Eggwise slowly paced. "When Ridiax opened the rift to the Higher Realms, the most powerful mages of Gê, representing each type of magic, came together to drive back its spread and destruction."

"The Devastation."

"Yes. They worked their charms and confined it to a place they called the Immortus. As they relocated the survivors, they created the Sentinels to hold the rift in place. Then began the centuries-long job of finding a lasting solution. Such was the origin of the Vigil."

Par knew this much, but he let Eggwise continue.

"Each mage contributed their special skills, but it was the Nowen among them who created the Thresholds to transport the survivors over the Ults to their current homelands, separating those born to lumina from those born to numena."

"Into Eloria and Arcana," Par said. "They were afraid mixing magics might create a second rift." This sparked a new thought. "Did they separate the people of the Lower Realms?"

"Ridiax relied chiefly on lumina and numena to open the rift. The Vigil left the Lowers alone."

"What about the Nowen peoples?"

"The Nowen were too powerful to be affected by the Vigil's whims. Besides, the Nowen believed that manipulating entire populations injured the balance of things. But they agreed to leave the Vigil to their own devices, if the Vigil agreed to remove all mention from their records that the Nowen ever existed. The Nowen then moved Meridon from the valley of Nux into this fold, effectively disappearing from the world."

That explained why even Vex hadn't known about them.

"However," Eggwise continued, "not all Nowen were happy with this outcome. Some still wanted to help the lands, even amid the Vigil's deceptions, or just make lives of their own. These chose to remain outside, keeping their presence secret, even from the Vigil. That choice, to stay in Meridon or live outside, is one every Nowen makes. That you must make."

Though Par would have preferred to learn this before coming here, at least it was still his choice. "And you chose Choga?"

"I did." Eggwise stopped pacing. He gazed at the trees across the river. "I was born in Choga. The fold to the Greening had been under my family's care for generations, and I understood the responsibility must one day fall to me. But, to tell you the truth, I often regretted not choosing Meridon."

Par might have too, considering the swamps and frogs near Toadwalk. "You liked Meridon better?"

"Choga is a lovely place once you know it. It was my home. But for most young Nowen, the choice is a formality. No one asked what I really wanted." He took a breath. "Sometimes, Choga felt like a box. We had to be careful, always keeping our secrets."

This sounded terribly lonely. And it brought another question. "Once a Nowen chooses, can they change their mind?"

"Not easily. Family pressures and expectations lay hard. Then there are questions, waiting periods, votes. And for Nowen outside, finding their own way back here is nearly impossible."

A heaviness grew in Par at the man's story. It reminded him of the secret he'd hidden growing up, that he couldn't invoke the gods, and the fear of being found out. A fear that had kept many things in his life beyond reach; beyond his own box.

Eggwise sat next to him. "I need to confess something. I helped you to Argent because I'd heard it hid a Threshold. I hoped if you could get me to it, I might return to Meridon for a second choice."

So Rafael had been right; Eggwise had his own motives. Yet Par felt no resentment at that. Without Eggwise and the folds, Par would still be lost in Choga. He'd never have gotten to Argent, or found other Nowen. Or discovered he might be one himself.

"Par," Eggwise said softly, "when your choice comes, don't choose based on what everyone expects of you. Choose—"

"The life I was born to?" Par said, repeating the man's words from the outpost.

Eggwise smiled. "Good ears make a good student. Let's get to it." He straightened. "Living in Eloria, you were instructed in the ways of lumina?"

"Of course. I also know a little about numena and the élan and—"

"Yes, you're very smart. Don't change the subject."

Par wished people would stop saying that. "I wasn't—"

"The most basic sigils deal with the fundamental physical elements. The more complex involve life: flesh and bone, plants and animals, then mind and soul. But there's one further level: the transcendent. While other sigils are bound by common limitations—not creating something from nothing, for instance, or affecting things not present—the transcendent ones go beyond those restrictions. These are the supreme sigils, the soul and spirit of reality, so to speak. This is the magic of the Nowen."

Par had forever failed at basic sigils, and now he had to learn a supreme, transcendent one?

He grimaced. Great.

Eggwise must have noticed his dismay. "Don't worry—we'll teach you an easy one. But first you must learn to use anima."

"What's that?"

"Elorians sense the lumina that flows from the divine realms. Arcanans, the numena of the cosmos. And so on. Nowens are sensitive to anima, the tension within the balance of existence itself."

Par might manage this after all: he had tension to spare.

"Now, close your eyes and clear your mind. Breathe. Relax. Find your balance."

Closing his eyes, Par quieted his thoughts. The river burbled nearby, and a gentle, warm breeze carried pine smells and birdsong: perfect ingredients for calm and balance. He remembered simpler times, like floating on the Greening with Enio. He remembered the vibrant yet peaceful balance when Lani had introduced him to the élan in the Urdel woodlands.

He'd come so far since then. And he had far to go. Yet here he was, sitting on a log by a river, safe from everything outside Meridon. And the new plan?

Relax.

"You're breathing like a fish riding a horse," Eggwise said.

Par tried again. Inhale. Exhale. Relax.

But worries had swarmed his mind like buzzing insects.

Dark armies, quakes in Argent, his friends in peril. The harder he pushed them away, the stronger they'd return.

After several long minutes, he was anything but balanced. He opened his eyes.

Eggwise had moved to the river-bank, looking at the water. Par came beside him.

"Any more balanced?" Eggwise asked.

"Still a fish riding a horse."

"True balance is holding fear in one hand and hope in the other. Let's see if we can at least channel that nervous energy. Want to try a Nowen sigil?"

At last. Par nodded firmly.

"It may be easiest if it's similar to something you've seen before."

"How about a flame sigil? Do Nowen have those?"

"Everyone everywhere has a flame sigil."

Par brightened, imagining the pure delight of showing his friends, his parents, the Abbot, every single person in Argent, that he could invoke a flame sigil.

Yet with all that was at stake, should he be spending precious time just learning to make a bit of fire?

He reconsidered. "Maybe one more Nowen-y?"

"Hmm. The hail and greet? You saw Zizik and I exchange that."

"What's it do?"

"It communicates a brief thought or emotion between two Nowen. Also helps loosen things up at parties."

That seemed even less useful. "Maybe something else? Sorry if I'm being difficult."

"It's your right. It's your first sigil." Eggwise pursed his lips. "What about the one you saw used on your diplomat friend?"

Par recalled Rafael's shackles falling off. That might have real value. "The shackle trick?"

"The pinch."

"It unlocks things?"

Eggwise shook his head. "A Nowen sometimes thinks of the world as a sheet or blanket. The folds fold that fabric, and the pinches pinch it. For an instant, the shackles weren't there. Well, they were there. But *there* wasn't."

"There wasn't there?"

"Not *there* there."

"Then *where* there?"

"Sorry," Eggwise said. "Nowen explanations take some getting used to. Where does a wrinkle go?"

"A wrinkle isn't its own thing," Par ventured.

"Correct. The Nowen did nothing to the shackles. They pinched the surrounding material. And that's the best I can explain with your current training." Eggwise chuckled. "When I was your age, we'd pinch out chairs as people sat."

Par had never imagined such a sigil. But if it could remove shackles, it was more useful than the hail. "Is it any harder than those others?"

"About the same, once you get your anima flowing."

"Sounds good to me, then."

"Very well. I'll bestow it on you now."

They leaned closer and pressed foreheads. Par had never had trouble receiving sigils; his problem had forever been using them. A wavy shape formed in the darkness of his mind. He pulled it in. Unlike most other sigils he'd seen, it had a pair of stalks twisting sideways.

Eggwise sat back. "When you invoke, your sigil will develop a reflection or shadow. That will be mine joining it." He found a pebble, gave it to Par, then left his hand out. "Nowen sigils, especially for beginners, can sometimes be strengthened with a physical connection."

Par held the pebble in one hand and took Eggwise's hand

with the other. He closed his eyes and summoned to mind the sigil he'd just received. He'd had plenty of instruction on how to use an Elorian sigil, but for everyone else learning those sigils, lumina seemed as abundant as sunshine. Never for him. But this time, it wasn't lumina he needed.

The sigil cast a shadow, deep and dimensional, the difference between a painting and a statue. It wavered slightly.

"I see it," he said.

"Good. Now let it fill with anima."

In the past, Par had only invoked a sigil when he hadn't supplied the magic himself. Like at the Immortus. He tried to recapture the same sensation.

Nothing.

He recalled when the Umbriarch had pumped him with numena in Arcana.

Nothing.

He brought back the sense of passing through the folds, the strange spinning and turning inside his body. But his sigil remained empty and faint.

Eggwise mumbled, "You're blocking."

"What am I doing wrong? Help me."

"A bird must flap its own wings."

"I'm flapping as hard as I can."

"But you're not letting go of the branch. Smooth and balanced, like a dance."

"So not a bird?" Par's exasperation grew.

"Or like a song. In harmony."

Par growled. "I see the sigils. They look just the same."

"Harmony isn't about singing the same notes. And squeezing my hand like a vise doesn't help. You're trying too hard."

"I'm not *doing* anything!" Par opened his eyes and let go of the man's hand. Burning with frustration, he flung the pebble into the river. Why had he believed he could do this?

As he got himself together, he remembered why.

Because he had to.

Eggwise sighed. "Well, a candle snuffed is once enough."

"What does that mean?"

"My own teacher used to say it." Eggwise rubbed his chin. "I'm not sure I ever knew."

Par smiled a little.

But Eggwise looked away. "Perhaps you were right. You need a better teacher."

There was little doubt in Par's mind that the failing here was in himself, not in Eggwise. And though Par had only known the man for a short time, he'd grown fond of him. Besides, if Eggwise gave up now, what would that mean for his chance at a second choice?

"I think," Par said, still bitterly disappointed, but refusing to give up, "I want us to keep trying."

Now Eggwise smiled too. "Good. In fact, we haven't tried everything yet." He reached into his pocket and removed the black stone on the silver chain he'd lifted from the museum.

The raw moon marrow.

Chapter Twenty-Nine

Eggwise examined the moon marrow. "I'm having second thoughts about this. There are risks."

"What risks?" Whatever they were, Par would take them.

"This amplifies not only magic, but emotions, mind, and spirit."

That's why it might help Enio too. "I have to try."

"Very well. We'll start by working on your anima." Eggwise snapped the black stone from its silver setting and handed it to Par. "Don't stare at this. Don't think about it. Moon marrow must become a natural part of you, like a weapon."

Par turned the smooth oval in his fingers. "I'm not very experienced with weapons."

"Then like a relationship. Don't force it. But don't fake it."

Not that Par was experienced with those either.

"Now, find your balance, relax. Let the anima flow."

Par closed his eyes and bowed his head. *Breathe. Relax. Find the balance.*

He sensed nothing new until, underneath his breathing, in

the deep space between heartbeats, he noticed an odd but subtle vibration. When he focused on it, the sensation faded.

"Don't get in its way," Eggwise whispered.

Par took another breath and began again, keeping his mind away from the small, powerful stone resting cool in his palm. The vibration returned, more structured, like the rhythms under music.

The rhythms brought images.

His home. Enio laughing. Lani smiling. Others, each dear to him.

The images brought feelings.

Peace. Happiness. Safety.

Eggwise's voice. "You're close."

Par let himself sink into the images and the feelings. But there was something uncomfortable mixed in; a quiet, nagging thought. What if he never saw his friends again? Had he ever told them how he felt about them? Or how much? And why not? Was he afraid they didn't feel the same?

The images drew back. The feelings thinned, except for one.

Fear.

"Careful," Eggwise warned.

Par couldn't let this fail. Everyone relied on him. He had to be a Nowen. He groped toward the images, but they had fled. Instead, he met a black wind, stiff and chill.

He pushed into it.

The wind increased, now ice cold to his bones.

He slipped backwards. He pushed harder.

"Don't struggle," urged Eggwise.

But the strongest blast yet obliterated any balance Par had left. His eyes flew open.

Eggwise was gone. The river and cabin were gone.

Par crouched on a pillar of rock in a raging sea. Waves crashed around him. Lightning flashed over a distant, grey shore. Everyone he'd ever known watched from there. The sea surged higher. Thunder boomed.

His fear turned to panic.

A monstrous black wave crashed upon the people, leaving nothing in its wake.

Par yelled out.

A blinding flash. An ear-splitting *crack!*

✳

The next thing Par knew, he lay in the grass under a peaceful sky.

Eggwise was beside him. "Are you hurt?"

Par's heart pounded. His face was wet. He wiped it. Sweat, not seawater. "What happened?"

"You fainted."

"There was a storm." Par's voice trembled. "I felt—"

"You felt power, and whatever lurks in your soul, amplified by the moon marrow." The black stone lay beside Par. Eggwise picked it up, snapped it back into its clasp and pocketed it. "You're not ready for this."

Par caught his breath, shaky and exhausted. "Didn't you say this was like a dance?"

"I didn't say a waltz." Eggwise helped him up. "We both need a break. Let's see how Rafael and Regent Zizik are getting along. And best not to mention this setback. We don't want Zizik to despair at our progress."

Despair was the right word. Par only hoped Rafael had made better headway.

The stroll beneath the ancient trees helped Par steady his nerves. To take his mind off his failure, he asked something he'd wondered about this giant fold.

"Eggwise, if Meridon is inside a fold, where does that river come from?"

"Outside, same as the sunlight." Eggwise gestured upwards. "This fold opens above, like a pocket, from horizon to horizon. Sun and moon and starlight peek in. Clouds and birds come and go. So does the river."

"Could someone ride the river in?"

"Well, it enters from underground, so not that way. As for the other end, remember, others can't even see it. Though in Meridon's case, and under proper conditions, the opening's immensity sometimes creates a rainbow among the Ults."

"Then we're still in the Ults?"

"We're in a fold. The opening is in the Ults."

The short conversation helped Par regain some focus, and they soon reached the patio of the ivy-walled Anthenaeum. Rafael was there, pacing, arguing, waving his arms. His hair was frazzled and his shirt untucked. Spit sometimes flew with his words. All very un-Rafael. At a table with a teapot, saucers, and a plate of muffins sat Zizik. He appeared relaxed, even amused.

"Uh-oh," Par murmured.

"What?" Eggwise asked.

"It's not going well."

"I see that. Does this Rafael feign more experience than he has?"

"I can't tell."

"Bit of a weasel, then?"

Par didn't reply.

Zizik set down a teacup and motioned them over. "How is our potential Nowen progressing?"

"We need more time," Eggwise said. Par added nothing.

"I see." Thankfully, Zizik left it at that.

Rafael halted, muttering to himself.

"What's wrong with him?" Par asked in a low, cautious voice.

"You tell me," Zizik said. "We were discussing—"

His eyes wild, Rafael spun to Par. "I'll tell you what's wrong.

I've presented my case in a dozen ways, offered every reasonable accommodation." He whirled again to Zizik. "And all you do is smile and say, *I see.* I can't even get a straight answer as to where Meridon is on the map! You just sip your tea, or eat a cracker, or—"

"I finished the crackers," the man said. "Would you care for a muffin?"

"No! Are the outer lands so worthless to you?"

"We have all the land we need."

"I don't mean the lands. The lives!"

Seconds passed. Par swore he heard teeth grinding.

"Well?" seethed Rafael.

"Well, what?" Zikik said calmly.

Before Rafael went completely mad, Par took his arm. "It's been a long day."

Panting, Rafael glanced at Par. A bit of sanity returned to his eyes.

"It has," Eggwise added. "Let's resume our efforts in the morning. Regent Zizik, might we trouble you for lodging?"

"Of course."

"If you don't mind," Par said to the Regent, "can we use that river cabin? I want to work on my sigils."

"That will be fine. But stay indoors after dark. While Meridon is safe from intruders, wild animals still populate the woods, and guards patrol elsewhere. I wouldn't want you to experience any difficulties."

Par figured that was Zizik's way of saying, *mind your business.*

"Oh, and Eggwise," Zizik said, "I wish a moment of your time. You can bring them supper when we're done."

"Yes, Regent. Par, you know the way. I'll meet you later."

His spirits low, Par led Rafael back into the forest. Rafael's lips still twitched in silent argument and his expression remained dark. Par gave him his space and held off any questions.

They reached the cabin by the river. The door was unlocked. Inside were two cots, a table, oil lamps, a dark fireplace, cabinets. Very rustic.

Rafael sat at the table and buried his head in his arms.

"Not going well?" Par asked at last.

"Argent chose the wrong person," he mumbled. "I'm a fraud."

"I'm the fraud." Par joined him at the table. "I tried my best and failed."

"That's not being a fraud. That's having hope. What about me? I failed with Zizik and I failed the Asrai's quest. I'm only here because the Borderlands couldn't find anyone else skilled with élan."

"But you had diplomatic training." Par hesitated. "Right?"

With a wry smile, Rafael sat back. "The Borderlands wants to be recognized as an independent country. For years they've sent diplomats abroad to create relationships, learn what every nation wants, or needs, or has, or fears. My *training*, as the youngest and lowest-ranking diplomat, focused on carrying luggage and tending horses."

Par winced as another shoe dropped. "But you handle yourself like a real diplomat." Par said it to boost the guy's spirits. He had no idea how real diplomats handled themselves.

"My supervisors padded my resume. I was their chance to get someone into the negotiations with the Asrai."

"So? No one else in Arcana or Eloria ever met the Asrai. She accepted you. No one had encountered the Nowen either, and you didn't volunteer. I pulled you here. You've dealt with situations no one could have been prepared for."

Rafael was silent.

"But look at me. Eggwise thinks I'm a Nowen. If he can't prove it, Zizik will throw us out with nothing. It will be my fault if we fail."

"You being a Nowen, Par, was never part of any plan. Our goal was to find them. And you did it."

"Because I jumped into the Mother Spring." Par sighed. "I was afraid of being left alone with the Asrai and Ornot."

Of being left alone, period.

"If you hadn't," Rafael said, "I'd still be in shackles. We'd be farther from the Nowen than ever. You were destined for this."

"I'm not sure I believe in destiny."

Rafael gave a slight, more sincere smile. "A teacher once told me that, whether we believe in it, or we make our own, just don't get in its way."

Par grinned a little too. Eggwise had said something like that. Actually, sometimes the Abbot also talked that way.

"So," Rafael said, and leaned forward, "you're having trouble with Nowen sigils?"

"Eggwise thinks I'm blocked. Not ready or something."

"It took me years to develop my sensitivity to numena and élan."

"We don't have years."

"Our friend Enio developed élan quite quickly, from what I hear."

"Yeah," Par said. "But he's a sensitive guy, couldn't you tell?"

Rafael made a small chuckle.

Par did as well. "I shouldn't joke. He's had a hard life and doesn't open up easy. Except when we were canoeing on the Greening. It was his favorite place. He says that's where he learned numena. It helped him with élan too."

"I wonder if there's something similar, special, in your own life."

"A river?"

"Anything. You and Enio have a tight friendship. Something there?"

For a moment, Par was quiet. Then he said, "Last year, at the Immortus, he helped me use the rift to invoke a sigil."

"How?"

"It's kind of silly."

"Tell me."

"Like I said, he doesn't let people get close. For a long time, he never called me his friend. That was… hard, since other than him, I kept to myself. But he didn't care I couldn't invoke and never told. Then at the Immortus, for the first time, he said it. He said I was his friend." Par still remembered the emotion of that moment, like dawn breaking. It still choked him up a bit.

"What's silly about that?"

"I mean, it's not as grand as destinies and magic."

"Love can be pretty grand, Par."

"Love? I didn't say—"

"You didn't have to."

Par couldn't deny it. Maybe as Enio had trouble admitting Par was his friend, Par had the same trouble admitting that friendships were sometimes like love.

"I should tell you," Rafael said, his eyes filling with concern, "he's not doing well."

"What? Last I saw him—"

"He worsened in the Ults. Our healing sigils gradually failed, until he took off on his own. I suspect to spare us the burden of his declining health."

"Sounds like something he'd do."

"Then the Dark Tribes found us. Their healings helped his body some, but not his memory. It's nearly gone."

According to the Asrai, that happened in Enio's final stages. Par's stomach dropped. "And Lani?"

"She's been… remarkable."

"Thank the gods."

"I don't mean to be nosey," Rafael added, "but when you speak of her, your eyes shine. Perhaps you and she have something special too?"

Par's face warmed.

"That's what I envy about you the most, Par. You have a lot of love in your life."

The warmth bloomed a moment longer, then cooled into resolve. "We have to help them."

"Yes, we do. But I suspect Zizik is toying with me, using me for his entertainment. Like they use the Gate."

"For entertainment?"

"He says they use it to watch the outer world. It's become a theatre. Anyway, Zizik likely has no intention of helping. Diplomacy is like barter, and I have nothing he wants."

"Did you ask if he'd give us some moon marrow?"

"You bet I did. He coughed his tea."

Then that was that. Par had come here to learn to be a Nowen, get moon marrow, help his friends. He'd failed, gaining for his efforts a cheap rock on a string. Except for rescuing Rafael, Meridon had been a complete waste of time.

"We're not doing any good here, Rafael. So we can wallow in self-pity, or do something."

"Do what?"

"Leave."

"Without finishing your training?"

"Even if I am a Nowen, Eggwise said I'm blocked. After what I experienced last try, it could be with fears and regrets. Staying here won't help those. But my friends might. Either way, I've had enough of Meridon."

Rafael nodded. He pushed his chair back and stood. "Very well. Do you know where we are? I mean, where Meridon is?"

"More or less. But before we leave, I need to see Eggwise."

"To say goodbye?"

"Maybe. But he's got a real moon marrow pendant. One way or another, it's coming with me."

CHAPTER THIRTY

As Par waited with Rafael for Eggwise to return, they planned their escape.

"I don't know whether I can open the Gate alone," Par said, "or if I need Eggwise to help."

"What if he doesn't cooperate?" Night had begun to fall. Rafael lit an oil lamp and set it on the table. "Or tries to stop us? He might not want to jeopardize his chance for a new choice or—"

Voices drifted from a corner. Par spun.

Eggwise stepped out of thin air with a tray of food and a bottle. "Pardon me. I'd have knocked, but my hands were full and the guards worked the Gate. Besides, it doesn't have a knocker. Or a door."

The Gate's guarded now? Par glanced at Rafael and saw the same realization. *Crap.*

Eggwise set the tray before them. "Try the wine. It's the Regent's own vintage. I'm rather full of tea myself, but I must have a taste. Are there glasses?" He walked to a cabinet.

At least it didn't appear he'd heard them plotting.

Rafael spread a piece of cheese with purple jam. "Good evening, Eggwise. Any progress with Zizik?"

"I'm not sure. We discussed several things and—"

"Eggwise," Par interrupted. "I'm leaving Meridon."

The man paused, his back to them.

Par sighed. "We're wasting time. You've got the moon marrow. We can bring it to the Asrai. Then she'll join our fight against the Dark Tribes."

Eggwise removed three glasses from a shelf and returned to the table. He sat next to Par and hesitated. "Are you sure you're not being hasty? You've only practiced Nowen sigils for a single day."

"I wish I had more time, but I don't."

"Of course you do. You're safe here."

"But my friends aren't. They need our help, and Enio will get worse without that moon marrow. The Dark Tribes are gathering—" Par stopped short. He'd said all this before. "Eggwise, I want you to take us through the Gate to the Asrai. Tell her you're a Nowen. Give her the moon marrow."

"Zizik will never allow that. Unlike your Asrai, Meridon has no interest in the problems of the outer lands."

Rafael dabbed jam off his lips. "And what about you, Eggwise? Are you a Nowen, or are you a Chogan?"

"I wasn't aware," grumped the man, "that I couldn't be both."

"Isn't that why you're here? To choose?"

Eggwise was silent.

Par pushed Rafael's point. "Even seeing the quakes in Argent, you still won't become involved?"

After letting out a long breath, Eggwise said, "Your own history shows the results of the Vigil's tampering with Eloria and Arcana. Centuries of war, and death. Compared to that, Meridon's choice to remain uninvolved has its merits."

"But more war and death are coming! How is Meridon's apathy

any better than the Vigil's interference? The results will be the same!" Par steadied himself. "Eggwise, are you going to help us or not? Even if the Gate's guarded, what about the river? Can we leave that way?"

"Possibly." The man's voice became softer. "But things have become more complicated."

"What things?"

Eggwise rubbed his face. "If I'm not granted a new choice, I must return to Choga. I'm old, Par, and one day I'll die there. But with no support from Meridon, who'll replace me? I am its last Nowen, and no one else can work the Channel, a fold on which Choga's economy depends. The people will be cast into poverty. My ancestors' dedication will come to nothing."

For a moment, Par was stunned. He hadn't considered that. He glanced at Rafael.

Rafael gave a very slight nod. He stood. "I need to lie down."

Eggwise reached for the wine bottle. "And I need a drink."

Right now, Par could use one himself.

But as Rafael left the table, a golden glory bloomed around his head. He passed behind Eggwise and touched the man's neck.

"What—" Eggwise began. The words trailed off, his eyelids closed, and he slumped forward.

Before Par could say anything, Rafael hushed him. Eggwise remained unmoving, his breathing slow and steady.

"You put him to sleep?" Par kept his voice low.

"Meridon's forgotten not everyone needs two people to invoke a sigil."

"Or they just didn't expect a diplomat to be so undiplomatic. Nice job."

"Thanks, though it takes little skill to coax a weary old man to slumber. If left undisturbed, he'll be out until morning. He can't stop us now."

Par nodded, saddened it had to come to this. But what else could they have done?

"So we're taking the river?" Rafael added.

"It's the only option left. But one thing first." Par eased his hand into the man's pocket and found the moon marrow on its silver chain. He lifted his own pendant, the fake on a string he'd gotten from Jeffrey. As Eggwise had done, Par snapped the real moon marrow from its setting. Jeffrey's stone came off the same. Then he swapped them, snapping both into the opposite pendants. When everything looked good, he put the silver chain with the fake stone back into Eggwise's pocket. He motioned to Rafael, and they left the cabin.

Outside, the actual moon overhead peeked into the fold, pale and vague. "I don't like deceiving him," Par whispered, looping the pendant on its simple string around his neck, "but as long as he doesn't notice we've taken the moon marrow, maybe he won't rush to tell Zizik we're missing. Or if he does, Zizik can't blame him, since we left on our own without his help."

"Clever. You're a smart—"

"Don't say it." They started along the bank.

The lights of other buildings, homes perhaps, twinkled on the hillsides. Soon small private piers appeared along the shores. At one there rested a little canoe, not unlike Enio's original *Sea Dog*. No one else was around, and in a few moments their walk became a river ride. The current was strong enough, and Par only needed the paddle to steer.

"What happens at the end?" Rafael asked as they drifted.

"I think we'll come out near the valley of Nux—that's where Meridon used to be." Par wasn't sure, but he couldn't let the uncertainty stop them now. "Might be pretty cold. Can you invoke fires?"

"No problem."

Slight problem: they weren't dressed for the Ults. But with Rafael's sigils, they'd make the best of it until they found the Dark Tribes.

They continued at least an hour into the night. No one else came into view, on the banks or in other boats. Chatting seemed like a bad idea during an escape, so there wasn't much.

Then, in the peaceful moonlight, a shadow slid across the water. Par looked up. Another raced across the waxy moon.

"Rafael," he whispered. "Do you see that?"

"What?"

A loud buzz sped over their heads.

Par ducked. "A bat?"

"Too big." Rafael's glory lit and grew to a golden globe, driving back the darkness.

A dog-sized scorpion with a thick barbed tail flew past. Its wings hummed like a swarm of hornets.

"Get down!" Par shouted. He held the paddle out like a sword. A skarix? The ones in the Citadel weren't much bigger than dragonflies, and Vex had once said the smaller the skarix, the deadlier its venom. But there were other kinds of deadly.

Another buzzed by.

"Put out your glory," hissed Par.

Just as the glory faded, another creature swooped by. Its tail whipped around and struck Rafael in the back. He cried out.

"Rafael!" shouted Par. He swung his paddle overhead. "Get away from us!" He found Rafael slumped and moaning. His shoulder was bloody.

The buzzing increased. Par shielded Rafael and blindly swung the paddle. "Go away!"

As he did, he spotted a glimmer back up the river. The shadowy creatures circled a moment longer, then broke off and headed upstream.

"Rafael?" Par whispered.

A gasp. "I'm… hurt."

"Hold on. I'll get us to shore." Digging the paddle into the water, Par hastened the canoe to the banks.

But when he reached it, someone stepped from the darkness. It was Eggwise.

This wasn't the time for questions. "Help me," Par said. "Rafael's hurt."

"I see that." Eggwise dropped a sack. "Quiet now. Let's get under cover."

Together they helped Rafael from the boat. He kept his moans subdued, though Par heard the struggle in his breath. They gained the trees and crouched together.

The unknown light continued to approach from up the river, swarmed now by the giant skarix. It was another canoe with a bonfire burning in its bed.

"Where did that come from?" Par asked.

"From me," Eggwise answered. "I lit it to distract those monsters."

The skarix circled the flames, following as the boat passed and finally disappeared downstream. Once the gentle sound of crickets had replaced the awful buzzing, Eggwise said, "We're safe now. The skarix enter Meridon from above, through the fold. There's speculation they grew that way near the Devastation."

Par was already examining Rafael's back in the moonlight. "You're bleeding. Can you heal yourself?"

"I'll try." A small spark of gold glory ran around one of Rafael's ears and fizzled. A smaller, briefer green arc followed. Then nothing.

He shook his head. "Too weak."

"Eggwise," Par said, "can you take him back to Zizik? I'll go after Enio and Lani myself."

"No," Rafael stated flatly. "I'll be fine. And you can't handle this alone."

Considering the unknowns, that was probably true. "But your injury—"

"He's still breathing," interrupted Eggwise, "which means the one that stung him wasn't venomous. He'll recover, but we need bandages." He glanced around. "Where's my sack? I brought us cloaks. Found them in the cabin."

Par turned to go look, but paused. "Us? You changed your mind?"

"Let's bind that wound and I'll explain."

Par found the sack, and after removing the cloaks they tore it for bandages. The wound was in the shoulder, thank the gods, not the neck.

As they worked, Par said. "I'm sorry, Eggwise. Rafael put you to sleep so you wouldn't stop us."

Eggwise nodded. "Well, if you'd let me finish explaining instead of knocking me unconscious, there was more to the story. I won't abandon Choga without someone to replace me. I'd hoped Meridon would take care of that, but their suggestion for a replacement took me off guard."

"Who did they suggest?" Par asked, tying the wrapping.

"You," Eggwise said.

"Me?"

"Ouch," hissed Rafael.

"Sorry." Par eased up on the bandage. "Why me, Eggwise?"

"Nowen or not, you can see folds, so you can guide boats through the Channel."

Take over the Channel? Par was too shocked to speak.

"And before you ask," Eggwise said, "yes, that idea crossed my mind after I began to suspect you were a Nowen. But it's not why I brought you to Meridon. You're too young to take on such responsibility. You have a life elsewhere."

Par wasn't sure how he felt about this, but he found his words again. "So this means you're leaving Meridon too?"

"Well, like you, I no longer wish to remain here. It's become more of a tomb than a refuge, and I may be old, but I'm not ready for burial. And don't feel guilty about Choga. There are Nowen beyond Meridon. I'll find someone."

Par nodded, letting it go for now—they had more immediate problems.

They rechecked the bandages, then sat back to catch their breath. Par asked, "Eggwise, how did you get here so quick?"

"The Gate, of course. I told the guards I needed to visit some old friends. Because I wasn't leaving Meridon, they let me pass. But they otherwise won't allow us to use the Gate without permission from Zizik, and he won't allow us to leave with this." He held up his pendant.

A fresh wave of guilt washed over Par at having swapped the stones. But he decided to keep the secret. For now.

Eggwise tucked it away. "As we travel, we might sneak in more training."

"Thank you, Eggwise," Par said.

With a muffled groan, Rafael stood. "Shouldn't we get going?"

They agreed and returned to their little boat, three now instead of two. The skarix were no longer in sight or hearing.

The man lifted a paddle. "I'll steer. Why don't you fellows get some rest? I seem to have had plenty." He eyed Rafael.

"Sorry," Rafael said and settled in. "But I don't understand. You should have slept until morning."

"Yes, well." Eggwise cleared his throat. "Tell that to a pot of tea and an old man's bladder."

Chapter Thirty-One

PAR AWOKE ALONE in the canoe. A foggy haze muted the daylight and blurred the landscape like an unfinished painting.

He was parked on the rocky riverbank. A campfire burned nearby, where Eggwise sat talking with Rafael.

"I couldn't get through to Zizik," Rafael was saying. "We needed a better diplomat."

"It's not your diplomatic skills that were lacking," Eggwise replied.

Par joined them. "That's what I told him."

Rafael looked up. "But remember, I've supervised luggage for diplomats. I can still apply as a political attaché."

Was that a sort of joke? Par wasn't sure. He smiled anyway.

"Nonsense," Eggwise said. "You're a thinker. Diplomats think more than talk. Politicians talk more than think."

Now *that* was satire Par understood.

"Besides," Eggwise went on, "dealing with the people of Meridon isn't easy, as we've all discovered. They've been closed in for centuries—by this fold, and by their apathy." He poked the fire. "Well, no use brooding over it further."

Par agreed. "Rafael, how's your shoulder?"

"I'll manage." Rafael touched it and winced.

"Still can't use a healing sigil?"

"I'm saving my magic. Might need it for the journey."

Par eyed the flames. "You invoked a fire instead of healing?"

"Not him." Eggwise patted his cloak pocket. "Me. The old-fashioned way. Flint and steel."

As long as Rafael was coping otherwise, Par didn't push it. He glanced around. "So, what's up with this fog?"

"That's not fog," Eggwise said. "It's fold. We are very near the edge of Meridon." He pointed downriver.

Before the haze swallowed the waters, two massive statues framed the banks. Ancient and worn, each formed the missing half of the other, as if the river had split one single sculpture. A rusty chain draped between them, bank to bank.

"It's too shallow for the canoe," Eggwise said. "We walk from here." He paused. "Par, are you sure you want to continue?"

"Why? Is the edge dangerous?" Par didn't recall him mentioning that part.

"I don't believe so, but that's not what I meant. Are you sure you want to leave Meridon? Regardless of its isolation, it's the best place to develop your Nowen abilities."

Par heard a question behind the question: are you sure you want to give up this chance of using sigils, like everyone else? Of being like everyone else?

More than almost anything, Par regretted losing that opportunity. But it would mean abandoning everything, and everyone, outside Meridon.

"Yes, I'm sure." Par forced a casual smile to hide his troubled spirit. "I bet I'm too old to become a Nowen anyway."

Rafael gazed at the river. "This doesn't end in a waterfall, does it?"

Par's smile changed to a grimace as he recalled his watery plummet into Choga.

But Eggwise simply stood and brushed off his hands. "One way to find out. Ready?"

Leaving the canoe, they strode past the looming grey statues. The half-faces were too weathered to show distinct features. That seemed a blessing: unblinking, watchful eyes would only add to the uneasy setting. Better that the figures should remain monuments to blind eternity.

Eggwise insisted on taking the lead, and Par followed last, keeping an eye on Rafael. Despite a restless breeze, the fog thickened like soup, until Par saw nothing beyond the shallow creek, then nothing beyond Rafael. The breeze increased to a wind, drowning the burble of water and Par's shuffling footsteps. It grew colder—thank the gods Eggwise had brought cloaks—and the ground became flat stone. That was easier to travel than unsteady rocks and pebbles, until it included patches of ice.

"I think—" Eggwise called back, when suddenly the mists seemed to explode with color. The wind gusted and howled, burying Par's shouts. He staggered into Rafael. They both lost their footing on what was now a slope of ice and tumbled into Eggwise.

All three plunged forward. In another moment they crashed into something solid and fell backwards onto cold, hard ground.

Par lay panting, catching his breath. They'd been rudely stopped by a granite wall. The wind had quit, the fog was gone, but even in bright sunshine, the air was freezing.

Rafael and Eggwise were beside him, moaning a bit, but beginning to sit up.

Par did too. "Are you guys all right?"

Eggwise rubbed his hip. "I'm not sixty anymore, but I'll manage."

"I'm all right," Rafael said. Fortunately, he'd fallen on his uninjured side. He was about to say more, but his cheeks bulged and his eyes widened. He turned to the side and vomited.

The symptoms were familiar; Pad had had them the first time he'd left a fold.

They had escaped Meridon.

"You'll recover in a minute," Par said. "Just breathe." As he helped Eggwise stand, he took in their surroundings.

The wall before them continued up and up, until its towering summit curved high overhead to almost touch its twin, forming an arch. A hint of a rainbow arced between the tips, but the sky beyond was solid blue, no longer the strange blue strip through milky white that was the sky in Meridon.

Rafael had gotten to his feet. He wiped his mouth. "Sorry."

"You traveled your first fold," Par said. "Tell that to those political attachés."

He nodded. "What happened to the river?"

Eggwise gestured to the rock and ice below their feet. "Underground. Or frozen."

Since they hadn't wound up that way too, Par wasn't complaining.

The ground where they stood was high up itself, overlooking a long, barren valley that stretched like a colossal scoop between frosty hillsides.

"I've seen this place before," Rafael said. "We're standing under the Horns of Nux. Below is the valley where the Horde held us captive. It looks like they've left."

As Par wrapped his cloak tighter, he noticed a path that circled one of the Horns, where the crusty snow showed shallow footprints. "That looks like a way down."

They readied themselves and, careful not to slip again, were soon descending a trail through crags and ice. Despite Rafael's shoulder wound, his legs worked fine, and late in the morning they arrived on the valley floor. The Horns now loomed high above, their lofty rainbow visible no more.

After a rest, they began the trek south across the valley. It was clear that a great host had passed this way, leaving all manner of animal, wagon, and people tracks.

Rafael squatted and examined a few. "They have about a day's head start."

"We'll catch up," Par said.

But Eggwise added, "And then what?"

"Diplomacy?" Par glanced at Rafael.

Rafael narrowed his eyes. "I'll try, but considering their reaction to strangers, I'd best try alone."

Par wasn't willing to sit that part out. "For now, let's keep following. Once we see them, we'll make a rescue plan for Enio and Lani."

"Whatever we decide," Eggwise said, "let's get to it before the Regent discovers we're missing, and figures out why."

They followed the army's trail through the abandoned valley. The highest peaks, the ones draped with snow, were back behind the Horns, which suggested milder terrain ahead. And though it was cold, the bright sun, the calm air, and the cloaks increased Par's confidence that they'd make good time.

As they walked, Eggwise said, "I've been considering your progress as a Nowen, Par."

"You mean my lack of it?"

"You did better than you think."

"Well, I wouldn't call it progress, what with the shouting and fainting."

"We haven't discussed it, you know."

Par grumped.

"Did I hit a nerve?" Eggwise asked.

"No... maybe." Par wasn't inclined to dwell on it anymore, and had never been a fan of laying bare his emotions. But in this barren, craggy valley, cut off from the world, an odd privacy wrapped him like a second cloak. So he shrugged and told of the images, the raging sea, and his panic.

When he finished, Eggwise paused their walk. "I once said that true balance is holding fear in one hand and hope in the other. For one so young, you certainly have an abundance of both."

"Is that good or bad?"

"Depends on the balance. Like a river, Nowen magic is most dangerous when troubled."

Rafael spoke beside them. "But how do you fix a river?"

"You don't fix a river." Eggwise resumed walking. "Its forces carve landscapes and bring life."

Par kept up. "So, what do I do?"

"Perhaps some dredging."

Hadn't he done enough already? Still, they were chasing an army, and soon to be chased by Zizik. They needed all the resources they could muster, and only Rafael could use sigils—unless Eggwise found a second Nowen. If Par became that second, it would improve their chances of success. So he took a breath and dug deeper. "I realize now that many of my past decisions came from fear. Fear of the Reckoners. Of the Asrai. Of being left behind and alone."

Rafael added, "And of people who hate you."

"I never said—"

"Enio did."

Par hadn't planned to discuss his past rejection as a feeble, but there seemed no use hiding it. "Back home, when people found out I couldn't invoke, they cursed me, and didn't want me around."

Eggwise huffed. "That doesn't mean they hate you."

"Why else?"

"They're afraid of you."

Par eyed Eggwise. "Afraid of a feeble?"

"You're different from them."

"That's not a good reason."

Then Rafael said, "Sometimes that's enough. Even though the Borderlands mix many beliefs, I made people uncomfortable when they saw I could use élan. I guess they couldn't tell where I stood, or if I wanted the same things they did."

"What is it you want?" Par asked.

"Just to be me. Whoever that is."

Par smiled. "It's Rafael, the diplomat."

Rafael smiled back. "Questing through far-off realms with Par the Nowen."

They both chuckled. It helped fill a hole in Par's spirits. "Who cares, anyway?" he said. "I'm stuck with me, either way. I don't really need to be a Nowen."

"Nor I a diplomat."

And that seemed to settle that.

Until Eggwise added, "What a load of rhubarb."

"What?" Par looked over.

"Poor Par. Poor Rafael."

"I didn't mean—" Par began.

"Feeling sorry for yourselves, eh?"

Par stiffened. "You don't understand, Eggwise. I don't know what else to do anymore. I've got nothing. I—"

Eggwise waved this off. "No need to be dramatic. Ups and downs are part of life. You've seen my shack, right?"

Starting to feel like a whining little lump of nothing, Par made no reply.

But Eggwise wasn't finished. "Look at yourself, Par. Hated by some, perhaps, but honored too, and by the Eminence himself. And with friends so dear, you'd sacrifice everything to help them. Is this the Par who has nothing?"

Eggwise was right. Par warmed a bit in his heart.

"And Rafael," Eggwise continued. "The diplomat of choice to meet the Asrai. First ever in Meridon. Succeed or fail, it's on your resume. Life isn't just the successes. You've tried harder than most and, I dare say, learned more than many. You've done well with your life, young diplomat."

Par glanced at Rafael and thought he caught a slight blush.

"Our lives," Eggwise said, "rarely turn out as planned. The trick is to be flexible, find your footing. But don't forever hop between lives, for you will be master of none."

"You speak wise words," Rafael said.

"They come with the years, son. As for you, Par, keep your chin up, and an eye out. We have a long walk, so a fold would be quite handy."

Par took a deep breath and eyed the wagon ruts that ran ahead through the valley toward his friends. Nowen or not, Par at last felt certain he was moving in the right direction.

The question now was whether he moved fast enough.

CHAPTER THIRTY-TWO

WITH HIS ANKLE chained to that of a golden-haired girl, Enio shambled down a ravine bordered by pine trees. A crowd surrounded him, but he kept forgetting who these people were and where they were all going. Whenever he asked the girl, her eyes filled with worry. He didn't like that.

Two men walked close ahead. Had he tried his questions on them? One had just called the other Keb.

Enio spoke up. "Hey, uh, Keb."

"What?"

"Are we there yet?"

Keb smiled over his shoulder. "Ask me again, and I'm stuffing you in the sack with Morty."

Apparently, he had.

"You doing all right, Enio?" the girl beside him asked.

"Sure." In truth, he was feeling steadily weaker, and sometimes the world went out of focus. But the pace wasn't fast, so he could still keep up.

She called ahead. "Keb?"

"Yes, Lani?"

Enio repeated the name in his head. Lani.

"What'll they do with us?" she asked.

"Question you, is all. Find out what you know of the enemy."

If anyone asked Enio, it'd be a short conversation. He didn't even remember waking up this morning.

"I've told all I know," she said.

Keb shrugged as he walked. "The Gorga will judge."

"Can you tell us," she added, "about this Gorga?"

"Not me. Hey, Hector, ever seen the Gorga?"

The other man shook his head.

"Figured. Well, there are rumors. Strong in presence and in magic. Some say fangs and burning eyes. Bah, I say. More likely a powerful necromancer, considering the plan to raise the sea dead."

"Sea dead?" Lani said, alarm clear in her voice.

"The *unclaimed* sea dead," Hector corrected. "For defense."

A voice ahead bellowed out, "Halt!"

The crowd shuffled to a stop. Talk began of an end to the hills and of shining waters beyond. People unslung their packs and settled into small groups. Lunchtime, Enio guessed. He wasn't hungry, but he'd feast on any relief from this hike. He eased to the ground, keeping his groans to himself.

The girl sat beside him. "I'm glad we're together again. After Rafael disappeared and they separated us, I worried about you."

"Rafael?"

She continued patiently, "He was a prisoner too, but a hand from nowhere spirited him away. I think it was Par."

Enio didn't recognize the name, but he'd play along. "Why did he only take Rafael?"

She chewed her lip. "I think that's all he had time for."

"Think he'll try again?"

"If he can. For now, we're on our own." She glanced around and lowered her voice. "Or maybe not."

Enio whispered back, "What do you mean?"

"When we get to the sea, I'll use the Sea Call that the Asrai gave me. She'll come or send help."

That sounded like good news—whoever the Asrai was.

"Great," he said, for lack of something better.

She eyed him. "Is your memory getting worse?"

He forced a smile. "I can't remember."

"Try not to worry." She took his hand. "We'll get you back to the Asrai. The Mother Spring will help."

"Good," Enio said. "I don't want to forget you."

She squeezed his hand. "You won't forget this."

He squeezed back. But her comforting words didn't fool him. He'd caught other whispers and side-glances, and now knew he was losing everything. Names, faces, days, hours, all vanishing like smoke. At least his feelings seemed to stick. Hopefully, they'd be the last to go.

Keb brought a skin of water and a handful of jerky. "Sorry it's not more appealing. Everyone's rushed. We're in sight of the shore."

Lani—was that her name?—peered at the dried strips of meat. "What is that?"

"Best not to ask."

Enio chuckled and sipped the water, but swallowed wrong and coughed. It took a moment to recover, but the effort brought a sudden thinness to his mind. Then his vision darkened at the edges. A wave of dizziness washed over him and the waterskin slipped from his fingers.

He didn't recall falling, but he lay on his back. Faces floated above and voices circled like noisy birds. He couldn't understand what they were saying. A golden-haired girl leaned close. A pretty green light shone around her head, then blinked out. She said something else. She seemed so sad, near weeping.

He opened his mouth—and didn't remember how to make words.

Time moved in strange jumps. People laid him on a stretched cloth and carried him. The girl held his hand. Her face and everything else faded into darkness, but she still held tight. That became his world.

Until it, too, faded with the rest, leaving him to sink into a night of blurry stars, all somehow familiar. And in the darkness, movement. A bright star, sailing closer, gliding along like a ship of crystal.

It was coming for him.

Chapter Thirty-Three

After a long day of walking, Par and his companions at last reached the valley's southern boundary. The snow-less land beyond trended downward through gorges and high hills, some dotted with trees. Par continued watching for the peculiar distortion that heralded a fold. As they passed around a rocky summit, he sighted a familiar shimmer dangling from a cliff. He pointed. "Eggwise, is that one?"

"Good eye," the man said. "But even if we got to it, it's flimsy and untethered and likely goes nowhere."

Rafael peered in that direction. "What are you two looking at?"

As they walked, Par explained the folds in more detail. Yet they found no others. When the dusk had pressed the hills into grim cutouts, Eggwise stopped near a huddle of boulders. "I suspect we're far enough from Meridon for the night."

Personally, Par wanted to press on. But they'd be no good facing the unknowns of the Dark Tribes while exhausted.

Other than their warm cloaks, Eggwise had also brought a small bundle of food, leftovers from their uneaten dinner. They gathered a bit of half-burnt wood and debris discarded by the army and nestled in the rocks.

"Shall I?" Rafael gestured at the kindling.

Eggwise withdrew his flint and steel. "Allow me."

As Eggwise made the fire, Rafael stood back and stared. He seemed wilted, but not from weariness.

Par came closer and lowered his voice. "Is your wound bothering you?"

"Not really. Just feeling a bit useless, I suppose."

"You're saving your magic. I think that's smart."

"I wish I could do more."

"Yeah," Par said. "Me too."

After they'd warmed themselves and finished a small meal of toasted bread and cheese, Eggwise said, "Shall we resume your exercises, Par?"

The previous attempts had been traumatic, but Par hid a grimace and nodded. Another thought struck him. "Eggwise, how long since you've had someone to invoke sigils with?"

"So long I can't remember." He brushed off his hands. "But I've gotten used to my life."

Par had known Eggwise long enough to recognize a regret. While Par had never been able to use sigils himself, Eggwise had lost an ability he'd been born with. How do you handle losing something so fundamental to your life? Still, if Par managed a sigil now, that would give Eggwise the second Nowen needed to invoke his own sigils again. It was the least Par could try, after everything Eggwise had done for him.

Eggwise removed the silver chain from his pocket. He offered the pendant to Par.

Knowing full well the real moon marrow was around his own neck, Par took it. And he decided right then that he'd swap the black rocks back again, but in secret, so as not to disappoint or hurt Eggwise. He now saw Eggwise as a friend, and friends didn't steal from friends.

Rafael watched nearby. "Can I help?"

"Not unless you've got a plunger," Eggwise said.

"A plunger?"

"He's blocked."

"My anima." Par wiggled his fingers. "My Nowen magic."

"Ah." Rafael narrowed his eyes for a moment. "A song comes from silence, and to silence returns."

Par stared. "What?"

"A proverb. Sometimes they clear your head."

That one hadn't. But Par would try anything. And Rafael seemed happier being involved. "Tell me another one."

Eggwise grumped.

"Oh," Par said. "Sorry. Should we start my practice?"

But Eggwise waved them on. "Witticisms never worked for me, but go ahead, get them out of your system."

Par turned back to Rafael.

Rafael said, "We often forget our burdens until we set them down."

Quite aware of his burdens, Par did not find that one very helpful. He nodded anyway.

"Our path is brightest walking through fire."

"Through fire," Par echoed, hoping something better was coming.

"Um, when climbing a tree, don't argue with the branches." Rafael tapped his chin. "If you're plucking apples, you're not in a wheat field."

Like the other sayings, those didn't help. In fact, the metaphors had become so at odds with their current surroundings that Par held back a grin. Trees and apples and wheat fields?

Eggwise huffed. "Wherever we are, it's certainly not a *wit* field."

A chuckle slipped from Par's mouth. He stopped it.

"I have to admit," Rafael said, "he speaks a *grain* of truth."

"*Barley* worth mentioning." Eggwise kept his tone flat.

Par snorted. He wanted to try one. "Isn't it *pasture* bedtime?"

They turned to him.

"Pasture bedtime. Past your…" Par trailed off.

"This is serious,Par," Rafael said.

"Very," Eggwise added.

"Sorry." Par sighed.

Eggwise and Rafael looked at each other and began to laugh.

Then Par laughed too. Regardless of how inappropriate it sounded in the middle of this wilderness, he needed to let it out.

But a sudden wave of sadness washed over him, and a sob choked him off.

"Par?" Rafael leaned closer.

Par swallowed a lump. "Sorry. It's just…" He took a deep breath. "Argent, the quakes, the army and Enio and Lani and… sometimes it's too much."

Rafael gently squeezed Par's arm. "Enio is in a bad way, yes. But you can worry less about Lani. She's from the Deep World, and they aren't an enemy of the Dark Tribes. When she gets to the sea, she can summon the Asrai for help to get home."

Par nodded.

"You know," Rafael added, "I never learned much about her."

"Oh she—" Par began. But he was supposed to be learning a Nowen sigil. He glanced at Eggwise.

"Go ahead," the man said. "Your past may yet hold part of your blockage."

"Well, she's not from the Deep World."

"No?" Rafael said. "Where then?"

"I first met her in the Urdel woodlands. Enio thought she was a forest witch." Par smiled at the memory. "Now she has to choose between the land and the sea. If she chooses the sea, she'll change, and stay there."

"So even if she escapes the Horde, you might lose her in the end."

Par hadn't considered the situation in quite that way, yet it changed nothing. "I only want what's best for her."

"I'm sure she feels the same about you."

Rafael spoke the words in a normal tone, yet they struck as if he had shouted, sinking deep into Par's ears.

Feels the same.

Feels what? He'd never asked.

Memories of her swarmed his brain, and he had the urge to reexamine each for clues. But Enio accused him of forever over-thinking. Maybe it was time to worry less about what she felt for him, and understand what he felt for her.

"You all right?" Rafael said.

Unable to help himself, Par hugged Rafael.

"Hey!" Rafael chuckled. "What's that for?"

"Your sayings." Par let him go. "They're appreciated. And so are you."

"Thanks. I'm not such a weasel, then?"

Par started. Eggwise had used that word back when Rafael argued with Zizik. "You heard that?"

Across the campfire, Eggwise cleared his throat. "I, uh, hadn't meant…"

"It's all right." Rafael said. "Diplomats learn to listen with both ears. Here's another saying: we see most clearly with eyes closed and hearts open."

Par turned to Eggwise. "I appreciate you, too. And I'm ready to practice."

"About time. And remember, don't focus on the moon marrow."

"And breathe?" Par said.

"Breathe."

So as the campfire's glow replaced the last of the sunlight, Par practiced his Nowen exercises. The subtle vibrations he'd felt before returned. This time, they sharpened the pinch sigil, gave it a bit more depth. And there was no nightmarish, raging sea. Yet his attempts did little of anything else.

"Very odd," Eggwise said when Par took a break. "I believe you have the anima, but blocked, not blocked?" His face darkened. "Honestly, I don't know."

Par still wore the real moon marrow around his neck and held the fake on a silver chain, planning to swap them into their rightful settings tonight. Still, he'd felt strangely empty during his practice. Had his earlier attempts frightened him so much that he feared trying harder, going deeper? Or was his problem not a blockage, but a void? Was something missing?

Eggwise went on. "I understand now why Zizik thought seeing folds wasn't definitive. However, since you've spent your life in a dark cave, so to speak, your Nowen eyes may still need time to adjust to the light of anima."

Rafael began, "Another proverb says that the light of—"

But Par raised a weary hand. "Thanks, both of you. I get it." He covered a yawn. "I'm exhausted."

"We need a good rest," Rafael said, peering into the distance. "I want to be fresh to plan my strategy."

"Our strategy," Par corrected.

"Our strategy, but my diplomacy. It will require a delicate hand. Let's not rush into it."

Par forced a smile. "I won't rush as long as we hurry. "

Rafael didn't smile back but gave a distracted nod.

"Eggwise," Par added, "can I keep the moon marrow overnight? In case sleeping with it helps."

"As you wish. But I agree, we need a good rest. Pleasant sleep, everyone."

They wrapped themselves up for the night. While Par lay awake listening for the sound of Eggwise slumbering, he realized the man had avoided mentioning another possible reason for Par's failure: that Par was not in fact a Nowen. He recalled something the wizard Vex had once told him, to never be afraid of the truth. Par would accept the truth, no matter what it was—once Enio and Lani were safe.

Chanting crickets joined the emerging stars. As the moon peeked over the eastern hills, he wondered if his friends watched it too. Soon, soft snoring drifted from Eggwise. Par sat up quietly. He laid the silver pendant with the fake stone beside the real marrow on its string, then snapped off both stones and swapped them. When Eggwise asked for the pendant back, he'd get the original, never the wiser.

Laying back again to sleep, Par glanced at Rafael. He was awake, watching, his eyes shining in the moonlight. Par nodded. Rafael winked and rolled over.

That night, whether from anxiety over the marrow, or over the morrow, Par drifted in and out of sleep. Once, he thought he was waking to a green sunrise and, perhaps, Rafael's low voice. Nothing after that.

CHAPTER THIRTY-FOUR

P AR SNAPPED AWAKE. The morning had come like a thief, the sun already sending cloud shadows lumbering across the hillsides.

"Par?" Eggwise sat up and yawned. "I was more tired than I thought."

"Where's Rafael?"

Eggwise looked around. "I suppose he slipped off for a moment."

"Rafael!" Par called. They waited as the echo faded. Par called again.

His suspicion grew. "Eggwise, do you remember, in the middle of the night, Rafael whispering something? And a green glow?"

"Now that you mentioned it…"

"Crap!" Par kicked the dirt. "He used a sigil to keep us asleep. He went on alone."

"Perhaps he feared we'd foul his diplomacy." Eggwise's eyes widened. "Did he take the moon marrow?"

Par checked. "No, it's here. Did you want it back?"

"You need it more than I."

Par was no longer convinced of that, but he nodded. "I bet Rafael didn't want to put us at risk if he failed. He's trying to protect us and redeem himself."

"How is running off into the unknown redeeming yourself?"

But Par understood. He'd felt the same, leaping after his friends at the Mother Spring.

They resumed their pursuit. As they tracked the Horde—and now Rafael—through lower ravines, they left the colder temperatures farther behind. At one rest, Eggwise sat on a rock and rubbed his ankles.

"Are you all right?" Par asked. He sometimes forgot that Eggwise, though often outspoken, was also rather old.

"Despite its name," Eggwise replied, "Kathnu by Toadwalk requires much less walking. I'll be fine, but you could make better time without me. Perhaps you should—"

Par cut him off. "We need each other. We stay together." And of course Par wouldn't leave Eggwise here alone.

But Eggwise smiled. "Yes, I think we do."

Around noon, they came to another overlook. The lands ahead dropped into rolling hills of pine forests. Far off in one direction, Par noticed a reddish haze.

"Is that smoke?"

Eggwise peered that way. "I think you're right. We're catching up."

That was the best news Par had gotten in days.

They hurried on, eventually reaching the treeline. The Horde's trail became more scattered, sometimes winding in and out of the pines, boot prints going this way and that, wagon ruts forced to easier paths. But Par and Eggwise cut straight through the forests and eased down the steeper runs, where the carts and animals couldn't pass.

With the trees now blocking most of their view, progress

became difficult to judge, but sometime in their long afternoon, a break in the pines offered fresh glimpses of the landscape. In the distance, between forested hillsides, something glistened.

"Look, Eggwise." Par pointed. "Water."

Eggwise shielded his eyes. "Yes. The Southern Sea, I imagine."

Par's spirits rose further.

After another densely forested valley, the air took on a slight tang of salt, until late in the day the trees ended abruptly at a drop-off. Over the cliff was the sea, choppy and rough, spreading to a horizon dark with clouds. The sand showed signs of a passing throng. There seemed to be no easy way down, so Par and Egg-wise continued along the ridge, toward the reddish smoke.

And finally, topping another rise, they stopped in their tracks. Tents, camps, and people—hundreds, maybe thousands—cov-ered the rocky beaches below. Lightning flashed across the water, where the clouds had darkened further.

Eggwise sighed. "Where do we even start?"

Par was too close now for despair. "That's not like any army I've ever seen. More of a traveling market." He studied the sweeps of tents, seeming very random and unorganized.

Except…

"There." He pointed to where flat rocky outcrops ran into the surf. The longest, like a ship's deck, rose higher than the rest. On the beach nearby stood several bright, colorful tents, very different from the shabbier masses.

Eggwise squinted. "Excellent. Probably their leadership. If Rafael is playing the diplomat, that's where he went. However, there's still an army between us."

"But I don't see any uniforms," Par said. "Just normal people making their camps. Besides, no one here is looking for us. We can blend."

"Well, we can try."

The hillside was still rough, but had become passable. Par

helped Eggwise down, away from any tents, choosing their final approach near a line of unattended wagons. With a deep breath, and as casually as if out for an evening stroll, they entered the camp. The sea and smoke smells joined with those reminiscent of the poorer spots of Argent, but not bad ones: rich stews and fresh breads blended with oils and soaps and animal musk. The occupants cooked and chatted, cleaned and repaired their possessions, and took care of their beasts—and their children. Invocations of dark red or purple or bronze reminded Par of the mages of the Lower Realms at the Immortus.

This was the Horde? The Dark Tribe army? The cause of the quakes and bringers of war?

Ignored by all, Par and Eggwise continued through the throng and soon reached the shoreline. The leadership tents there were roped off, and guards with actual weapons stood before them. Par could just see inside the central, largest tent. People there paced and talked over each other, the conversations too muddled to make out. They held staffs, some with dangling bones, and their robes bore strange symbols, but Par saw no sign of Rafael. Or Enio and Lani.

Two smaller tents sat just past that one, both closed tight, both guarded.

"We have to see inside those," Par said.

"How do you propose we do that?"

While the front of the tents faced the bustle of the camps, their backs were more secluded, set up near the rocky shore. "Let's try the far side. We might need to cut an opening."

They faded back into the crowd. With all the cooking throughout the camp, snatching an unguarded kitchen knife was the least of their challenges. Then they returned by a wandering route to a corral of horses close to the shoreline rocks. Their goal was nearby. They ducked low and made the short dash.

A horse gave a jolt and a startled neigh. Par lunged with Eggwise behind the tent and crouched, listening for shouts or threats. None came, and the animal calmed.

When Pad had caught his breath, he pressed the knifepoint into the tent material. It was thick, made of skins, but he managed a small puncture and peered in. The hole was frustratingly small, but he made out an arched roof, supported by a thick tent post.

He strained to see lower, but nothing else came into view. When he was about to give up and switch tents, he heard something rattle.

Chains?

The peep hole was at the limit of what it could reveal. He sliced the material further. He looked again.

Near the base of the tent post lay two shackled figures.

Enio and Lani.

CHAPTER THIRTY-FIVE

PAR NEARLY SHOUTED with relief. There were no guards inside the tent. As loudly as he dared, he hissed through the rip, "Lani!"

She looked up. "Par!"

Enio remained curled on his side, unmoving. Rafael was not with them.

"I'm coming." With his hand trembling, Par sawed through the thick material until the gash reached the ground. He pushed through and hurried to Lani's side. Like Enio's, her hands were shackled together, and her ankle was chained to the post. "Did they hurt you?"

"No, but—" She turned her gaze on Enio.

He seemed asleep, yet his breathing was as thin as paper and his face as pale. Par lay aside his knife and jostled him gently. "Hey. Enio?"

"His memory worsened," Lani said, "as the Asrai told us it would, until he finally collapsed. The healers here tried their magic on him, but nothing has helped, not even my élan. Their diviners said his mind was as silent as…" She looked away.

Par's mind finished the sentence: silent as the grave. His relief, and his stomach, slid off a cliff.

Eggwise cleared his throat.

"Who—?" Lani began.

"Sorry," Par said, having briefly forgotten about Eggwise. He helped the short old man into the tent. "This is Eggwise. He and Rafael helped me get here."

"A pleasure, madam." Eggwise rose from his crawl.

Lani gave him a polite nod, then spoke again to Par. "So it's true? You were the one who took Rafael?"

Par examined her chains. "I tried to take you all—I'll tell you about it later. We've been chasing after you, but last night Rafael ran off on his own. I think he came back here."

"If he did, I haven't seen him."

The shackles were solid bands, fastened and sealed. "Have they hurt you?" As Par looked up, he noticed the blue shell still hung from her necklace, the one from the Asrai, allowing Lani to delay her ultimate choice between land and sea. He focused on it, wondering how much thought she'd given to that decision.

"They've only questioned us," she said. "They're bringing us to their leader, the Gorga."

The name interrupted Par's stare; Rafael had mentioned it too. But Par had the moon marrow now, which completed the Asrai's mission. He needed to get it to her if they had any hope against this Gorga and the quakes—and healing Enio.

He turned again to the chains, searching for any loose bolt or weakness. "Lani, can your Sea Call get the Asrai to rescue us?"

"Maybe, if I can reach the sea. What about Rafael?"

"We'll try to find him. But first, I have to get you out." He traced her chain to the post and tugged. It was driven deep. "Eggwise, can we remove their shackles?"

"Can you pick locks?"

"I mean, can we try a pinch?"

Eggwise hesitated. "We can try."

Lani watched questioningly, but now wasn't the time to explain the whole Nowen thing. Par laid his hand on Eggwise's, careful not to let the moon marrow pendant still in his own pocket distract him. He closed his eyes and began his breathing exercises, trying to calm his hammering heartbeats.

Curls of clear, wavy anima spiraled around the sigil, stronger than before—yet unsteady and confused. Unbalanced.

Please. Please let this work.

Rather than an answer, his brief prayer brought more questions. Why was he appealing to the gods of Eloria, the granters of lumina, for help with anima? Should he ask the numena-giving stars of Arcana? He might as well ask the mountains for bread, or the sea for wine. Each was master of their own realm, not of anima. And if the gods were listening, maybe Par's prayer should instead be to heal Enio.

The sigil had faded.

"Par." Eggwise's voice came quiet and resigned. "That's enough."

Par opened his eyes. The shackles remained solid, tight, as if choking his soul.

Then Lani said, "Let me help."

"How?" Par asked, hiding his despair.

She moved to the post. "I can still use élan. I haven't tried to escape because I didn't want to leave Enio." An emerald glory circled her head. She touched the post where the chain was spiked. The wood began to swell, fattening slowly like a sponge in water. As the wood expanded, it cracked.

"That's it," Par said. "Keep going." Her wrists were red from the shackles, her face smudged, her hair tangled. But beneath it all, even behind her élan, shone an unquenchable spirit. Par smiled. "Lani, you're wonderful."

Lani smiled back at him. Their eyes met. Her glory flashed brighter.

The wood expanded faster.

"Wait," Eggwise hissed. "I think—"

Snap! The entire tent shuddered. As the post expanded, it had stretched upward and ripped something.

A guard pushed aside the front flap. A purple glory burst around his head. He drew his sword. "Intruders!"

Par raised his hands. "We're unarmed!"

Another guard arrived behind the first. A third stuck his head in. "What's going on?"

"Get Yantra," the first ordered.

They didn't have to wait long. A grey-haired woman entered, robed in red, with small bones clacking from a staff like dry wind chimes. Rafael walked behind her, unbound, but with an ugly bruise across his cheekbone. As his eyes met Par's, his pained expression worsened.

"I am Yantra," the woman said. "And you must be Eggwise and Par."

"We are," Par replied, holding back his frustration. Yet hope was not completely lost. They still had the Sea Call.

Yantra gestured her staff toward Lani and Enio. "We have examined your friends. Assuming they hide no deception—and lies are not easily hidden from diviners—I know your purpose already. But I will waste no time on your feeble attempt at rescue. The Gorga approaches." She motioned to the guard. "Bring them."

With swift conjurations, the guards detached the shackles, then used a simple stretcher to carry Enio. Yantra ushered them out, keeping Lani and Enio before her, and Par and the rest guarded behind. Outside, the clouds hung heavy, veiling the late sunset and brushing the sea's horizon with grey rain. Yantra led them to the beach, toward the large stone outcrop and up smooth, worn steps to the flat top.

Two older men waited there, each holding a staff. One man wore robes of dark purple. A long, thin mustache, as black as night, hung past his jaw. White hair and a beard framed the second's face, and snowy eyebrows climbed his forehead; his robes were a dull bronze. Par guessed that with Yantra they represented the three magics of the Lower Realms.

The outcrop stretched like a stone tongue over the water. The sea splashed and foamed against its rocky sides. Yantra spoke with the two others. They gestured down the shoreline. Crowds had left their tents and were congregating on the dim beaches, some creating small, glowing red pits.

Rafael spoke from beside Par, his voice low. "Welcome to the Horde."

"Yeah, thanks." Par eyed the bruise. "What happened to you?"

"My diplomacy didn't come across as delicately as I had planned. They knocked me around a bit."

"Can't you heal yourself?"

"It's not bad. Besides, I think it makes me seem less of a threat and leverages up some sympathy."

That was Rafael, all right. "Listen," Par said, "if Lani gets to the water, she'll call the Asrai. If can we distract—"

Just then, Yantra held aloft her staff. Down the shore, long metal horns glinted briefly in the glow of the red pits. Full, round notes sailed seaward.

The sound died away. The Horde fell silent and still. Thunder and green splinters of lightning answered from the horizon.

"Gorga!" Yantra shouted. "We await you! We call you up!"

Suddenly, a flash burst through the clouds overhead with an ear-splitting *boom!* that nearly sent Par to his knees. Then, farther out, a wave approached like a great moving mound. As it neared the outcrop, it fell away, and out of it rose an enormous beastly head on a neck covered in black scales.

Par gasped. He'd never seen a dragon—except in fanciful pictures—but this could only be a dragon of the sea. Steam shot from nostril slits. Black fangs, as long as his arm, dripped in its massive wolfish snout. Its eyes, however, had not the mad fury of a beast. They burned with green fire—and with intelligence.

The creature glided closer. Par only stared and tried to keep breathing. Yantra and her companions held their places.

The monstrous face now loomed before them. Par reeled, not only at its frightening appearance but at the sour smell wafting from its slime-coated tongue. Then its skin began to shimmer with a greenish glow. Par blinked to dismiss any trick of the shadows. Yet he had not imagined it. Nor was he imagining that the beast had begun to shrink. The snout drew back. Its scales smoothed. Strange wing-like fins reached onto the rock, pulling the creature from the water before curling in on themselves. The visage of a monster faded.

Before them now stood a man-sized worm, still forming, shaping. A sheen of sparkling seaweed wrapped its body. Legs and arms defined themselves. So did a head of green hair. It lifted its face to the group.

Yantra bowed.

The guards bowed.

Par couldn't move. He couldn't believe his eyes.

It was the Asrai.

CHAPTER THIRTY-SIX

Par's hope for rescue crumbled. The Asrai was the Gorga, leader of this army.

Lani was the first to speak. "Asrai? How... why?"

As the Asrai shifted her gaze to Lani, then to Par and Rafael, her composure wavered. A brief tremor touched her lips.

"Welcome, Gorga," Yantra said. "The Horde has gathered."

"Anyone care to tell me," Eggwise murmured to Par, "what's going on?"

"It's her, Eggwise. The Asrai."

"What? The ruler of the Deep World?"

Rafael whispered, "Say nothing. We may yet find some leverage. I don't think she expected us."

"The feeling's mutual," Eggwise said.

Her poise restored, the Asrai stepped forward, trailing a glisten of slime behind her seaweed gown. "I see we have guests."

"From enemy lands," Yantra said. "We've brought them for you to question."

"If I may?" Rafael raised a finger.

The Asrai glared at him. "Be silent until questioned, lest I cast that one into the Deep." She nodded towards Enio on his stretcher.

Rafael bowed. Par dared say nothing.

The Asrai spoke to Yantra. "You did well. I will examine them in private."

"Our tent is at your disposal." Yantra hesitated, her eyes flicking down the shore to the watching crowds. "But the people await."

"And I will not disappoint them." The Asrai blazed an emerald glory. From below the outcrop, a bolt like lightning shot silently away beneath the waves, reaching beyond the shoals. But where it disappeared, a line of surf formed, like a great scar ripping across the sea. It headed landward.

The crowds murmured and drew back.

Yet when this long, rolling wave reached the sands, it did nothing more, nothing spectacular. After a brief visit, it retreated and dissolved.

Par was almost disappointed, considering such theatrics, to invoke a simple wave that—

That had left something behind. Small piles of somethings, up and down the beach. Broken and white. Driftwood?

No. Bones.

The crowds had halted their retreat. Some returned to inspect the piles. One trio lit their glories. Again Par spied blackish-purple, red, bronze. The bones before that threesome trembled.

And then rose. In a moment, a skeleton stood upon the sand.

More dark glories flickered and more skeletons rose, their jaws and teeth frozen in death's last grin. Par shivered, and suddenly recalled Enio's dreams. He glanced at his friend, still unmoving on the stretcher. "Gods," Par muttered. "I thought you'd dreamt all this."

Dozens more formed until the bone piles were exhausted.

Yantra said, "Thank you, Gorga. But... did you not promise many thousands? And transport for us across—"

"Did you bring me moon marrow?"

Par stood as rigid as the graveyard ghouls, and breathed as little. The guards hadn't had time to search him. But here he now stood, the moon marrow in his pocket.

"We searched where you asked," Yantra said, "but found none."

The Asrai frowned. "Send some to search again. Soon I shall deliver you more of the sea dead. Until then, let the fear of us spread. That fear will feed our victory." She turned to Par. "For the moment, I have guests to entertain."

Yantra motioned to the guards. As they escorted Par and his friends from the stone outcrop, he shuffled closer to Lani. "Why is the Asrai—?"

A guard shoved him. "Quiet."

Lani shook her head, just as bewildered.

They were taken to the larger tent, empty of the assembly Par had seen earlier. Inside, the floor was thick with carpets and pillows. A smoking bowl on a tripod breathed sweet incense. The guards set Enio gently to the side, and Yantra invited the Asrai to a tall chair draped in colorful blankets.

The Asrai sat. "Thank you, Yantra. Please leave us."

With quick bows, Yantra and the guards left. Par glanced at Rafael, hoping he'd try his diplomacy now.

But Rafael's lips were tight. He seemed to be studying the Asrai.

She gestured first at Eggwise. "Who are you?"

"I am Eggwise, from Choga."

"Choga? You're quite far from home."

"Aren't we both?"

She ignored this and addressed Lani. "What of your mission, daughter of the seas?"

"I don't understand, Asrai. You are the Gorga?"

"There is much you don't yet understand. Answer the question."

"We traveled from the high lake to the Valley of Nux but found no city and no Nowen."

The Asrai leaned impatiently forward. "I ask of the moon marrow, girl!"

"Also none."

Again Par held his tongue, though they might soon examine his mind and discover he had exactly that substance. He glanced at Enio, still pale and unconscious. Hadn't she pledged to use the moon marrow to help heal him? Should Par beg she make good on that now?

But if she'd lied about who she was, and about helping the outer lands, what else had she lied about?

He needed to find out before handing it over.

The Asrai sighed. "I had hoped that you, Alehilani, one of my own, would prove more capable at that task than this unwashed Horde. I am disappointed."

"May I speak?" Par asked.

"If you must."

"Do you side with the Dark Tribes?"

"I side only with the sea."

"Then why do they call you their leader?"

"Yes," added Lani. "Asrai, what's going on?"

She focused on Lani. "You will understand better than your companions. For millennia, we, the nymphs, have witnessed the humans ravage the world. They opened the Immortus rift, unleashed the Devastation and destroyed the fair lands of Gê. When they fled to other lands, they drove our kind from the forests, lakes and hills by the endless growth of their towns, and their commerce. Now, after centuries of war among themselves, their nations find common ground and befriend each other, and so their greed not only expands, it is emboldened!"

Par caught true hate in her tone. She took a breath and smoothed her voice. "As their alliance strengthens, the Lowers, the people of this Horde, now fear their own persecution will increase. That presents a unique opportunity."

"Then the quakes," Par said, beginning to understand. "They're not from the Dark Tribes. They're from you."

Her lip curled into a slight grin. "You're smarter than you look, boy. Your lands rest upon the foundations of the deep. I've walked their silent floors. I've touched the ancient pillars. And I shake them at my pleasure."

Rafael took over. "So you deceive our countries to believe we are attacked by the Dark Tribes, kindling a new war that we may destroy each other? Your plan is clever, Asrai, but perhaps too ambitious. We would discover your treachery. The survivors would hold you accountable for your crimes."

"Yes, the survivors. I did indeed learn that my attacks, my quakes, were most destructive only along your coasts. The people farther inland would continue to fester and increase and return, like a stubborn plague. Hence my plans for war. Yet still I searched for a more thorough solution. Something to extend my will to the corners of your world."

The words jumped from Par's mouth. "Moon marrow? But it can't be that powerful." Otherwise, considering Par's own missteps with it, he'd be a smoking lump of cinders.

Her eyes shone with cold delight. "That is the genius, and justice, of my plan. It is not my power alone that the moon marrow shall magnify. Through the Mother Spring, it will harness one of the greatest forces known: fear. And before I begin, I will make sure your people's fear is abundant."

"Our *people*," Rafael said, "are not so easily frightened."

"You're wrong." She grinned. "Fear is always easy."

"Asrai," Lani said, almost begging. "You can't do this. What you are planning, it's evil."

"Theirs is the evil, daughter of the seas. Evil against the balance, against nature."

"But we are *all* creatures of nature! Just because you are of the sea—"

The Asrai laughed. "I am not *of* the sea. I *am* the sea. And the moon is thirsty!"

Par started at mention of a thirsty moon. He had heard it before, again from Enio, on the shores of Argent.

Yet Enio continued to slumber.

She went on. "Once I have the marrow, I no longer need lure your rulers from their strongholds to the sea with offers of negotiation, or the people of this Horde with promises of a limitless army. I shall whet the moon's thirst, and it will draw near, and my quakes will increase a hundredfold. A thousand! It will not matter who walks the coasts or hides in caves. For my seas shall rise, and the lands will crack as when their foundations were laid, until my domain, the Deep World, is all that remains."

The Asrai's words filled the air, souring the sweet incense and choking all reason. Icy silence reigned until she broke it. "But Alehilani, you no longer have a role here. Return to the sea, where dwell those who love and accept you."

"No, Asrai. I can't. Not if you do this."

"Then perhaps you will change your mind once you see how I deal with my enemies."

Par couldn't let this go any further. Before she discovered he had the marrow, he had one last chance to use it himself. But the only Nowen sigil he knew was the pinch. Could that help them escape? Open a fold? Attack the Asrai?

Feigning fear, he grasped Eggwise's arm, then bent his mind to the pinch sigil.

Eggwise got the hint. An instant later, Par sensed the tremor of the man's anima.

The Asrai shouted, "There is moon marrow at work in this tent!"

Just then, something yanked Par from behind. He lost his

concentration, and his hold on Eggwise. The tent and those before him disappeared down a white corridor.

He fell before the Meridon Gate. It shimmered and closed.

Zizik bent over him and smiled. "Got you."

CHAPTER THIRTY-SEVEN

PAR SCRAMBLED TO his feet. Two Nowen guards stood behind Zizik. The Meridon Gate had closed, and the tent, the Asrai, and his friends were gone.

"Open!" he shouted at the Gate. "Reopen!"

But the arch remained empty and dead.

He spun to Zizik. "Save them!"

"Save?" Zizik seemed genuinely surprised. "You stole moon marrow from Meridon. I traced it to the Horde's camp. To you. I want it back." He held out his hand.

"Then take it!" Par dug the pendant from his pocket and tossed the hateful thing, sending the stone on its silver chain skittering across the marble floor. "Just save my friends."

A guard chased after it.

"Careful," Zizik said. "The stone's power may be unbalanced. Return it to the museum."

The guard eased it up by the chain.

Zizik nodded to the other. "Inform the Assembly that we've secured the marrow and one of the thieves, the young potential Nowen."

As the guards left, Zizik turned to Par. "Regarding Eggwise and your friends, I am forbidden from doing anything more—without permission from the Assembly. Your fate now depends on whether you are a Nowen. Tell me, were you able to use one of our sigils?"

Par glanced at the empty portal, trying to figure out what to do next. "No, but—"

"However, not only can you see folds, but the moon marrow roused in your presence, which enabled me to find you. Your Nowen birth may yet prove true."

There was no more time to ponder these things. "Listen to me, Zizik. The Asrai hates humanity and wants to destroy the lands beyond her realm. We have to stop her."

"Her actions will not affect Meridon. We are safe."

"But Nowen still live outside."

The man hesitated. "They've made their choice. Choices have consequences."

"They didn't choose to die, Zizik! Neither did the families they've made since. Don't you care about anything besides Meridon?"

"I care about many things. But such is the balance."

"Balance?" Par's patience was gone. "The Asrai uses the same word. But that's not balance! It's frozen, petrified, like the Horns of Nux. Like Meridon. If that's what it means to be Nowen, I want no part of it."

A small voice spoke from the doorway. "Papa?"

It was Jeffrey, the boy Par had met upon arriving with Eggwise. But Papa? Indeed, he now saw the resemblance.

Zizik turned. "Jeffrey? What are you doing here?"

"We came for theater." Several small faces peeked low around the corner.

"No more theater today. Run along, children."

A wave of disappointment swept through the little group. They began to disperse.

But Jeffrey stepped forward. "Par isn't staying?"

"I can't," Par said. "There are people outside who need me."

"Oh." The young boy sucked his lip, then held out the wooden frog Par had given him. "Do you need your luck back?"

Regardless of Par's new disgust for Meridon, he couldn't help but smile. "No. I think the little girl who gave it to me would want you to have it."

"We'll discuss all this later," Zizik said. "Say goodbye, son."

"All right. Goodbye, Par. Will you thank the little girl for me?"

"Goodbye, Jeffrey. I'll try."

Once the boy left, Par added softly, "If she survives the Asrai."

Zizik stood silent, looking after his son. Then he spoke slowly to Par. "You think me harsh. But you don't understand. Even if we wished to intervene, we have no army. We've never needed one. The sigils we once used for defense have passed less and less through the generations until they've been forgotten. We'd be useless in battle. We are vulnerable anywhere but here."

So whether it was their laws that kept Meridon uninvolved, or even their apathy, underneath was a good helping of fear.

And that gave Par another idea.

"Zizik, you're afraid for the safety of your people, for those you care for. For your children. I get it. Maybe I can help."

"You?" Zizik said. "How?"

"The last two stone Sentinels at the Immortus are great Nowen mages from the time of Gê. I have the sigil to release them."

A flicker sparked in the man's weary eyes. "Indeed?"

Par nodded. "They could stand with you. Or at least they must have the sigils you've lost."

The man's face showed a stirring of thoughts, like dust awakened in a long-sealed attic. He gazed again at where his son had been. "Believe that I do not wish the Asrai's violence upon the world. Neither do I wish to continue as we are, isolated and hidden, never to stroll in an unfamiliar meadow, or sail the open seas, or lie beside our children beneath a sky full of stars. And to never meet the outer world's people, many of whom we have admired through the Gate, and even loved. All Meridon deserves this, and more." He rubbed his chin. "The legendary Immortus mages were powerful and wise. If you could give me the sigil to release them—"

"I would, but…" Par sighed. "I'd have to be able to invoke a sigil to bestow one. Can you pull it from me?" The Umbriarch of Arcana had once managed that—and nearly split open Par's head.

"Such a skill is also lost."

That was not a deal breaker. When Par had failed to bestow the sigil on the wizard Vex, the Umbriarch had empowered Par to give it to Enio.

"Zizik," he said, "Enio also has the sigil. He's one of my friends still held by the Asrai. But he's very ill and needs help. If you want to release the mages, I need you to rescue him." He paused. "All of them."

"How does he possess a Nowen sigil?"

"It's a strange sigil, with many roots. It worked for the other Sentinels when invoked with the proper magic."

Again the man was silent. Then a new resolve formed in his face. "Very well." He addressed the Gate. "Reopen."

The space flashed. But instead of the tent, there was only the glowing green outline of the Asrai facing the Gate, her arms raised.

With a panicked shout, Par pushed Zizik aside. A blast of lightning shot out, striking a pillar. A section of marble exploded, just missing them.

The portal closed. Par helped Zizik up. "Are you injured?"

"I am not. You may have just saved my life."

But the bolt had been off center. Par shook his head. "I don't think she wanted to kill us."

"No?"

"She now knows I have moon marrow, and she has my friends. She was making leverage to negotiate a trade."

Zizik raised an eyebrow. "That's quite insightful. And here I thought Rafael was the diplomat."

"A better one than me, I'm sure."

"Perhaps, but that leaves us at an impasse. The moon marrow is not negotiable."

If it could cause the destruction the Asrai claimed, Par had to agree. But there were still the mages.

"Zizik, Enio's not the only one with that sigil. He shared it with Alexander Vex, a wizard from Arcana and the last surviving member of the Vigil. Can the Gate find him?"

"The Gate cannot locate individuals. I found you because you were using the moon marrow. But we can search in likely places."

Par considered. "I last saw Vex in the Vigil outpost in Argent, near the Threshold."

Zizik again addressed the Gate. "Open to the Argent Threshold."

It did. The room showed more damage: one wall had cracked open to the sky beyond the cliffside. The monitor still twinkled with its sparks of magic, but no one was present.

"Let's try the Citadel," Par said. "Vex mentioned he'd been visiting there."

"The ancient Vigil stronghold? Very well. Gate, open to the Citadel of the Vigil."

It opened to a panoramic view overlooking the grim yellow sands of the Devastation. In the distance rose the dusty domes and towers and stout walls of the Citadel, nestled before jagged black mountains.

"The Citadel is sealed," Par said. "But Vex has the Luminary's ring. It allows him inside."

"I doubt the seals would hinder the Gate, since the Nowen created those charms. Where inside should we look?"

Par didn't hesitate. "The vault."

"Gate, show us the vault."

In an instant, the view leapt into a tight, round room. Niches along the walls swelled with boxes and jars and other odd objects. A man sat on the rim of the central low-walled well, reading a scroll.

"Vex!" yelled Par.

The wizard fumbled his scroll and dropped it into the well. "Par?"

"I'm in Meridon, the city of the Nowen. The Asrai has Lani and Enio. She's the one causing the quakes, not the Lowers. She's the enemy of us all. She wants to kill us all."

The wizard's face darkened. "The hells you say."

Par nodded. "Will you help us?"

"You have to ask?" The wizard stood. He tapped the Luminary's ring, black and glistening, against the well. With a flash of light, the shelves emptied, their contents returning to the well's hidden depths of forgotten treasures.

Just a few days earlier, Vex had reached his hand through the Argent Threshold and brought Par into the outpost. Now Par returned the favor. He held his hand through the Gate. Vex took it and stepped into Meridon.

Chapter Thirty-Eight

PAR WAS THANKFUL beyond words for Vex's arrival. The air itself seemed to brighten with hope.

The wizard scanned the Gate room, its shattered pillar, its empty pews. "Meridon, you say?"

"It's a lot to explain. This is Zizik, the Regent. He's in charge."

Zizik bowed. "Along with the Assembly, who will be furious that I'm acting without their consent."

Briefly, Par told Vex everything that had happened since disappearing from Argent with Eggwise.

"You're a Nowen?" Vex said at last, his heavy brows raised.

"That remains to be seen," Zizik answered.

Par side-stepped the issue. "Our plan is to release the Nowen Sentinels at the Immortus. We'll ask them for help."

"And you want me to give the Sentinel sigil to Regent Zizik?"

"Yes."

Vex eyed the man. "Considering I know nothing of Meridon or the Nowen, that seems..." He shifted his gaze back to Par. "But your instincts have long proven their worth. This is your best plan?"

"It's our only plan, Vex."

"Very well." The wizard addressed Zizik. "Sir, will you accept this sigil?"

"I will." The two men leaned together and touched foreheads. With a brief flash of silver numena, Vex bestowed and stepped back.

Zizik stood with his eyes closed. "You're right, Par. It is quite complex."

"The different magics," Vex said, "trace their own routes through that sigil. We were each able to invoke it after several hours of practice."

But Zizik opened his eyes. "In your vocabulary, I am a Sigil Master. I'll manage. Nevertheless, Nowen use sigils in pairs, and rarely learn new ones after childhood. We will likely need at least that time."

Time they didn't have. Par took a breath. "Let me try."

"You?" both men said.

"I've failed with Nowen magic until now, I know. But I've had that sigil in my head for a year, I've drawn it for Vex, I've traced its loops and curves, and the Umbriarch of Arcana once helped me bestow it. If I can't invoke it, then you can get someone else."

"It's worth the attempt," Zizik said. He addressed the Gate. "Open to the Immortus."

With a brief flash and a stale, dry cough of wind, the Gate opened on the yellow sands of the Devastation. Ahead stood the ancient stone platform of the Immortus and its two sigil-covered monoliths, the last of the original eight Sentinels.

"Gate," Zizik said, "remain open." He stepped through. Par followed with Vex. They strode across the sands to the monoliths. Vex scanned the desolate, grey horizon. "I'll keep watch. You two get started."

Zizik moved to the base of one Sentinel, Par to the other.

Unlike his practices with Eggwise, Par couldn't reach to grasp Zizik's hand. But Eggwise said that wasn't always necessary, so Par closed his eyes and brought the familiar Sentinel sigil to mind. Then, as Eggwise had taught him, he summoned anima. It boiled, it sputtered, but like the pinch sigil, never filled in. He relaxed, he breathed. When that didn't help, he strained, he pushed. He fought not to scream with frustration.

At last, sweat trickling down his forehead, Par opened his eyes and gave a soul-draining sigh. "I'm sorry. We need a real Nowen."

But Zizik was staring at him. "When you were with Eggwise, I assume you also tried the moon marrow?"

"It made me panic. Eggwise said I was blocking. He said…" Par still felt the sharp echoes in his nerves. "He said I had a lot of fear."

"What is the source of this fear?" Zizik pursed his lips like an abbey monk listening to confessions.

"Of losing people. Of being alone."

"Can you be any more specific?"

That was as specific as they'd gotten. But wasn't it obvious? "Enio is getting worse and—"

"No," Zizik said. "Something as strong, but deeper."

"Deeper?"

"Or perhaps a better word would be *buried*."

"I don't understand."

Vex eased closer. "Um, maybe I can help."

They turned to him.

"Par, remember our time together last year, when you allowed me to look into your soul?"

"How could I forget?" Par forced a smile. "You said my failures at invocation weren't because of a curse. You said I was just born with a thick soul."

"Yes, well, I'd never heard of the Nowen, so couldn't suspect you of being one. But to delve as deeply as I did—and I tried not to rummage around too much—with such a profound examination, I couldn't help…" Vex cleared his throat. "This may be rather personal."

"Shall I stand away?" Zizik said.

Par hesitated, as if pondering a reach into a murky pond. But this wasn't the time for timidity. He shook his head.

Vex went on. "Regardless of the configuration of your soul, I noticed another wall. One of your own making."

"My making? For what?"

"The same as any wall. For keeping things in, or out."

That was a truth Par couldn't deny.

"You can't be blamed," Vex added. "You've spent your life hiding your condition, your feelings, from the Elorian Hierarchy and your teachers. Even from those closest to you."

Par grimaced at the memories, many embarrassing and painful. "But the Eminence has since changed the laws, so—"

"Laws change more easily than hearts, even our own. Your wall remains."

"Then what should I do?"

A slight amusement seemed to gleam in the wizard's eyes. "There's no easy solution. Perhaps examination and treatment by your Reckoners. Or a period of retreat and meditation. Or…" He paused, waiting.

"Or what?" Par asked, impatience obvious in his voice.

"Or," Vex said, his voice steady and kind, "just tell her."

Par's thoughts skidded to a halt. He knew what Vex meant. Tell Lani how much he wanted her to choose life on land. And tell her why. Par had always seen Enio as the one with the walls, never calling Par his friend until they'd almost died at the Immortus. But Par had built a barrier just as thick. Even while he longed to be closer to Lani, he'd never allowed her closer to him.

Everyone was staring. He looked down, his face warming. "I've tried. It's all so complicated."

Vex patted Par's shoulder. "Yes. The most complicated thing in the world. And the simplest. But I suspect you'll remain blocked until you figure it out."

Par nodded, though it wasn't like he hadn't tried.

"However," Zizik said, "now you know, and knowing may help. Ready to try again?"

"As much as it takes."

On their following attempts, the anima seemed a little more energetic, more alive and flowing. Par's hopes grew.

And each time, it fizzled.

After several minutes of tempting successes and ultimate failures, Zizik stood back and shook his head.

Par looked away. He felt empty, used up, and his friends were imprisoned, and Enio was dying, and the Asrai was the Gorga and… "I'm sorry," he managed.

"Don't blame yourself," Vex said. "These issues are not easily resolved."

"We'll return to Meridon and I'll pass the sigil to another Nowen," Zizik added. "While they become familiar with it, we can open negotiations with the Asrai. Perhaps stall her plans until we can release the mages."

Sadly, that seemed their best hope.

They left the Immortus and returned through the wavering portal.

"Now, if you'll excuse me," Zizik said, "I know a skilled teacher to whom I can trust this sigil."

But Par stopped him. "First, we need to make sure my friends are unharmed, and that the Asrai knows we'll bargain."

Zizik eyed the damaged pillar.

Par got the hint. "It should be safe. She'll assume we've taken her warning to heart."

"Very well. Gate, reopen to the tent."

It did. The Asrai sat on the makeshift throne with the dignity of a queen. She was alone.

"Welcome back," she said. "I assume you've returned to discuss terms."

"We have." Zizik stood forward.

Par joined him. "Where are my friends?"

"Safe and sound. Except, obviously, for Enio. We've continued to sustain him, but our efforts are of less and less effect. Now, I believe you know my simple request."

"The moon marrow," Par said. "What will you do with it?"

"Protect my kingdom."

"By destroying everything else?"

She waved him off. "A small demonstration of the moon marrow's power will restrain humanity's vice. Only those who continue their ruinous behaviors would be in peril."

Par wasn't having it. "You lied about the quakes and pushed everyone to the edge of war."

"For a greater end. When I have the moon marrow, there will be peace."

"Why should we believe you?"

"My word is enough. But I am in no hurry. Let us talk and learn more of each other, our favorite foods, whatever you wish. And while we do, your armies grow restless and the Horde raises more sea-dead. Soon there will be blood."

"Not if we tell everyone your true plans," Par said.

Her brief laugh held no warmth. "You would fan the world's fear, which is the very power I need." She clasped her hands and leaned forward. "And remember, even now your friend runs out of memories, and strength, and breaths."

Par's stomach sank even to his boots. Everything else she'd said might be truth or lie, but Enio's fate was clear.

He had one last idea. "Then I request a good-faith prisoner exchange. Me for my friends."

Vex laid his hand on Par's shoulder. "Now wait—"

With a half-step forward, Par shrugged it off. "Asrai, if during your negotiations, Enio… if he dies, the Nowen will never agree to your terms. I'll make sure of that. So a trade. Me for them."

Certainly, no one had appointed Par the official diplomat for Meridon, and he doubted his words carried any weight with their assembly. So, standing just ahead of Vex and Zizik and with his back to them, he tugged aside his collar, revealing the fake moon marrow on the string he'd gotten from Jeffrey.

Her eyes flicked to it and widened.

He lowered his hand, letting the shirt again cover the pendant.

She gave a nearly imperceptible nod. "I had chosen Lani to represent the Deep World, once I'd learned of her friendship with you, Par, and of your own esteem by the outer lands. So I will agree to your terms, since my current prisoners offer me no better advantage."

Par was the reason for the Asrai to employ Lani? That nearly gutted the relief of the Asrai falling for his moon marrow deception.

"And," she added, "in case of duplicity, I will keep the one named Eggwise."

"But—" Par began.

"Surely, that is not unreasonable."

Vex stepped forward. "This entire *proposal* is unreasonable."

"Why?" she said. "Is it not Par's decision?"

"He's under duress."

"Asrai," Par said, certain his plan now was the only option, "would you give us a moment?"

She smiled. "I will soon leave the Horde and return to the Deep World, where I will not allow the likes of your Gate to open. So do not take long."

Par gathered aside with Vex and Zizik.

"Par," Vex said darkly, "you mustn't do this."

"I have to. There's too much at stake. And Enio is dying. Nowen magic is all that's left to try on him."

Vex and Zizik said nothing.

He continued, "Rafael once told me that diplomacy involves finding the balance between things of unequal value. This is a three-for-one swap. Nothing in the power balance otherwise changes." He sighed. "I just wish Eggwise was part of the trade."

"It is a risk I think he'd accept," Zikik said. "As a Nowen, he may be useful in negotiating from that side."

Of course, no one knew that Par was bargaining with fake moon marrow. What would the Asrai do when she found out? Ornot had already threatened to cast him into the sea. But no matter what happened, at least the others would be safe in Meridon. At least Enio would have a chance.

"If I can't persuade you otherwise," Vex said, his words heavy, "then after the exchange, I'll return to Argent and notify the Eminence of these developments. And Par, take this." Vex discreetly removed the Luminary's ring from his finger.

Zizik leaned in. "That looks like moon marrow."

"If it is," Par said, taking it, "it's not raw, so it's not what the Asrai needs." Yet Par knew Vex didn't do anything without thinking it through. "But why give it to me? What if she finds it?"

"The ring is useless beyond the Citadel, except perhaps…" He paused, and his words became even heavier. "To capture a message."

Now Par understood. When he'd first found it among the long-dead Vigil, the ring had spoken. The Luminary himself had placed his dying words in it. If worse came to worse, Par would make his last message as useful as possible to whoever later heard it.

He dropped the ring in his pocket. Then, with a last nod to Vex and Zizik, he turned to the Asrai. "I'm ready."

She called to someone out of view, "Bring them."

Guards appeared with Eggwise, followed by Rafael and Lani. Lastly, they brought an unmoving Enio on a stretcher.

"To show my good intentions," the Asrai said, "I'll make the first gesture. Lani, step through."

Par reached his hand through the Gate.

But Lani spoke to the Asrai. "What's going on?"

"The others will follow. Do as I say."

Lani glanced at Rafael. He nodded back. Then she took Par's hand, and arrived in Meridon.

"Are you all right?" Par asked her.

"Yes. But what's happening?"

"Par," the Asrai said. "It's your turn."

He slipped his hand from Lani's. "Trust me." Before she responded, and before he lost his nerve, he passed from Meridon into the Asrai's tent, again flashing her the pendant.

She glanced at it, then motioned to Rafael. "You may take Enio."

Par joined Rafael lifting the stretcher. Enio remained still, except for the slight rise and fall of his chest.

"Take him," Par said to Rafael. "Make the Nowen help."

Rafael nodded. Par whispered, "Don't you die," in Enio's ear. Vex and Zizik received the stretcher through the Gate. Rafael followed with it, and the portal disappeared.

Eggwise came beside Par. "Prisoner exchange?"

"I'm sorry you weren't part of it."

"But something else was," said the Asrai.

Par lifted the stone and its string from around his neck.

"Par," gasped Eggwise. "You didn't!"

She snatched it from his hand and held it up. "Exquisite," she said. "Beautiful."

"I thought so too." Then Par gave an ugly chuckle. His friends were safe, and she was about to discover his deceit anyway, so it was pointless to hide it further. Besides, he couldn't resist seeing her face when she found out. He added, "Beautiful, for a toy."

"Par…" hissed Eggwise.

She peered at it closer. "A toy?"

"It's fake," Par said, confident he'd at last done something useful.

"Fake?" She bloomed an emerald glory. The rock sparkled like starlight. Her face turned radiant. Joyful.

But Eggwise gave a deep sigh.

Par glanced at him, at her, confusion growing in his mind, apprehension in his heart.

The Asrai smiled. "This is quite real. But you thought to deceive me? Well, enough of childish games."

Her glory blazed. An instant of searing pain, and the blinding green light threw Par into numb oblivion.

CHAPTER THIRTY-NINE

PAR AWOKE UPRIGHT, wrapped in vines, dangling against a rock wall like a portrait. The air was heavy and wet. He blinked away the sweat blurring his vision.

He was back at the Mother Spring. The Asrai stood below him, on the very spot from which Par had made his fateful leap to the *Sea Dog*. She faced the boiling lake. On the surface floated a skeleton.

Eggwise? Par nearly shouted with horror. But a groan beside him came from that man himself, also held by vines.

After a quick gasp of relief, Par said, "Eggwise?"

He opened his eyes. "Par? Where are we?"

"The Deep World. The Mother Spring."

"I hadn't imagined it quite so tropical."

The Asrai studied something in her hand. It was the stone Par had gotten from Jeffrey. He strained again to free himself, but he was held tight.

"Eggwise," he said, abandoning his struggles for now, "you told me Jeffrey's rock was fake. Were you wrong?"

"I may have made a mistake, but I wasn't wrong."

Maybe it was the heat, or the vines stiff against his pounding heart, or the prospect of imminent death, but that answer made no sense. "What do you mean?"

"Jeffrey's stone was indeed an imitation. But the first time you used the moon marrow in Meridon, after you fainted, I, um…" The man cleared his throat. "I swapped it."

"*You* swapped it? Why?"

After a fruitless wriggle, Eggwise said, "I warned you not to focus on it. But when you failed with your anima, I tried to help by exchanging the stones, so you'd still have the marrow, but not where you thought. I should have trusted you more. I'm sorry."

Par sighed. "I appreciate your intentions. But I'm the one to apologize. In the cabin, when Rafael put you to sleep, I swapped it myself."

"You did? Wait, let me think through this."

But Par went on. "Then during our walk to the coast, I swapped it back. Which means I wasn't returning the real one to your pendant: I was keeping it."

The Asrai continued to peer at the stone in her hand. The air wavered around it, such as Par had seen around the folds, and around Nowen during their invocations.

"This moon marrow situation," Eggwise said, "seems as tangled up as we are. In any case, she has the genuine item now."

Par's secrets were again making a mess of things. But dwelling on them was pointless. He kept his voice low. "Our plan was to stall the Asrai using negotiations for the moon marrow while another Nowen learned the sigil needed to free the last Sentinels. Even though the Asrai has the marrow now, maybe we can still slow her down."

"How?"

Taking a breath, Par shouted, "Asrai!"

She looked up. "Par. Just in time. I am about to begin. You shall be my witness, that this moment be remembered in legend."

Again Par struggled. The vines remained unyielding.

"You're safe there," she said. "But I had to dispose of my advisor, Ornot. He did not agree with my plans." She nodded toward the skeleton in the waters. It was sizzling into pieces.

In disgust, Par looked away from the sight. "Can you help me understand? How does destroying the world save it?"

"Not destroying." Her attention returned to the rock in her hand. "Merely removing a limb to save the body. For millennia, the outer lands and its hateful people have been a scourge upon the nymphs, upon the world. That ends today."

One thing about the Asrai—she liked to give long explanations. Par went with that angle. "I don't think that's the real reason you're doing this. You say the people are hateful. But you don't hate them. You fear them."

"Fear?" She again peered at Par. Amusement flickered across her pale, narrow face. "I am no coward, boy. I have led legions."

"It's not fear that proves a coward. It's lies. All you've done is lie."

"The world no longer recognizes truth. It would not recognize mine."

"What truth?"

"That only my vision can restore the balance."

"Who are you to decide such things?" Par's idea to keep her talking was working. Now if Zizik could just get his part done…

She answered with the boastfulness Par had expected. "I am uniquely qualified. I myself witnessed the Devastation. The Vigil considered many solutions to prevent another rift, including mine: to flood the lands and let the balance return on its own. Yet they spurned my foresight and instead relocated the survivors. And just as I predicted, your people built your cities and your nations and trampled the world unrestrained. Except here, in the sea. But the Vigil has at long last perished, and it's time for the rest of humanity to join them so the balance may return and the lands may heal."

"The people of the outer lands," Par said, "have made mistakes. But we've learned from them. There are hopes of friendship between Arcana and Eloria. We'll extend that to the Lowers and the nymphs. We can be better. The balance isn't lost. Together we can regain it."

The Asrai sighed like a frustrated parent. "You still don't understand. You've built your civilization upon the sands. You depend on the sea, not the sea on you. We are the world's foundation. We are the fulcrum of the balance."

Par hesitated, running out of ammunition. "Please, Asrai, listen to me. You can't restore it through mass murder. Bring your grievances to the nations. As new coalitions form, they'll give you a seat at the table and—"

"I have heard enough from you. Now be silent and bear witness." She turned again to the Mother Spring. Her glory brightened and grew. Then she began to rise, floating into the air, out and over the center of the roiling waters. She raised the black stone.

The waters spit and boiled. Steam thickened and swirled. And as when the Mother Spring had sent the *Sea Dog* to the Ults, images appeared within the mists. First only stretches of moonlit sea, then islands and distant shores, then forests and rivers and plains. And overhead, the moon itself, porcelain white.

The Asrai hung before it all, glowing now like an evil green star.

"Listen to me!" Par yelled, out of ideas. "We can—"

"I said be silent!" she boomed back. "Now you shall see how easily your towers are toppled, how easily your dreams denied."

"I won't!" yelled Par. "I—"

His vines tightened, choking off his words. Her voice rang louder. "Hear me, people of the lands. I am the sea, and I call the moon to your ruin. Make your peace, for the reign of humanity is over."

As she spoke, the moon itself reflected her glory, turning a sickly green.

"The moon is thirsty," she continued, her words echoing like thunder. "See? Even now, it comes to drink of your crimes, and of your souls. Surrender to destruction, and above all, embrace your fear, for it is all you have left."

Par felt the same terror that must be sweeping all those within reach of her powers. But after a gasp for air, he managed to shout, "Don't listen to her!"

The Asrai spun, fury on her face. "Since you cannot be silent…" She gestured toward the solid ground below Par. The rock there shifted and moved aside, creating two shallow furrows.

Or graves.

"In final honor of my late advisor," she said to him, "I hereby enact his sentence of imprisonment, but in my own way. You shall remain there, unless I think of a better use for you." Then she smiled. "But don't count on it."

With another wave of her hand, the vines holding Par and Eggwise carried them toward those dark holes.

"No!" Par tried to fight as the vines pressed Eggwise flat into one and Par into the other. Before he could scramble out, the vines snapped away and the ground above flowed like mud, then hardened overhead like the roof of a coffin, cutting off the light.

"No!" Par pounded on the rock.

But he was alone.

Trapped in the dark.

Buried alive.

CHAPTER FORTY

THE WALLS OF Par's pitch-black tomb slammed back his shouts. He twisted and kicked. His fingers clawed for any opening or seam, the roof too cramped for him to sit up. But it was no use. At last he stopped his struggling, his ragged breaths the only sound. Somewhere above, the Asrai had begun her attack on the world, and Par had provided her the means to do it. And here he lay like a corpse. Or soon to be one. What now? Wait for the air to run out? Slowly starve? Which would be better? Or worse?

Some questions shouldn't have answers.

His drumming heart sent tremors through his bones. As he slowed his breathing in hopes to last longer, the worst of his panic eased. Still, it was all too much, everything. There had been many other times when he'd questioned his decisions; despaired at what he'd gotten himself into; asked, why him? But buried alive? Nothing like this. Nothing as forsaken and alone as this. And what had he thought he could accomplish? He should never have leapt for the *Sea Dog*. He should never have left Argent.

Staring wide-eyed into the dark, he remembered that Enio

and Lani were now safe in Meridon. He should take comfort in that. Easier said than done, given his situation. Yet thoughts of his friends further steadied his nerves. No, he wouldn't give in to his fear. That's what the Asrai wanted. That was her weapon, and her victory.

So blindly, he again searched his tight burial chamber, in case he'd missed a crack or fissure. There was scarce room to turn or reach, and his clammy hands met only rough, cool stone. He made a quick squirm and winced at a sharp poke to his hip. A rock? He reached down—he'd lose his mind if the thing moved. But it was in his pocket. He drew it out: the Luminary's ring.

His hope stirred. Was this any help? He tapped the ring on the roof of his stone coffin.

Nothing.

He recalled the center being moon marrow. He rubbed his thumb over it and focused on his anima, trying to prompt some reaction. It had no effect. As Eggwise said, once bound to a purpose, moon marrow had no other use.

And as Vex had said, the ring had no real powers beyond the Citadel. Par was a long way from there.

Even so, Vex had also reminded him that the ring could store a message. And here was Par, buried alive, thinking perhaps his last thoughts. If nothing else, he could commit his last words to the ring. If whoever found his forgotten bones still fought the Asrai, even in some distant future, the things he'd learned might help them.

Par touched the ring's center stone. "Ring," he whispered, "remember what I say."

In his pit of deepest night, a very faint light sparked between his fingers. That small bit of illumination nudged up his spirits. They rose further when the ring's surface mirrored his own dim image.

Par cleared his throat. "Hi."

He grimaced. Terrible start. He began again.

"I'm Parynius Ignatious of Eloria. Par to my friends. Heard of me? Unworthy of the gods, feeble, abomination? I didn't ask to be born that way. Or to be so handsome." He made a nervous smile. "Sorry, dumb joke. I'm short on air, so I'll get to it. The ruler of the Deep World calls herself the Asrai, but she's also the Gorga. She lied to Eloria, the Dark Tribes, her own people, everyone. The quakes hitting our cities are her doing, to destroy and remake the world. She hates the spread of humanity. Or she fears it. Maybe the difference doesn't matter."

Even as Par said it, something rang wrong. There was a difference. And if these were his final words, he better get them right.

"For a thousand years, since the Devastation of Gê, the Asrai has hidden her people away. She convinced them it was for their safety. But as in Eloria and Arcana, isolation grew into fear. Same with the people we call Lowers, who use magic of the Lower Realms: they hide in the hills and mountains so they won't be persecuted. I've listened to plenty of theories over who hates who and why. The other day, someone recognized me and tried to drop a flowerpot on my head. But I don't believe we really hate each other. It's mostly fear. Except for the Asrai. She's ancient, and over time her fear twisted into an awful hate. Now she's using your fear. That's what she needs to destroy you."

Was that clear enough? Maybe, but something was still missing. He kept going.

"I don't know much about hate. I guess it helps us feel powerful, or tough. But believe me, I know about fear. My friend Eggwise says fear is strongest at the edges. It's true. I've lived on those edges, unable to go back, afraid to go forward. Afraid of what people would think if they learned I wasn't like them, that I couldn't invoke. I know fear isn't easy to shake off, but to fight the Asrai, we have to try." Par reflected for a moment. "Or we need to replace that fear. I'm not sure what best counters hate.

Hate divides, so just… stop… that. Sorry. Rafael probably knows a better word—he's a diplomat. But fear is different. Fear goes deeper."

Par's heart beat faster with the growing realization that he was putting things together. Hopefully not because of suffocation. He'd better speed this up.

"Sometimes, fear is justified. Like fear of losing those we care for. But sometimes it hurts more than it helps, like when we're afraid of people we've never even met, or who just seem different from us. And we wall ourselves away from them. That causes the isolation I talked about, cuts us off from each other. Pretty soon, we're all alone."

Like Par was now. His friends returned to mind. Friends? A tomb had no room for lies. They were more than friends.

A lump in his throat slowed his next words. He swallowed hard. "And being alone has always scared me more than anything. It's foolish, I know, because being afraid is exactly what cuts me off in the first place. But you know what? My friends make my fear go away."

He wiped a growing dampness from his eyes. "Sorry if I'm rambling: it's hard to concentrate in here. What I'm saying is that the opposite of fear must be love. I may be an idiot when it comes to love, but for a minute, one stupid minute"—he sniffled—"can we see those we're afraid of as just people with families and friends and fears like our own? Is that so hard? Let me tell you, it isn't when life looks short. But fear locks us away and gives the key to our real enemies, gives them power over us. Right now, that's the Asrai. So remember what you love, and who you love. That's how you defeat her. If you don't, everyone loses. Everyone dies."

He swallowed again; thank the gods the air had lasted. He'd said what he needed to say.

That is, to those fighting the Asrai. He still needed to say something directly to Enio and Lani. For his own sake.

Par smiled, teary-eyed. In truth, Enio didn't need to hear it. Somewhere in that stubborn, broken-toothed, stick-skinny body, Enio knew it already. Besides, if Par said it, Enio might punch him. But there was someone else Par needed to tell.

He took a deep breath of precious air.

"One last thing. I've learned that sometimes we keep our heart secret because we're afraid of it getting broken. Walled-up hearts might be safe from breaking, but not from shredding. So, Lani, I love you." His voice cracked. "I should have told you sooner."

With that, Par closed his hand over the ring. If nobody ever heard what he'd said, at least he'd said it. And he'd discovered what he truly feared. It wasn't being alone. It was being alone with himself, with the feelings he kept hidden in silence, the ones others might see, and reject him for.

His tears now weren't from fear or grief. In that moment, as if sunlight had reached through the seas above the Deep World and into his private darkness, Par experienced a freedom he'd never known.

Even buried alive.

Chapter Forty-One

Par wiped his eyes and lay back in a strange peace. With everything he'd said into the ring, and to Lani, he'd used his last breaths well. He'd revealed the truth about the Asrai, and admitted a truth to himself. Now he felt he could accept his fate. He could even sleep—except it might be the last time he'd close his eyes. Besides, he didn't want to lose this feeling. He'd keep it alive, as long as it lasted. As long as *he* lasted.

The seconds carried him along, each handing him off to the next, each here then gone into eternity. He found if he listened hard, he heard distant noises. Rumbles and murmurings moved beneath him, around him, through the rock. Perhaps from the breath of timeless, hollow abysses; or the weight of waters that flowed high above, covering the Deep World; or other powers no surface creature understood, or imagined. Whatever their source, they made him feel less alone.

Then, hidden among the others, he noticed a faint, sharper sound, brief and rhythmic. He pressed his ear against the side.

Tap tap.

Eggwise was buried in that direction. For all his eccentricities, he'd been a good friend. He'd taught Par many things, not just the Nowen stuff. He'd said the greatest balance of life was to hold fear in one hand and hope in the other. Eggwise never explained how to fix that when it went awry. But Par had figured it out on his own: love tipped the balance.

Tap tap.

If Par had known that truth earlier in life, it might have saved him the lies and isolation his fears had brought. Eggwise's lonely existence as the last Nowen in Choga hadn't sounded much better. Strange, how two people from such different beginnings arrived at the same end. Maybe that happened more than Par realized.

Tap tap.

Each time the same: two taps, then silence. It was a gift of company. He raised his ring to tap back.

And he realized something else.

Nowen used sigils in pairs. In twos. They often needed to touch, but not always. How much space was allowed between them?

How much rock?

Tap tap.

Par had nearly given up on anima, but he still had the Nowen pinch sigil. He summoned it to mind, and let his anima flicker around the edges.

Two extra loud taps, and the sound stopped. If Par guessed right, Eggwise was signaling, prompting him to try again. Par concentrated on the sigil. This was their last chance. He tried harder than ever to fill it with anima.

But his sigil dimmed.

Eggwise had said not to force it. Find the balance. Hope and fear.

Par had known the fear; he'd found the hope. What was he missing?

Eggwise had tapped twice.

Like the Nowen used sigils. In twos.

Because a balance has two sides.

And love tips the balance.

Par might still be vulnerable to fear of the Asrai, not to mention his own entombment, but he wouldn't let fear win. He countered it with the best source of hope he knew: his feelings for his dear friend Enio, and his newly admitted love for Lani. Tears again threatened his eyes, and warmth filled his heart.

And the sigil brightened beyond anything he'd seen before.

Par laughed, though his joy was tinged with irony. His block was gone, but it had taken his burial to go as deep as he'd needed—and say what he'd needed.

Then, beyond his sigil, he saw its mirror image. That must be Eggwise doing the same.

Par regained his emotional balance as his sigil turned and moved like a boat under sail. Eggwise's sigil glided toward it. The two met, and with a glorious flash merged into one.

"Good, Par!" Eggwise's voice came through the solid stone—not so solid anymore.

With the sigil bright in his mind, Par hissed back, "Now what?"

"Now, up and out!"

Par threw himself upward, half expecting to slam into stone. But he didn't. He passed as if through a brief fold and tumbled onto the ground above. Eggwise landed at his side.

The Asrai, engulfed in a globe of green light, floated high above the boiling Mother Spring. The steaming, billowing clouds beneath her still showed images of spreading forests and cities, even the ghoulish green moon. Still holding aloft the moon marrow, she continued to spew her cruel, booming words. "You see your end! Humanity has made an enemy of forest and hill, mountain and sea. They are your accusers. The moon has watched and now it judges!"

As she spoke, countless threads of thinnest shadow, like black veins or arteries, had begun to stream from all the lands. They flowed to the Asrai. She was collecting her power: the fears of the people.

Par had little time. If she noticed him, he'd be entombed again, or else join Ornot as a dissolving skeleton. He might try to jump, crash into her, disrupt her witchery. But even with a full running leap, he'd never reach.

He turned again to Eggwise. The man lay motionless. Par shook him. He didn't rouse, but still breathed, perhaps having overtaxed himself. Par considered dragging him out of here. He sighted the Asrai's guards outside the Mother Spring's entrance, blocked by some misty green force. That way seemed useless. He turned again to the spring. It was said to take things where they needed to go, as it had taken Par to meet Eggwise. Yet, assuming it still did that during the Asrai's evil invocations, Eggwise was unconscious and might not survive a push over the edge into the spring, or wherever it sent them, like Par's wild river ride and waterfall.

Par had one last idea. He grasped the Luminary's ring, reeled back, and sent it soaring over the ledge. It plummeted into the clouds above the spring, hopefully back to Vex, where it would now be most needed. Though the wizard had no way to rescue them, he might find Par's message, or return to the Citadel vault for something to use against the Asrai.

After a brief flash and crackle of lightning, the ring disappeared. But that flash sent ripples through the clouds. The images there flickered.

The Asrai turned. The fury on her twisted face needed no words. With the twitch of an eye, she sent Par and Eggwise flying. They slammed once more against the stone walls, so high and hard it took the breath from Par's lungs. He was held this time not by natural living vines—his new bonds were of mere shadow, yet steel-cold and unyielding.

The images before the Asrai steadied and sharpened. She resumed her speech, her voice thundering into the mists. "Fear this day. Fear your fate. Fear me!" The shadows collected thick around her. Then, from her raised arm, from the moon marrow, a claw of shadow reached out, directed toward the moon itself.

"The moon is thirsty!" she called again. "I call it down, to drink of your souls!"

If Par flung himself into the spring, a last act of defiance, he might disrupt her magic like the ring had. He struggled harder, but it was as if he were held by icy iron chains.

Yet he could still breathe. So he could still speak.

"She's lying!" he yelled out. "Don't listen to her. Hear me!"

His shadowy bonds squeezed. Searing pain stabbed his chest. Then *Crack!* A rib snapped.

He screamed, blinded by white pain. When he recovered enough to focus, he could barely draw breath.

"Hi. I'm Parynius Ignatious…"

The words came not from him, but from the Mother Spring.

For a moment, the frightful streams of shadow that flowed to the Asrai faltered. She peered down, disoriented, searching for the source of the voice.

"…ruler of the Deep World calls herself the Asrai, but she's also the Gorga. She lied to Eloria, the Dark Tribes, her own people, everyone. "

"Who dares!" she shouted.

"The quakes hitting our cities are her doing, to destroy and remake the world."

She turned to Par, her eyes burning with hate. Par's chest squeezed tighter. Another rib cracked. The pain was so great that the scream died in his throat. He grasped at consciousness. It came and went in piercing fragments, but his words still flowed from the Luminary's ring.

"…she's using your fear. That's what she needs to destroy you."

"…the opposite of fear must be love."

"…remember what you love, and who…"

"That's how you defeat her."

"Lies!" screamed the Asrai. "I cannot be stopped!" Her voice rang with fury. "Fear me! Fear all!"

But the shadowy threads being drawn from the world, the fears feeding her magic, and the claw reaching toward the moon were breaking up. The pressure around Par's chest drew back. His head cleared.

"Stop this!" she screamed. Her fury turned to panic—her spell, no longer feeding on the world's fear, had found a fresh source: the Asrai herself. Her skin, her body, now steamed, bleeding shadow. Bleeding fear.

"No!" she shouted again, fighting against the very magic she had summoned.

The green globe holding her above the spring sputtered and was gone. With a shout she fell, plunging into the Mother Spring's boiling waters. She thrashed and fought, and her last screams were terrible, only dying away as her flesh sloughed from her bones.

Suddenly, Par was free of his bonds.

And falling from the wall.

But something caught him. The pain in his sides roared and dragged him fully into unconsciousness, but not before he glimpsed the Asrai's guards rushing forward.

PART FOUR

DESTINIES

Chapter Forty-Two

Fitful visions of reaching vines, of being lowered.

Then the voice of Eggwise. "I think our Nowen here broke something. Easy now, Par."

Par rode a wave of pain back to the light. He lay on the ground above the Mother Spring. He tried to speak, but merely breathing lit fires in his chest. A single word made it out. "…Asrai?"

With a gentle smile, Eggwise said, "She's dead. I saw the end."

"As did we." A new face bent overhead, pale but rugged, one of the Asrai's guards. "We owe you a great debt, son." Others like him stood nearby.

"You might begin to repay it," Eggwise cut in, resuming his familiar crankiness, "by healing this boy's hurts."

The guard's glory glowed emerald. He reached out. "If I may?"

Par grimaced and managed a nod.

The touch healed Par's pain like cool water quenching a savage thirst. He took a full, easy breath. Below, the Mother Spring had boiled away, leaving a large rocky basin encrusted with bruised minerals and shriveled weeds. There was no sign of the Asrai, or the moon marrow, or the Luminary's ring. He wrinkled his nose at the trace of something burnt, yet the odor was already being replaced by the fresh, living scents of the Deep World. Of the vibrant élan.

As he gazed upon the ruin of the spring, he noticed a shimmer growing near the center. It widened into a doorway. Zizik stood in its mouth.

The guards raised spears and invoked their glories.

Par scrambled to his feet. "It's all right! He's a friend."

The portal, with Zizik framed in its entrance, rose into the air, glided forward, and came to rest beside Par and his group.

Zizik stepped out. "Par, what has happened?"

"It's over," Par said. "The Asrai is dead. How did you find us?"

"It wasn't easy." The man glanced around. "We discovered that the moon marrow you gave us was fake, and as I searched for you through the Gate, I heard the Asrai's words and witnessed their effect upon the lands. I traced the epicenter to here. But the Gate wouldn't open to this place until now."

"I didn't know I had the real moon marrow," Par said, "but it was destroyed with the Asrai."

"Yes, I sense that." Zizik sighed. "Well, that being the case—"

Par didn't hear the rest. Lani stepped from the shimmering doorway. The sight of her was spring air and sunshine.

"Par!" she said. "Are you all right?"

He stepped closer, ready to embrace her. "I am now."

But her expression stopped him cold. It was empty of joy.

And Par realized. "Enio?"

Her face darkened. She shook her head.

A pain worse than any fractured bone threatened to puncture Par's chest.

The guard bowed before her. "Thank the thundering seas

you've come, Lady Alehelani. With the Asrai and Ornot gone, our armies are in disarray. You know the outer lands better than any. We need your counsel, lest we fall into chaos and violence."

"Yes, of course," she said, her eyes on Par. She took his hand. "Go to Enio." She squeezed. "Hurry."

Jumbled thoughts and emotions rushed Par's brain, but there was no time to sort them out. He squeezed her hand back, nodded, and stepped through the portal into the Meridon Gate chamber. Eggwise and Zizik followed, and the Gate closed.

A group, some of whose members Par recognized as Meridon teachers, gathered around one of the pews. Rafael was among them. The shadowed carvings of ancient faces frowned from the walls and pillars.

Par pushed forward. Enio lay there, his breath as dry and lifeless as the Mother Spring.

"He hasn't moved in hours," Rafael said.

A bowl of water sat beside him. Par reached for it. "He needs to drink, he—"

Rafael stopped him. "He'll choke, Par."

Zizik added, "We've done all we can. He slips away."

But Par wasn't giving up. "Zizik, what about the mages at the Immortus?"

"Even as we speak, a most skilled Nowen struggles to learn that sigil."

"We can't wait any longer," Par said. "Take me to the Immortus. I'll invoke the sigil myself."

Zizik eyed him. "We tried that already."

"There's no time to argue. Take me."

Eggwise answered from behind. "Yes, take him."

"Very well," Zizik said. "Gate, the Immortus."

The Gate opened to the sands of the Devastation. Par and Rafael lifted Enio and carried him through, with Eggwise and Zizik close behind. Ahead lay the last two looming monoliths, the Nowen Sentinels, rising like broken black teeth into the grey sky. Every other time Par had come here—first as a prisoner of Cronus, then as a tool for the Ortu—someone had died.

No. Not this time.

They crossed the sands and lay Enio between the towering stones. Rafael and Eggwise stood aside. Par gazed at Enio's limp body one last time, then moved to a monolith and touched its dark surface. He turned to Zizik. The man did the same with the other.

With a final breath and swallow, Par closed his eyes and brought to mind the strange, twisted sigil he'd gotten from the mage Ridiax. Balancing his fear and his hope, he directed his anima into the sigil. Waves of Nowen magic traced its loops and curves. A second sigil appeared in his mind as Zizik invoked. And with both now brimming with anima, the sigils merged, radiating clear and strong.

"Look!" Eggwise shouted.

Par's eyes flew open. The monoliths steamed as with morning fog. He stood back. So did Zizik. The steaming increased, and the Sentinels seemed to melt until a veil of mist hid them completely. When it dispersed, two robed figures had replaced the tall stones.

Thank the gods. It had worked.

The two figures drew off their hoods. A man and a woman stood there, ancient and noble, hair long and white. They faced each other.

"You were right," the old woman said. "Our sacrifice was well made. Though I expect the years have not been as kind to me as to you." She reached out a hand.

The man stepped closer and took it. "The years have never been more kind. You're as lovely as ever."

"Please," Par interrupted, spoiling the reunion, but in too much need to avoid it. "Can you help my friend?"

Before Par explained further, they lowered their eyes to Enio.

His chest trembled with what barely seemed breath. Par waited, breathing not much better. "Please," he said again. "He doesn't have much time."

"No, he doesn't," the woman said. "His journey ends here." The mages stood unmoving and said nothing more.

Par watched them through welling tears, tears getting hotter. Angrier. The words burst out. "Help him!"

"We have," the mages said together.

But they had done nothing, no magic, no anima. Par knelt, pressed his ear to his friend's chest and listened, the thumping inside so very slow. He raised his eyes to the mages. "I don't understand, he's still—"

"Possessed," said the woman.

That was the last word Par had expected. When Enio had fought the Ortu in this very place, he'd briefly allowed Cronus to take over his body. Yet wasn't Cronus dead and gone?

"But not by another," the woman added. "He possesses himself."

That made even less sense.

She went on, "He has been protector and protected. Ailing and healer. Dreamer and dreamed. But all dreams must end so that new ones begin."

The man spoke, his voice strong and formal. "Know ye now the Nowen, the people of the now and of the here, of where and nowhere. The Nowen, sail and anchor, salt and sea, morrow to morrow. Three above. Three below. Two the balance, then and fro."

As Par stared, lost and confused, the two mages lifted their clasped hands to form an arch. The space beneath shimmered, then opened into darkness. Were they creating a fold? But deep in that void, there appeared a distant glimmer, followed by others: small swirling lights or strange stars. Par had seen them once before. It was the Higher Realms.

Something approached from beneath the stars: a boat, shining as if made of crystal. Rainbow winds filled its sails.

A low, dry rattle came from Enio.

Par spun to his friend. The chest stopped moving.

Before Par shouted his horror, a vapor rose from the body. Par fell back. It swirled into the shape of Enio and drifted beneath the mage's arms, through that portal to the boat—which looked suspiciously like the *Sea Dog*. The vessel drifted off.

"Enio!" Par called.

But the woman said simply, "He has gone."

Par's heart became as stone. This couldn't be. Not after everything they'd been through. He lay a faltering hand on Enio's body. The tears Par could no longer stop ran down his cheeks. Had he spent too long in Meridon? Too long chasing his Nowen dreams? Could he have done something sooner? Their victory over the Asrai was now ash in his mouth.

"Is there nothing more you can do?" His voice trembled.

"There is nothing," the woman said gently.

Just before Par fell apart, she added, "But there is something you can do."

Par looked up. "Me? What?"

She smiled. "Two the balance, then and fro. Your friend's journey is nearly finished. He must complete his circuit to return whence he began. You, Par, must guide him."

"How?" Without waiting for an answer, he shouted at the void, "Enio!"

"Not with words," she said.

Par didn't understand. "Do I need a sigil?"

"You need nothing you don't already have. Find him within you, that he may find himself."

Within? But Par would try anything. Peering after the vessel, he thought of Enio, coal-bright eyes, wild hair, and the broken teeth that the wide smile never hid. That brought other memories: Enio's beloved *Sea Dog*, born as a canoe, grown now into a fine sailing ship; Par's time with Enio on the river, and their studies and misadventures in the abbey; Enio's occasional hints for a supper invite when he had none at his own home; and the stories he'd told no one except Par, stories of his mother before she'd died. These things and more filled Par's heart. He prayed they were enough.

And just in case, he summoned a memory of them sharing bowls of thick, pungent crawtad soup.

Rather than turn, the vessel sped faster into the night. Into the void! Par was about to call again when a second ship appeared, sailing straight at it. A collision seemed imminent, but the portal vanished. The mages had dropped their arms and ended the vision.

"Wait!" Par shouted. As he struggled with an urge to leap forward without seeing anything to chase, a great gasp escaped Enio's lungs.

Par spun. Enio's chest expanded with deep, full breaths. Color was returning to his face.

With a yelp of joy, Par dove toward his friend, stopping at the last instant from crashing on top of him.

Rafael joined them. Par had to hug something, so he hugged Rafael and whispered, "He's alive."

"Two the balance," Eggwise said, his words tinged with awe, "then and fro."

Par wiped his eyes and looked up. "What does that mean?"

"It means," the woman answered, "he's back where he belongs—with you then, and with you now. Returned is Enio the healed, who has journeyed to help Enio the ailing, who himself returns."

"I warned you," Eggwise murmured to Par, "about Nowen explanations."

Enio's eyes flickered open. "Where am I?"

With no more hesitation, Par fell upon his friend and hugged him. "With me."

A small chuckle of surprise came from Enio's throat. "I can see that."

Par still hadn't quite digested what the lady mage had said. But it didn't matter, as long as this Enio was Enio the healed. Enio the returned.

Zizik addressed the mages. "I bow to you, ancient and powerful Nowen, Sentinels for the Immortus. You will be welcomed in Meridon with honor and—"

The Nowen male raised a hand. "Our power is spent. We must move on."

"Move on? But great mages," Zizik stammered, "Meridon needs you. We've lost much since the days of Gê and forgotten many of our ancestor's sigils, such as those for battle and defense."

The man nodded. "Then use your Gate for that which we intended. Not as a wall, but a door."

Zizik paused and sighed. "Yes. We've isolated ourselves from the world. We will try to remedy that."

"As for your sigils," the woman gestured to Par, "ask him."

"Me?" Par said.

"Did not Ridiax give you many gifts?"

When Par had returned from the Higher Realms, he'd received a cloud of sigils from Ridiax. He could do little with them before. Now he could bestow any that were Nowen. Perhaps he could use them himself.

But that prompted another question. "I met soul to soul with Ridiax. He must have seen I was a Nowen. Why didn't he tell me?"

"Perhaps," said the woman, "he felt you were not yet ready to know."

Par couldn't argue with that. He nodded and said, "Thank you for your help," though his words seemed small after what the mages had done. He added, "But I'm still uncertain what happened."

She smiled once more. "Your love tipped the balance, Par." She reached out and again clasped hands with her companion. Their eyes met, and their faces shone with such perfect peace that it left Par speechless. Then, like the other Sentinels Par had seen released here at the Immortus, their forms began to waver. Their eyes never unlocked as they faded, became transparent, and were gone.

Out of wonder or reverence, no one spoke. Where once the rift to the Higher Realms opened by Ridiax and restrained by eight mysterious monoliths had raged, now only that bare platform remained. The surrounding yellow sands looked somehow less alien, just an unremarkable desert. Even the grey clouds that seemed always to choke its sky were breaking. This was the site of many of Par's trials. Of victories, of death—and if he never saw the place again, it would be too soon.

Close by in the sands, the shimmering Meridon Gate still waited. Others had gathered beyond the entrance, even a few children. All watched with wide eyes.

"Hey," Enio said, sitting up. "Is anyone going to tell me what's going on?"

Par and Rafael helped him stand. Par said, "There's a lot to explain. Even to me. Let's get out of here."

"Good, I'm starving." Enio looked around. "Where's the closest tavern?"

Rafael laughed. "Yeah. I could use an ale."

"Ale?" Eggwise said, coming over. "Count me in too."

Zizik joined them. "And me three."

Par wrapped an arm around Enio's shoulders and they walked toward the Gate.

Enio placed his own arm around Par. "And I've got this sudden craving for crawtad soup."

Chapter Forty-Three

Par returned with his friends through the Gate to Meridon. Enio seemed stronger with every step. The waiting Nowen offered to heal Enio further, but he insisted he was fine. When the people saw his stubbornness, they focused instead on Zizik, showering the Regent with questions.

He raised his hands. "I'll tell you everything once I've addressed the Assembly. Now, please, one moment." He gathered Par, Enio, Rafael, and Eggwise for a private talk. "It would honor me to present you before the Assembly. They will have many questions and, I promise, much praise."

"Thank you," Par replied. "But last I saw Argent, it was under attack by the Asrai's quakes. I have to get back, tell them what's happened, and help if I can. Also, I want the healers to check out Enio."

Enio grumped.

Par ignored him. "And, Zizik, I've made my Nowen's choice. I choose the outer world."

But Zizik smiled. "The Nowen Ceremony of Choice has outlived its purpose. You may return to Meridon anytime." Then to

Eggwise, "And you, sir, will you stay? We have many changes to make, and your help would be most valuable."

"Well,"—Eggwise moved a hair bead—"I have responsibilities in Choga. The Channel—"

"We will assist in your duties there, if you wish."

"Ah. Very kind."

Zizik turned to Rafael. "And I can think of no better diplomat for our engagements with the outer lands."

Rafael also seemed hesitant. "Thank you, sir. You don't know how much your offer means to me. But like you, I have testimony to make elsewhere. After that, however, I'll ask to be assigned here, if that's acceptable."

"I'll insist on it."

Rafael raised his chin. It heartened Par to see the guy's confidence returning.

Zizik glanced at the Gate. "Now, where to first?"

Before everyone went their separate ways, Par turned to Eggwise. "I haven't thanked you for—"

"I owe you more thanks than you owe me." Eggwise laid a hand on Par's shoulder. "Because of you, this grumpy old swamp fart is part of a larger world. Let's call it even."

Par chuckled. "Does that include the cost of Jont's Channel ticket?"

"Consider that ledger balanced."

In a surge of affection, Par threw his arms around the man.

"Yes, well." Eggwise cleared his throat and patted Par's head. "The sentiment is mutual. Now, get out of here."

Par nodded and faced Zizik. "Argent outpost, please."

"Argent outpost," the man repeated to the Gate. It opened to that familiar chamber, cleared now of rubble and largely repaired. Vex was there, examining the monitor's twinkling globe.

With a last wave, Par, Enio, and Rafael left Meridon and entered the outpost. "Vex!" Par called.

The wizard jolted. "Par? Someone should really hang a bell on you. What's happened?"

"Everything's all right." Par made a quick explanation.

Vex looked more relieved with each word. At last, he said, "Come, we must find the Abbot."

"And the Eminence," Par added.

But Vex led them out of the chamber as if not hearing.

They traveled the outpost's secret corridors and up to the High Temple. The damage there was extensive. Rushing guards and frantic workers helped the injured and reinforced crumbling walls and pillars. Vex led them out of the grand golden doors to the central plaza where, though still night, the lantern-lit activity was just as intense. Cracked walls and broken statues were everywhere.

"There." Vex pointed out the Father Abbot, healing a woman's leg. She thanked him and hurried off.

"Cornelius!" Vex called.

Weary and haggard, the old Abbot glanced over, but his face brightened as they approached. "Ah, thank the gods you're all safe! The quakes here have stopped. Is there news?"

Par repeated the explanation he'd given Vex, then asked the question he dreaded. "How bad is the damage?"

"Extensive, but repairable. However," his voice faltered, "the Eminence has died."

"Oh no." Par's spirits sank. "What happened?"

The Abbot gazed sadly into the distance. "During the last of the Asrai's attacks, the sea rose like death's own shadow, threatening to drown all those evacuating across the mainland causeway. The Eminence stood in its very center and made a great invocation, sacrificing himself to hold off the flood while the crowds fled."

Besides his position as Fondiscate, closest to the gods, Par had thought the Eminence wise, honest, and kind. He had helped Par more than once. Par couldn't find any words.

Vex asked, "How many others?"

"Many wounded, but I pray no more deaths. We're still searching. Then will come time to mourn and rebuild." He eyed Enio. "Speaking of the wounded, mind if I check?"

"He doesn't," Par said.

Enio rolled his eyes but didn't object.

The Abbot laid his hands on Enio's head and invoked a sunny Elorian glory. When he'd finished, he said, "Seems he's back to being good old Enio."

"Damn right," Enio said.

The Abbot cleared his throat.

So did Par. "Uh, Father Abbot, how can we help?"

"I think everything's in hand. And you look ready to drop. Let's find you a room. We'll meet again in the morning, and you can tell me the rest."

Par realized he was, indeed, as tired as he'd ever been in his life. They crossed the plaza, where the fountain's leaping, burbling waters no longer burbled or leapt, to the palace, the late home of the Eminence. A great black banner hung from the highest balcony, and one of the large ornate doors had fallen off. Otherwise, the structure seemed intact. After a word to a palace guard, the Abbot bid them goodnight.

The guard led them to a room Par recognized. Pink marble walls, elegant furniture. Par had awoken here when he'd been captured at a wedding and brought to first meet the Eminence—not so long ago, though it felt like another lifetime. He settled on a velvet couch. Enio paused at a table of candles, and amused himself by flicking the flame from wick to wick. Even his ability to invoke had returned.

And as Par watched, he drifted into a deep, exhausted sleep.

*

He awoke to sunlight blushing through the saint-painted windows. The Abbot, Vex, Rafael, and Enio sat around a table arrayed with breakfast foods. Par sat up, yawned, and smiled. Everyone together again.

Well, almost everyone. His smile wavered. Lani was still in the Deep World. Had she decided between life there or on land? Until he knew, his heart would find no peace, but at present there was nothing he could do about it. He'd make the best of his time here in Argent.

"Good morning," he said, joining the others.

"Par!" they called, except Enio, whose mouthful of muffin muffled his greeting. It cheered Par to see him eating again. Enio was skinny at the best of times. Now, after his illness, he had the body mass of a sneeze.

Par scooped himself a plate of fried potatoes. "How long have you guys been up?"

"Some of us," Vex said, glancing at the Abbot, "I suspect the entire night."

The Abbot waved this off. "We've healed the injured and thankfully found no more serious casualties. Rebuilding will take far more time. But now, Par, we need your insight. We're trying to work out what happened with Enio."

"I thought," Vex said, with a hint of impatience, "that I just explained it rather well."

Rafael dabbed his mouth with a napkin. "You were quite detailed. But in truth, much of your Arcanan terminology went over my head."

"Mine too," said the Abbot.

"Then let me try it this way." Vex took a plate from near Enio, stacked with crackers and salami slices. "May I?"

"But I'm still—"

"Imagine this is Enio's body." Vex placed a cracker on the tablecloth. "And this is Enio's soul." He set a slice of meat on top.

Par nodded. "My friend. The soul of a salami."

Enio eyed him.

Par grinned.

Vex continued. "Back before this business with the Asrai, Enio's soul was ravaged during his possession by Cronus. So the Abbot committed Enio to the Mercy House to heal. There he lay bedridden and unresponsive." Vex flipped the cracker over, the salami now underneath.

"Until the Summer Festival," Par said. "He hadn't recovered yet, but I'm sure he invoked and lit the crowd's candles."

Enio pulled over a bowl of olives. "I remember riding a crystal boat under strange stars and past people holding candles. I think I helped light them, but I don't remember the festival."

The Abbot raised a finger. "Soon after, he communicated through the projection sigil I bestowed on him, then awoke and left his bed."

"Which made us think he was on the mend," Par added.

"At least, for a time," corrected the Abbot. But I wouldn't have let him out of my sight, much less sail to the Deep World, had I truly known how quickly he would relapse."

"As he did in the mountains," Rafael said. "But this still doesn't explain—"

"Bear with me." Vex placed a second cracker beside the first and set a slice of salami beneath it too. "As Rafael points out, even after Enio's apparent recovery, he again struggled and faded. But at last, after all our trials and travails, Par brought him to the Immortus. This second cracker represents the later Enio that arrived there, his soul having had time to rest and heal. The Nowen mages sent this mended soul back to the Summer Festival, to protect his earlier soul as it did that healing." Vex removed the meat from the bottom of the second cracker and placed it on top of the first, so that cracker was now sandwiched with salami.

The Abbot eyed it. "You're saying that Enio's body was—or had been, or would be—indwelt by two Enio souls?"

But Par remembered the mage's words. *He has been protector and protected. Ailing and healer. Dreamer and dreamed. But all dreams must end so that new ones begin.* "Then the dreams he told me of quakes and skeletons and the rest weren't dreams, or even visions, but memories from the soul that had already traveled that path, and returned to help him heal."

"Very good." Vex again indicated the salami-sandwiched cracker. "This is the Enio that Rafael traveled with through the Ults. That you, Par, brought to the Immortus, to the mages. One body, two souls. One Enio safe below and healing, and one above, the one you could talk to. The Enio below at last healed enough so that the mages could send it back to become the top Enio, and finishing that task, remain the final Enio." He moved the salami he'd just placed on the first cracker onto the second. "A risky undertaking if you ask me. Considering his difficulties, I'd say two souls don't integrate well. I understand it played havoc with his memory."

"Not to mention," the Abbot said, rubbing his temple, "with verb tenses."

"But what about the two crystal boats?" Par asked.

"I suspect," Vex said, "they were an interpretation, a manifestation, of whatever his soul needed for its journey—two souls, two boats. The same way he perceived the crowd at the Summer Festival sailing their own small boats. Anyway, we now have before us one fully healed Enio."

Rafael was tracing small loops in the air, apparently trying to figure this all out.

But Par looked from the crackers to his friend. "Two Enios?" He shook his head. "As if the end of the world hadn't been enough."

Enio was about to eat an olive. Instead, he threw it at Par.

Par dodged. But the twisty explanation sounded as good as

any. Still, after everything he'd learned from the Nowen, another possibility occurred to him. Perhaps the mages had *folded* Enio.

He kept that theory to himself.

Now Enio was eating the crackers and salami, which seemed weirdly appropriate.

"And what of the Asrai?" Rafael asked, giving up on Enio's soul. "I'm still a bit vague on her demise."

Vex pursed his lips. "From the way Par described things, she used the moon marrow and the Mother Spring's reach to gather people's fears and amplify them, focusing that power upon the moon to draw it down and remake the world. But the words Par put into the Luminary's ring countered her own. When she could no longer supply to her charm the fear it required, it drew upon her own energies, her hate, resulting in her destruction."

"Her hate consumed her," the Abbot said.

"I believe I just said that." Vex clasped his hands. He again wore the ring. Par was happy to see it had found its way home.

The Abbot continued. "I'm just surprised that while Par's words were inspired, they changed enough minds to make such an immediate difference. The fear she provoked I would not believe so quickly overcome."

"Yes, well. I wanted to mention something about that." Vex cleared his throat. "As the Asrai's voice began to spread through the lands, the Mother Spring also sent it, along with Par's words, to the monitor. I was in the outpost at that moment and heard them. And in an effort to help…"

He paused.

"What?" Par said.

"I, uh, I had the monitor redirect your speech to the Vigil's web of pendants, within reach of the Mother Spring and the Asrai's fearmongering, or beyond."

Par felt a gnawing uneasiness. "How many people are we talking about?"

"Everyone."

Par narrowed his eyes. "Everyone in Eloria?"

"Yes, and, well, I'd never done this before, you understand, so I had no fine control over—" Vex cleared his throat again.

"Vex?"

The wizard sighed. "I'd reestablished the connections between the other monitors, so your words flew through them to every Lustering pendant of Eloria, and to every token of Ascendancy in Arcana, and to every Relic of Rising within the Dark Tribes, wherever they were in all the lands, around necks, through noses, in boxes, on mantels, in shops. Each and every one spoke what you'd said."

"Everyone?" The word still stuck in Par's mind.

"Perhaps not everybody paid attention, but enough that their reaction to your words helped tip the balance."

Par tried to remember if he'd said anything embarrassing.

Then tried to forget that he had.

Had Lani heard it too?

Did he hope she hadn't?

Did he hope she had?

He'd begun to sink in his chair when the Abbot delivered him from his self-conscious death spiral. "So, Par, I understand you're a Nowen."

Par gladly grabbed the lifeline and sat back up. "I can't show you without a second Nowen here. But, yeah, seems so."

Enio spoke between bites. "Can't wait to see."

"In retrospect," Vex said, "it also solves the puzzle of how you've always been able to pass through the Citadel seals. My assumption that your thick soul confused them was incorrect. The ancient Nowen probably designed them to admit their own people. To admit you."

That made sense—the same way the Meridon Gate had been able to reach Vex inside the vault.

Enio let go a bone-rattling burp. He wiped his mouth, then caught everyone staring. "So, what's the plan for today?"

"Glad you asked," the Abbot said. "We've still much work to do in the city. And Alexander, can you assist me with the Threshold? We must assess the damage along the coasts and ask if Arcana needs our aid."

"Of course."

"We should also check Jod and the Borderlands," added Rafael.

"And," Par said, "the Deep World."

And Lani.

The Abbot stood. "We shall. But I meet now with the High Council to discuss the Eminence's passing."

Par sighed sadly and nodded.

"So please continue to help in any way you can." With that, the Father Abbot was out the door.

Chapter Forty-Four

Fter breakfast, Vex left for the Argent Threshold to assess damage to the other lands. The Deep World lay at the bottom of that list, since the Asrai hadn't attacked there. Par wouldn't ask for it to be moved higher for his personal interests—to see Lani. Besides, she must be busy dealing with the leadership vacuum the Asrai left behind. So Par joined Enio and Rafael and hopped a wagon bringing aid from the ruling quarter down to the city. When the eastern cliffs swung into view, Par tried to locate the secluded spot he'd once pointed out to Enio as a nice place for a cottage. He realized he couldn't find it because it had crumbled into the sea.

A steady increase in shops and street traffic eventually took them to the busy central district. The healers had already been through the area and treated most injuries. And while the damage was less severe than Par had feared, leaking aqueducts, upthrust cobbles, crumbling chimneys, overturned carts, loose animals, and shattered wits created chaos. Enio and Rafael were pulled away to use their invocations for critical repairs. As a lone Nowen with no sigils, Par applied himself to manual labor. It was hard work, mostly lifting and carrying, but involved no magic portals or walking skeletons or sea monsters. He was happy to help that way.

Near midday, he joined workers in a tented courtyard preparing food for the volunteers. After much chopping and stirring, he spied Enio and Rafael.

"Hey, you layabouts," he called, grinning, "this isn't a picnic. Get back to work."

They waved and hurried over. Par ladled them bowls of steaming stew.

"Take a break, son," said the hefty but energetic woman in charge. "You've done plenty."

Rafael leaned toward Par's ear. "They have no idea."

Without argument to either, Par scooped himself a bowl and joined his friends. They grabbed mugs of ale and settled on a street curb.

"Where are you helping next?" Par asked as they ate.

"You tell us," Rafael said.

"Me?"

"You have a knack for winding up where you're most needed."

Par laughed at what seemed an obscure joke.

But Rafael was serious. "It's true. At least, it sounds that way from Enio's stories."

"You've been talking about me?" Par glanced at Enio, who grinned through a beer-foamed mustache.

"You once believed the gods had cursed you," Rafael went on. "But consider: last year, if you hadn't fled your town, fought for your friends and the things you felt were right, you'd never have met Vex, or Lani, or defeated Cronus."

"Twice," Enio said between spoonfuls.

"And," Rafael continued, "you'd have never received the sigil from Ridiax to release the mages, or traveled to the Deep World—"

"As a stowaway," Enio corrected.

"—then to Choga, leading to the discovery that you're a Nowen, and finally to the Asrai's defeat. Imagine the world today if you had sat home. Given up."

"I can't take credit for Choga," Par said. "The Mother Spring dropped me there on its own."

"Exactly." Rafael swirled his ale. "On the path to bringing the nations what they most needed—your message. Hate isn't the opposite of love. Fear is."

Par smiled a little, having learned that the hard way.

Enio stood. "Or maybe going where you're needed is just more weird Nowen stuff. I need a refill."

When Enio was out of earshot, Rafael said, "It surprises me you two are such close friends. You're very different."

"Yeah, but we balance each other out." Par sipped his ale. "He comes across as rough sometimes, but no one has a truer heart."

Enio was arguing with the person working the kegs. "That's not the top!"

"Same stout hearts," Rafael said. "Very different livers."

Par chuckled.

Rafael eyed the sun. "I should be getting back. I need to ask Vex for transport through the Threshold to Jod, but first I must prepare for an appointment with your High Council. We're laying the groundwork for the Borderlands to become its own nation, with Jod as its capital."

"I've never been to Jod."

"It's lovely, Par, and one of the most ancient cities this side of the Ults. It's an era of new beginnings, and new things are often built on old foundations."

Par raised his tankard. "You'll make a fine diplomat."

They clinked.

Enio returned with a sloshing mug.

"Don't overdo it," Par said.

"Are you kidding? It's the cheap stuff. Practically water."

Rafael stood. "And now, gentlemen, I must go."

"We'll miss you," Par said, rising with him.

Rafael held out his hand, but Par pulled him in for a hug. Rafael stiffened for a moment, then hugged back.

"Get used to it," Enio said. "Par's a hugger."

When they'd separated, Rafael turned to Enio. "We had a rough start. I hope, maybe, I can call you a friend?"

"Nope," Enio said. Then, after an instant of awkward silence, he smiled and added. "No *maybe*."

As with Par, Rafael offered a hug.

"Hey, no mush." Enio held out a hand.

Rafael took it, added a friendly slap to Enio's shoulder, and turned again to Par. "That speech you gave touched many hearts. Ever considered a job in diplomacy?"

"I didn't really plan out the words," Par said. "And like Egg-wise said, diplomats think more than talk, politicians talk more than think. I doubt I'm cut out for either."

"You might be surprised," Rafael said. "Like life, it's always two steps forward, one step back. The trick is to keep walking. See you soon, my friends."

He started off. Three steps later he stopped, looked down, and wrinkled his nose at a brown lump under his boot. After scraping it on a cobble, he disappeared through the crowds.

Par had to chuckle. He couldn't imagine a better metaphor of himself in politics.

"He's not so bad," Enio said. "Did you know he was raised by llamas?"

Llamas? Before Par asked, Enio added. "Oh, crap."

"What?"

"I forgot to ask him to trade sigils."

"I bet the Abbot will give you any sigils you want."

"Yeah?"

"If it's nothing too dangerous. Or rare. Or guild-only or—"

Enio snorted. Then he seemed to realize something. "While I was sick, I couldn't use my sigils. Now I know what you've been through your whole life."

"It's not like I haven't told you."

"Well, now that you're a Nowen, I can't call you thick anymore."

"Not for that, anyway."

They both laughed and drank.

Par said, "We've come a long way since St. Livius."

"Twice for my soul. The worst was losing all my memories. Not knowing anyone."

"The mages told me to guide you back—find you within, they said. So I thought of our times together. I guess you still remembered a few of those things." But did he find Par at the Immortus, or back at the Summer Festival? Or both? It still hurt thinking about that Nowen *then and fro* stuff.

Enio lowered his ale. "Remembered? No, I don't think I did. I didn't even see or hear you. But the feelings—I knew those. I followed them."

Feelings without memory? One more thing to keep Par awake at night and wondering. He laid a hand on Enio's arm. "Whatever happens from here, I'm just glad we're together."

Instead of responding to Par's heart-felt comment, Enio didn't turn, didn't smile. He said, "The *Sea Dog* is still stuck on a mountain. How do you suppose I can get it back?"

That's where the Asrai had sent it, through the Mother Spring. "Maybe someone from the Deep World—"

Par paused mid-sentence.

Now Enio smiled. "Yeah. I wonder who we know to ask? Anyway, come on. This city isn't going to rebuild itself."

Par followed. Enio not only sensed Par's feelings like no one else, he also sometimes knew what he was thinking.

Chapter Forty-Five

P AR WORKED ALONGSIDE Enio for the rest of the day. When the critical repairs dwindled and the sun dropped low, they caught a wagon back to the ruling sector. They were the good kind of tired and talked little during the return trip. When they arrived, Par heard low somber singing coming from the High Temple. They decided to peek inside.

The damaged roof had been stabilized enough to admit people safely. An assembly had gathered, all holding candles that glowed solemnly throughout the long, arched chamber. Incense, earthy but sweet, smoked in censers. Everyone there wore their finest ceremonial robes and faced the far altar, where lay a linen-wrapped body. To its side was a portrait of the regal, kind-faced Eminence.

Par was dirty and sweaty and didn't feel right going farther in. So he stayed with Enio in the back, silent, their heads bowed. One of the Eminence's last acts had been to change the laws of Eloria to no longer persecute those who couldn't invoke the gods. The world would be poorer without him.

Soon, the incense and the lengthy day took its toll. Par stifled a yawn and leaned to Enio. "We should check on Vex."

They slipped down a side corridor to a secret alcove—not so secret anymore—that lowered to the Vigil outpost. The guard recognized Par and let them pass. They found Vex at the Threshold.

Vex turned, and the portal blinked closed. "Come in, my friends."

"How are things looking?" Par asked. "Much damage?"

"As much as you'd expect. I've spoken with the Aubade of Arcana. They are in similar shape as we are. He and the Umbriarch were quite saddened to learn of the Eminence's passing, and plan to visit for a later memorial. Also, a gathering of nations is in the works, and you're both invited. I'll let you know as that progresses. They—"

"Have you checked on the Deep World?" Par said, the words tumbling out.

"I've never seen the Deep World, so I can't open the Threshold there. Perhaps you could help?" He held out the keystone. "Or does a Nowen even need one of these?"

Instead of using the keystone, Par tried touching the sigil that Eggwise had shown him, on the Threshold's step. "Deep World, please."

The portal remained dull and dark.

"Maybe it needs two Nowen." He took the stone and brought the Mother Spring to mind.

The Threshold shimmered and changed. Workers, human, though some a bit fishy-faced, bustled around the dry lake bed. Several invoked enchantments toward its bottom and at its stone walls where patches of moss and vines hung thin but tenacious.

Lani was among the workers.

"Lani!" Par called.

She turned.

Some there raised spears.

"It's all right!" she called and hurried over.

Par reached out. But his fingers only touched the cold stone wall beyond the Threshold.

"Sorry Par," Vex whispered from behind. "I already used it for passage today."

Enio came to Par's side. "Hi Lani!"

She stopped before the portal, panting. Relief flowed from her eyes. "Enio! You're healed."

"Yeah, I—"

"What about you?" Par said. "Are you all right?" Her face and hands were soiled, but she looked every single kind of awesome.

She brushed back sweat-tangled hair. "Could be better. But with care and time, we think the Mother Spring will recover. Same with the rest of this place. The Asrai messed things up pretty good, but we're hopeful."

She'd said *we*. Did that mean she was staying there with the others? Or was Par overthinking again?

"Uh," he said. "Do you have a second to talk?" He glanced at Vex.

Vex nodded and took Enio's arm. "Come over here a moment."

"Now?"

"Right now."

"But—" Enio glanced at Par, at Lani, back at Par. "Oh, *right.*" As he left, he mouthed, *Tell her.*

But Par had to ask something first.

Lani continued, "We think if we—"

"Did you decide?" Par said.

A shadow of confusion passed over her face, then understanding dawned. "That's going to take a longer conversation, Par. There are still… things you don't understand. It's complicated."

Why was it always complicated? But at least it wasn't over. He took a breath. "Lani, I wanted to say this in person, I mean *in person,* in person." He leaned as close to the Threshold as possible. "I want you to choose life on the land. Life with me."

Someone called from behind her in a language Par didn't understand. She looked back and answered with similar words. The tone seemed argumentative.

She turned again to Par, her grin rushed. "I have to handle this. We'll talk again later. I promise."

Unsure what else to say, Par nodded.

She paused. "Oh, and Par, I heard your words with the Asrai."

That sent such a ripple through Par's brain that his concentration broke and the portal closed. He remained staring at the blank rock wall beyond.

Enio spoke from behind. "Did you tell her?"

Par didn't move or blink. "I think so."

"And?"

"It's... complicated."

Chapter Forty-Six

THE FIRST GATHERING of every nation and magic, the first in a thousand years, was being held in Jod, nestled on the westernmost shores of the Silver Sea. Par had never seen such an ancient city. The main keep loomed like a large, squat hill overlooking a busy bay. It boasted thick, sloping walls, and dozens of thin, rugged towers, the stones rubbed smooth by the centuries and discolored by as many years of sea birds. Its foundations had been laid before any in Eloria or Arcana, back in the days of the Vigil's greatest works. And its greatest deceits.

Par hurried now through a crowded corridor, passing dignitaries, diplomats, and mages. Some speculated on subjects new to their ears, like the Citadel and the Immortus rift. But many spoke instead of human rifts, those born of old suspicions and fears. The very rifts this gathering was meant to heal.

Or if not heal, at least recognize. That was a start.

He paused at an intersection, unsure which way to go. A hand grasped his shoulder. It was the Father Abbot, dressed in the flowing white and gold of the Elorian Hierarchy.

Par smiled, relieved to see a familiar face. "Good morning, Father Abbot."

"Par, glad I caught you. I assume we're looking for the same thing?"

"Enio's class?" Enio had been asked to describe how he invoked sigils of multiple realms. Par wouldn't miss it for the world.

"It's just ahead," the Abbot said. "Follow me."

Par had spent most of his time here bestowing the Ridiax sigils on Zizik. Now, rushing to see Enio, Par had gotten himself lost because he'd also been looking for Lani. He hadn't talked to her since the Argent Threshold, several days back. Was she here, representing the Deep World? If so, that was an important job, and he probably shouldn't bother her. He should really stop thinking about her until she was ready to talk to him.

But he couldn't.

Two more corners and they arrived. The room sloped like a steep amphitheater, the seats nearly filled. The variety of robes and hats was remarkable. Many resembled the Abbot's attire, others the blue and silver of Arcana, and still others the somber colors Par had seen throughout the Dark Tribes.

The class hadn't yet started. The Abbot found seats high in the back, gathered his robes and sat. "Before I forget, Rafael sends his regards."

Par joined him. "Is he here?"

"He was, but I believe he's left again for Meridon. Always busy, running from place to place. He added that Eggwise sends his greetings, but is occupied with training duties in Choga, if that means anything to you."

Scanning the room, Par nodded. No Lani here either, but he spotted Enio down front, standing beside the small lecture stage with his arms crossed as two saggy-faced men showed him open books. One man was dressed like the Abbot. The other like Vex, in Arcanan wizard's garb and a pointed hat.

"The official diplomatic sessions don't begin until tomorrow," the Abbot said. "Today is for preliminaries. Later there will be an official introduction of the Nowen by Regent Zizik. Then Alexander will lay out the history of the Immortus and the Vigil's rise and fall, all leading to recent events. It would be an ideal time to introduce you, Par."

Par winced. "I already introduced myself, by accident, to the entire world. I'd rather stay in the background for now."

"I can sympathize. I myself have been trying to keep a low profile, but being High Sigil Master obliterates one's privacy."

Par kept forgetting that the old Father Abbot, the man he knew from St. Livius, was the new High Sigil Master of Eloria, one of the Eminence's last promotions. Maybe Par should bow to him more often, or at least call him by his proper title. But it felt like calling a family member *mister*.

The Abbot interrupted his thoughts. "I think they're starting."

The wizard in blue stepped to the lectern. He sparked a silver glory around his head, on-off, on-off, to quiet the room. The chatting settled.

"Thank you," he said. "Once again, I want to thank Necromancer Shaad for her enlightening perspectives on mushrooms. And now Master Enius Marius will give us his insights on sigil interaction between realms and relevant variation of compass and gyre." He motioned Enio to come forward.

Enio did, but only the crown of his bushy hair rose behind the lectern. The man in blue helped him onto a box.

"Thanks," Enio said, not loudly, but the sound carried. He glanced over the audience, hesitated, turned to the man who'd introduced him. "The what with the what?"

"What we just discussed. How you invoke sigils from different realms."

"Oh. Why didn't you just say that?" Enio again faced the packed room. "Well, um, when you get down to it, different sigils aren't as different as people say. The lumina ones, the ones Elorians use, reach more up. I mean, the root thing does. The numena ones are bent—"

"Bent?" someone from the audience said.

Enio leaned his head sideways. "Slanted. Crooked and—"

"Crooked!" someone else said, more shocked.

"Here we go," mumbled the Abbot, shaking his head.

The wizard near Enio raised his hands to again quiet the audience. "I'm sure he didn't mean that in a pejorative sense, right, son?"

"The what sense?"

"You meant its compass is oriented—"

"The way the root thing goes?"

"Fine, yes, the way the root thing goes."

Par wished he had something to snack on while he watched this.

Enio began again. "So, yeah, they don't really go different ways. It just looks like it sometimes, because the magic they use comes from different places. The ones with more than one root—"

A woman in dull red near the front raised her hand.

Enio noticed. "What?"

"More than one root?"

Enio brightened. "Isn't that something? The one from Ridiax had roots growing likes weeds, lumina, numena, élan, Ortu—"

"In the same sigil?" she said.

"Yup. And—"

Another spoke out. "The Upper Realms mixed with the Lower?"

"The Ortu is not *lower*," someone said.

Someone else: "The gods are above—"

Another: "Gods? Humph! The cosmos—"

"Blasphemy!"

"Please!" shouted the man in the pointy hat. "Let's keep this civil."

The Abbot leaned towards Par. "They wanted Rafael to give the talk, since he also can use sigils of variant realms. He was busy, so I recommended Enio. I admit, a diplomat might have been more sensitive to, uh, cultural diversities."

"Should we help?" Par asked, his amusement shifting to worry for his friend.

"No. I stand by my decision."

Once more, the people had quieted. The pointed-hat guy nodded to Enio.

Enio eyed the room for a moment. He sighed. "Look, I was born in Eloria, where they only taught the magic of the gods. I mean, lumina. But I spent more time in my canoe than school. I don't know the right books. The right words." A humble golden glory, the lumina of Elorians, bloomed around his head. "I spent loads of time alone on my river, mostly at night after the barges docked. Just me, the moon, the stars. And I found there was more magic than what I'd been taught. One day, I cast my first Arcanan sigil." As he spoke, his golden glory shifted to silver, to numena magic, as if the sun had passed and surrendered to moonlight. Small gasps moved through the chamber.

Enio frowned. "Eloria locked me up for it."

But Par had to smile, remembering their escape last year from the abbey.

"And the élan, nature magic, is another kind, and it's everywhere—in the leaves, and the animals, and the bugs, and the rivers." His silver glory shifted to emerald green. More gasps. "Where there's life, there's élan. I learned that from my nymph friend."

That would be Lani.

"Some people," Enio continued, "say the three Lower Realm magics are bad. Evil." His glory darkened to a blackish purple.

This time, the room was stunned into such silence that Par could have heard shadows bump. Most people had never seen anyone use two kinds of magic, much less three. Four? Never. It was also the first time Par had seen Enio channel Ortu magic while not being possessed by Cronus.

His purplish glory dimmed and winked out. Par thought he caught a streak of bronze and red, the other two magics of the Lower Realms. Perhaps just a trick of the light.

"The Nowen stuff," Enio said, "I guess is in the middle, balancing everything. I don't know much about it, but it works in pairs. What was that saying?" He scratched his nose. "Three above, three below, two the balance, then and fro. Anyway, no single magic is the right kind. Or the wrong kind. It depends on how you use it."

The Abbot squeezed Par's arm. Par nodded and understood now the Abbot's choice of speaker.

The crowd remained silent. Enio scanned the room and shook his head. "But knowing the magic, the sigils, isn't the most important thing. It's something else." He lay his hand on his chest. "The will, the heart. Everything comes from there, and through there. If you want to know about that stuff, ask him." He pointed straight at Par.

Every head turned.

"Crap," Par muttered.

"Might as well stand," the Abbot said and rose beside him.

Par didn't move.

With a slight chuckle, the Abbot tugged the back of Par's collar and helped him to his feet, then cleared his throat and addressed the room. "Allow me to introduce Parynius Ignatious. Par for short. Yes, *that* Par."

Like a low breeze, whispers moved through the seats. "Par?" someone said. "Par?" People stood for a better view. A woman in brown removed her hat and bowed. Others near her followed. Soon, the entire chamber had bent like wheat in the wind.

"What do I do?" Par side-whispered to the Abbot.

"I'd suggest," the Abbot said, "you bow back."

So awkwardly, Par did, since there was nowhere to hide. And Enio was too far to strangle.

Chapter Forty-Seven

FTER THE BOWING and whispering, Enio's class resumed. He spoke of his experiences with the different magics, in his own simple language, and he answered questions. The room became less argumentative, yet there seemed little meeting of minds between teacher and students. Perhaps Enio didn't quite understand how he did what he did. Par figured it was as likely the audience was a few steps behind Enio.

When the class ended, Enio received polite applause. As some approached to speak with him further, Par slipped out with the Abbot. They stood in the shadows near the door, Par's back to the passing crowds.

"Think he did all right?" Par asked. Then he bowed. "High Sigil Master."

The Abbot lowered his voice. "Don't you start too. But yes, I'd say so, once the audience saw past his lack of schooling to his natural talent."

Par nodded and said half in jest, "Maybe someday he'll become a Sigil Master."

But the Abbot remained serious. "Not a Sigil Master. *The* Sigil Master."

Par grinned. Gods help us all.

A tall, thin man tapped the Abbot. "Pardon me, Master Cornelius. May I have a word?"

"Of course. Excuse me a moment, Par."

Shortly after the Abbot stepped away, Enio came out. Par waved him over.

"How'd I do?" Enio said, seeming a bit haggard.

"Except for pointing me out, you did great."

"Thanks."

"Indeed, he did." The Abbot returned. "Up for another class?"

"I'd rather go fishing," Enio said.

"Speaking of fishing, I've just received news. The *Sea Dog* has been returned."

Enio's face lit. "Where is it?"

"It's moored in the harbor. Left there by the Deep World delegation."

"Come on, Par!" Enio grabbed his arm and yanked.

Par stumbled a few steps and stopped. He looked at the Abbot. "Delegation?"

But the Abbot winked. "She's waiting on the battlements." He nodded the other direction.

Enio tugged again.

Par stood rooted in indecision. He needed to see Lani, and he needed to see her alone. But the *Sea Dog* was Enio's heart. He focused helplessly on his friend. They locked eyes. And there came over Enio's face a strange, subtle change.

"Oh…" Enio said. He released Par's arm, lowered his gaze, looked at his boots. Though he still smiled, his words came haltingly. "You know, Par, I've been thinking. Sure, we always talked about sailing the *Silver Sea*. But when I lost the *Sea Dog,* you don't know how much… how much I missed it." His smile faded.

Par was pretty sure he did.

Enio went on. "After what I've been through, after everything that's—" He took a breath. "I need to sail alone awhile." He shrugged, eyes still down.

Par hadn't planned that far out. "Give me some time, Enio. I'll—"

"You need your time. I need mine." He looked back up. His eyes had a damp shine. "Tell her I said hi."

Before Par answered, Enio turned and bolted into the crowd.

Par reached out. "Enio!" But his friend was gone.

And Par didn't follow. He'd never thought he'd have to choose between Enio and something else. Or someone else.

The Abbot placed a hand on Par's shoulder. "Everyone must find their own destiny."

Par stared at the spot where Enio had disappeared—and without even a handshake.

"Now go on, Par. Someone's waiting."

Destiny was something Par had never dwelt on either, much less one without Enio. He took a deep breath, and feeling like his own mooring lines had just snapped, set an unsteady course for the battlements.

CHAPTER FORTY-EIGHT

As Par hurried up the worn, twisting steps to the battlements, his thoughts twisted too. Enio was on his way to the harbor, to leave in the *Sea Dog*. No fold or Threshold could find a moving boat. And Lani waited ahead. More than once, Par considered dashing back, arguing with Enio to stay, make plans together, like old times.

Yet Par could barely think, much less plan. He kept climbing, one anxious footstep after the other.

He came to a wooden door. Should he rehearse what to say? But like his legs, his hand decided. He pushed the door open.

Lani stood alone at the parapets, stark and lovely, gazing toward the sea. The early sun cut pale shafts through scattered clouds. Did that mean a sailor's delight, or a sailor's warning?

One way to find out.

Par took a breath. "Lani?"

She turned. She smiled.

He stepped forward.

"Wait, Par."

He stopped, puzzled.

Her fingers gripped the string of shells always around her neck. She singled out the blue one. "Do you remember this?"

"From the Asrai. To postpone your *chela élande*. Your decision."

She removed the shell and again faced the sea. Par waited for her to say more. The sharp screeches of gulls and the low rumble of waves echoed below.

"I was born in the forests of the Urdel," she finally said, "but the sea took my heart. Have you ever seen anything more beautiful?"

Par watched her in silence. He had.

When she said nothing more, he stuttered out, "Is the Deep World—are you—did the—"

She rescued him from his floundering. "For centuries, the Deep World knew only the Asrai as its leader. She may have been worthy at first, but pride and ambition rotted her heart. The so-called government she left behind is in shambles. They're forming a new council. They've asked me to be on it."

Par's mind again found its legs, and it sprang into a gallop. "I see. Right. Well. I've been thinking how nice the Deep World was when I visited. I can see myself living there. We were worried at first I might have trouble breathing, remember? But I didn't, thanks, I guess, to the élan. I can help with the council and—"

"I'm sure you'd be happy there," Lani said. "But I'd miss you."

His racing thoughts barreled face-first into her words as if he'd hit a wall. It took a moment to recover. "Did you say *miss me?*"

"I turned them down."

Par swallowed, careful not to scare off the joy stalking his heart. "Then you chose the land?"

"I did not choose the land."

His joy stumbled. With his jaw clenched and his toes curled in his boots, he struggled to remain expressionless.

She added, "Nor did I choose the sea."

"Oh… What?"

Her eyes dropped again to the blue shell. "I once told you I might have more choices than anyone thought. The heart of the élan does whatever's best for the balance. It often gives male nymphs a new form, or female nymphs a home, wild and untamed, to nurture and protect. For me, that seemed a choice between land and sea. But because I'm only half-nymph, my fate remained unclear."

Par remembered. "You once joked you might end up as a codfish." He forced a smile, desperate to get wherever this was going.

She went on. "But at last I realized I had a third choice. And I wanted you with me when I made it." She hurled the shell over the parapet.

For an instant, Par's eyes followed its arc through the air toward the sea.

The sounds of Lani's receding footsteps drew back his attention. She'd moved several paces away. An emerald glory now flowed over her entire body, engulfing her like green fire.

Par started toward her.

"Stay back!" she commanded.

He froze.

She raised her arms, her entire body brightening, blazing, until Par could no longer see her. Suddenly, an explosion of light and air blasted him back against the parapet. "Lani!" he cried into its fury.

But the tempest calmed and passed. Par blinked his eyes clear and scanned the battlements. Lani was nowhere in sight. Panicking, he searched the crashing waves below.

"Here!" roared a voice. From above.

Par spun and snapped his gaze skywards.

A great beast, long and winged, larger than any horse or skarix, hovered overhead.

He recoiled, fearing for an instant it was the Asrai. Yet no steam shot from its nostrils, nor did it have fins, and its scales were not slimy and black. They sparkled like hammered gold.

Par's alarm turned to wonder.

Lani?

As Par stood like a tent post, she descended. Her outline blurred, shifting like a cloud, shrinking, reforming. The familiar Lani settled again before him.

Her grin, forever a little too wide for her face, seemed to waver. "Better than a codfish, right? But I warned you it was complicated."

Still Par stared. In the past year, he'd traveled distant lands, some beneath the sea, some within a giant fold; he'd learned of the Vigil and the Immortus, the Thresholds and the Citadel; he'd witnessed a world of different magics; and he'd discovered he was born a Nowen. He couldn't conceive of his life getting any more complicated. Yet, of all the outcomes he'd imagined for Lani's *chela élande*, this was in none of them.

Her expression sobered. "The élan decided that besides land or sea, I had a third choice. The air. I wonder if that's why the Asrai kept me close? Perhaps she sensed what I would become, and hoped to use me to rule with her, land and sea and sky."

Par said nothing, a new resolve growing in his heart.

She hesitated, then looked away. "So that's my new nymph form. I felt you should know, Par, before—"

"Lani."

She turned back.

Deep in his stomach, Par felt the stir of old fears. Yet they didn't stop him from taking the last step between them.

Or from pressing his lips to hers.

The few other kisses he'd experienced had seemed like donations or charity, given out of concern, reassurance, friendship. Each a short little tale with a tender but thin plot. This one was different. There was nothing one-way about it, and if the others were short stories, this was a novel.

As gently as he'd begun, he parted. He watched her for a moment. She had closed her eyes.

With his heart warm and pounding, he said. "What does the *chela élande* want next?"

She opened her eyes. They sparkled like jewels. "The rest is up to me. But the sea, land, and air get along in perfect balance. What about a half-nymph with a dragon form and a Nowen named Par?"

"So you'll stay here?"

"By 'here' you mean—?"

"With me."

This time, there was nothing unsure in her smile. "Oh, Par. I was hoping you'd say that."

Par leaned forward and they kissed again. Unlike the books he'd read, the sequel was even better.

A symphony of heartbeats later, they separated. "Wow," Par muttered, a little dizzy.

Lani laughed. "I was thinking the same. By the way, where's Enio? We should tell—"

The spell broke for the moment. "Enio! He's trying to leave." Par hurried to the parapet.

Jod's harbor spread from the wharf like its own busy town. Ships, many of them barges and merchant vessels, toted their wares back and forth, in and out, forever using Jod as a go-between for trade among the lands. Some stood out as especially fancy, flying the colors of visiting dignitaries. But Par only cared about finding the *Sea Dog*.

At last, he did.

It was already beyond the harbor gates.

CHAPTER FORTY-NINE

Under full sail, the *Sea Dog* sped into open waters. Enio stood at the bow, facing the morning sun, the course given to wind and wave.

Par now watched from the deck several paces behind. He cleared his throat. "Nice day for a cruise."

Enio spun. His surprise crinkled into a scowl. "If you're going to Threshold onto someone's boat, ask the captain first."

Par hadn't Thresholded—if that was a word—but he'd explain later. He stepped forward. "You ran off. We need to talk."

"What happened with Lani?"

"She chose…" Par kept a straight face, "not the land."

Enio's voice rose. "Why didn't you go with her? To the Deep World?"

"She—"

"You think being a Nowen is better? Grow old and weave beads in your hair like Eggwise?"

"No, I—"

"All you wanted was to be with her, Par. Like all I ever wanted was to sail the *Silver Sea*."

This conversation was going wildly off track. "But you don't have to do it alone, Enio. We wanted to sail the sea together, right?"

Enio's frown weakened. For a moment, he said nothing. Then he stepped to the side rail, leaned on his elbows, looked out over the passing waves. He heaved a deep sigh. "My whole life, the world has thrown me trouble, put stuff in my way. Another storm, another mountain. But look." He motioned toward the horizon. "Clear sailing now. I won't lose this chance. But I won't let you lose yours, either. Even if I have to turn this boat around."

Par joined his friend at the rail. "We've both had our mountains. I guess everyone does. But we've faced them together. And together, haven't we even moved a few?"

"Yeah, well, wind moves boats." Without turning, Enio shook his head. "You're still overthinking. You don't get it."

"Get what?"

"I'm in *your* way now.

"*My* way?"

"You've got important things to do, places to go. And you can't give up on Lani. You're supposed to be with her, not with—" He swallowed the last words.

So that was it. After all their happy plans of sailing the sea, Enio was willing to give up their companionship, their friendship, and be alone again, if it would get Par back with Lani. Par had never loved the guy more than at that instant.

"I've been trying," Par said, his throat a little tight, "to tell you something." He waved a hand above his head, like brushing away a gnat.

"Tell me what?"

"Wait a moment."

They did.

"Well?" Enio said.

"Just a moment."

"You said that six moments ago."

Then a shadow.

A downrush of wind.

A roar.

Enio snapped up his head.

Lani, in her magnificent golden dragon form, hovered above the boat.

"Purple hells!" Enio threw himself to the deck, never taking his bulging eyes off the creature. As on the battlements, it blurred and reformed as it descended, settling on deck as the beautiful half-nymph that Par loved.

He helped Enio back up. "She didn't choose the land. She chose the air. Which means—"

"Which means," Lani said, stepping to Enio, "no one is turning this boat around."

Enio reached out a tentative hand, a finger. He poked her shoulder.

But she grabbed his wrist, yanked him close, and wrapped him in her arms. "I've missed you, Enio."

With an unconvincing yelp of protest, he melted and hugged her back. "Me too," he murmured.

Then she squeezed tighter. Enio gagged. She said, "Wandering off in a blizzard? Half frozen when they found you? If you had died, I'd have killed you worse." She loosened her hold on him.

Yet Enio stayed in the hug. "Sorry. I got... lost. But I'm better now. Right Par?"

"It's a long story and involves the Nowen mages and Enio's soul," Par said.

"And crackers and salami," Enio added, still enfolded.

Par stepped closer, amazed at Enio's marathon hug. "Hey. I thought you didn't like the mushy stuff?"

Enio side-eyed Par and, without a word, pulled him in. Par gladly joined.

When they separated, Par turned to Enio. "The Abbot said everyone must find their own destiny. We'll find ours together. Lani and I have decided to come with you—with the captain's permission."

Enio's face brightened like the dawn. He gave a grand, welcoming bow. "Granted." He straightened and added, "But I should tell you, they want us to stay."

"Who does?" asked Par.

"The robes and hats. We're famous, I guess. They made offers."

Par had everything he wanted right here. But he was curious. "Like what?"

Enio curled his lips as if judging a barter. "Let's see. A guy from Eloria said they'd put up statues."

"Of us?"

"Yeah. But not as saints. I asked. We'd have to be dead first."

Par suppressed a grin. "I'll pass."

"And someone from Arcana offered to name towns and stuff after us. Like, Eniopolis."

"You're kidding."

"I'm not."

"What for me?"

"Something about a Parthenon."

Par liked the sound of that.

"Anyway," Enio said, "if you're giving all that up, are you giving up your Nowen training too?"

Now it was Par who turned to the rail, watching the sunlit waves that paved a shimmering road to the horizon. "I know I could learn a lot in Meridon. I can't even invoke without another Nowen. But…"

"But with them," Enio said, "you're worried you won't be special anymore."

"Special?" Par turned back.

"Yep. You've always moaned about being different. That you can't use sigils like everyone else. Oh, woe, I'm cursed! Cursed!" Enio drew a dramatic arm across his forehead.

Par nudged him. "Cut it out."

Enio dropped his arm. "And in the Urdel, when we first met Lani? You hid behind it so you didn't have to tell her how you felt. That you loved her."

Lani chuckled.

Warming now, Par shook his head. "I remember when I didn't say that."

"Doesn't matter," Enio said. "It was true."

It was.

"And then there was that crap about having a thick soul. You sounded proud of it."

Again Enio saw something in Par he hadn't seen himself. Or, at least admitted.

Enio continued, "But you can stop all the lying and denying and speechifying, because you'll never be normal. Nobody's normal. Besides,"—he grinned—"you'll always be a feeble to me."

Par stifled a snort. "Lani, help."

She reached out her hand. "I, for one, think you're still pretty special."

"Thank you," Par said, taking it, "even if I am the only one on board who can't fly."

"Enio can fly?" She looked at him.

"Vex bestowed me the sigil," Enio said. "But I can't use it right now."

That gave Par a hint of worry. "Are you still healing?"

"Nope." Enio patted his stomach. "My weight ratios are off. Too many desserts."

Everyone laughed at that and Par added, "Maybe Lani could give you a ride. That's how we got on board." He skipped describing his quiet terror during most of that trip.

"Hey!" Lani bumped Par playfully. "I'm a dragon, not a wagon." Then she lifted her gaze to the sails. "But I've got another idea." She released his hand and stepped back.

Par watched her curiously.

She raised her arms. Emerald light coursed over her body. Was she dragon-forming again? Instead, she stood firmly on deck with the light flowing out from her, along the floorboards, up the mast, into the sails and rigging. The timbers groaned. The boat tipped.

Along with Enio, Par dove to a railing. And with the sails aflutter and a swirl of wind and spray, the *Sea Dog* rose from the water.

Gasping, Par gripped the rail tighter and peered overboard. They continued to rise, up and up. Jod and its harbor shrank until the vessels were marked only by broken white lines in the sparkling sea. At last, the boat leveled off.

Lani came beside him. "Are you all right?"

"I've never been great with heights." Par caught his breath. "How long can we stay up here?"

"Until my élan runs out."

Enio eyed the sails approvingly. Par remained huddled over the rail, fortifying his grip on it, and on his breakfast.

But Lani said, "Don't worry, I'll land well before then. Shall we try forward?"

"Yes!" Enio hooted and ran aft to the helm. He grabbed a rope, invoking with his own green glory. The sail swung, the *Sea Dog* veered to starboard, the wind rushed by.

Lani laid a hand on Par's. "But if you'd rather, we can—"

"Really, I'm fine," he said, doing his best to sound convincing. Then, with fear in one hand and hope in the other, he released the rail; in truth, with his friends there was no room for fear.

But there might be for another kiss. He leaned in.

Enio's shout from the helm interrupted. "About damn time

you stopped overthinking that. Um, need some privacy? Want to use the cabin?"

"Enio!" Par shouted back, embarrassed.

"What? You winked at me."

"No, I didn't."

"You did. Both eyes."

Par gaped. "Both eyes is a blink!"

"It was a double wink. I figured you were desperate."

Before Par ran up and tackled his friend, Lani again saved the day. "Ahoy, Captain Enio, what's our heading?"

"Oh, right." Enio's faced sobered. "Nowhere." He licked his lips. "Everywhere."

Par met Enio's eager eyes, saying with his own, *At last.*

In the same intimate silence, Enio answered with an easy nod: *At last.* Then, his broken side teeth peeking through a wide smile, he turned his attention to the horizon.

Par watched his friend a moment longer, free now of any mountains, sailing the *Silver Sea* in a way they'd never imagined from their small canoe. As if Par's heart weren't full enough, it swelled a little more.

Finally, he said to Lani, "You know, he's right about no one being normal. Look at us. I can see folds. Enio can use gods-only-know what magics, and my girlfriend is a dragon nymph." He considered. "Though among us, I'm still the *least* normal."

"Just because you can't fly?"

"Worse. Without another Nowen, I'm still the only one who doesn't have any magic at all."

But she chuckled. "Of course you do. Haven't you figured that out yet?"

"What?"

"Love is magic. You've always had that."

Par squeezed her hand and made no argument.

But it occurred to him that she was wrong.

Enio had been near the truth during his class, saying magic had never been the most important thing. Enio had even lost his for a while, but he'd carried on. And Par had lived most of his life without it, feeling cursed and unworthy. But his friends had helped him through the dark times.

The sails snapped and billowed, carrying the *Sea Dog* through gulfs of sunlit air high above the sea. Par couldn't deny the power of magic, of course. But be it lumina, numena, anima, élan, or every sigil and realm, even a Sigil Master could gather only so much each day.

Lani leaned against him, her head on his shoulder, and together they watched their friend steer the *Sea Dog* into uncharted tomorrows. And Par smiled. Because he was now certain that love wasn't magic, like she'd said.

Love was better.

You never ran out of that.

The End

Dear reader,

I hope you enjoyed the story of *The Sigil Masters: The Last Nowen* as much as I enjoyed telling it.

Sweet sailin's and fair landin's

Rick

ABOUT THE AUTHOR

Rick Duffy writes to discover new worlds and wander from the familiar. He grew up on the boundary of street-lit suburb and shadowed forest, reading second-hand fantasy and science fiction books often out of order. He now writes them himself (in order) and is best know for his award winning *The Sigil Masters.*

Rick lives in Colorado, is never far from a biking trail or a cup of tea, and hopes we all find time everyday to explore.

Connect with him at *rickduffy.com*

www.ingramcontent.com/pod-product-compliance
Lightning Source LLC
Chambersburg PA
CBHW021245190726
48289CB00005B/1490